ROGUE MALL

by the same author
Disappearer
Colin Cleveland and the End of the World
Girl's Rock
The Eternal Prisoner
Rogue Males

Mark Hunter series
Beautiful Chaos
Sixty-Six Curses
Trouble at School
Mysterious Girlfriend
The Beasts of Bellend
Countdown to Zero

Rogue Males

Chris Johnson

Samurai West

Published by Samurai West
disappearer007@gmail.com

Story and Art © Chris Johnson 2024
All rights reserved

This paperback edition published 2025
ISBN-13: 9798293402267

Prologue
A Brief Descent into Hell

The girl had always wondered about the sad-looking man who lived on her street. She wondered why always looked so sad. She wondered why he lived in a house by himself instead of with a family like other people did. She wondered why he wasn't friends with any of the other people on the street. If she said hello to him, sometimes he would say hello to her and then sometimes he wouldn't, and she wondered why he did that.

But most of all she wondered where he went when he went down that footpath, the footpath that started at the end of the street between the gardens of two of the houses and took you right out into the countryside. Nearly every day the sad-looking man would go down this path, sometimes in the morning, sometimes in the afternoon, and he would be gone for hours and hours. Mum said he was probably just going to work, but the girl wasn't convinced of this because when other people went to work got in their cars and drove off, or if they walked, they walked into the middle part of town, which was the busy part of town; they didn't go out into countryside, which was where that path went. In the countryside there were only trees and fields, there weren't any shops or schools or other place for people to work in. Yes, she knew that they had farms out in the countryside, but the girl always thought that people who worked on farms lived on them as well, and anyway, the sad-looking man didn't look like a farmer.

So the girl wondered a lot about where the sad-looking man might be going to when he walked down that path that went into the countryside. Perhaps he had some secret place deep in the woods that he went to, a special place that only he knew about, and perhaps there were magic people who lived there and who were friends with the sad-looking man.

Or perhaps it wasn't people at all, and it was just the animals of the woods that he went to see, and the animals were the man's friends and he knew the secret of how to talk to them. Perhaps the sad-looking man liked animals more than he liked people, and that was why he never talked to the other people in the street.

And so the girl wondered, and she kept wondering until one day she decided she would find out for herself where the sad-looking man was going to when he went down that path, and she would follow him the next time he went, she would follow him without him seeing he was following her and she would find out where he went to. The little girl knew that she wasn't supposed to do this, because her parents had always told her never to go far from the house on her own, and they had told her that even with her friends she shouldn't go too far out into the countryside, because there were dangerous things like cliffs you could fall down and deep pools you could fall into and drown, and even if you didn't fall down a cliff or drown you might get lost and if you didn't get found in time it would get dark and in the dark you would be even more lost. And there could be bad people in the countryside as well. It wasn't always safe to be in lonely places where there weren't any people who knew you around to see that you were okay.

So the girl knew her mum and dad wouldn't want her to follow the sad-looking man down the path into the countryside, because the place he went to was probably a long way away and not close to the town and the houses where people could see you and it was safer. She knew this, but she just wanted so badly to know where the sad-looking man went to and if the place he went to was a place where he was happy instead of being sad like he was the rest of the time, so she decided she would go without telling her mum and dad.

And one day, one bright sunny morning when it was the school holidays, she decided that today was the day. She followed the sad-looking man when he came out of his house and she followed him to the end of the street to where the path started. There was a signpost pointing to the path, a signpost that told you the path wasn't private property and anyone could walk down it. And so, on her little bike she followed the sad-looking man along the path and out into the countryside, always keeping at a safe distance behind him so that he wouldn't turn round and see her.

She followed him along the windy path, further and further into the countryside until they must have been miles and miles from anywhere, or so it seemed to the little girl, and she wondered if they were ever going to get to the sad-looking man's secret place. If they didn't get there soon, she would be too tired to go on and she'd have to stop and have a rest, and if she stopped and had a rest, the sad-looking men would get too far ahead of her and she'd never be able to find him again.

But before the girl could get too tired, they came to the place the sad-looking man was going to; and it wasn't at all what the girl had been expecting, because the place was a big building made of bricks and concrete. The girl was surprised to find a big building like this standing all on its own in the middle of the countryside. She wondered what it was for. The building had hardly any windows, so at first she thought it might be a sports and swimming pool place like they had in town, or one of those big cinemas. But what would one of those places be doing out here in the middle of nowhere? And there ought to be people around and a big sign telling you what the building was for, but there were no people around at all and there was no sign telling you what the building was for.

From the edge of the trees, the girl watched the sad-looking man as he walked up to the building and went in through the door, and it wasn't a big, important-looking door, just a normal, door-sized door, looking very small in that big wall.

So, was this building the sad-looking man's secret place in the woods, the place where he kept all his friends? The girl had imagined the secret place as being outdoors, a hidden place in the woods that only he knew about and that you had to crawl through lots of tunnels in the bushes to get to—but instead of that, the secret place was this great big building.

Well, there was only one way for the girl to find out what the big building was and what the sad-looking man was doing there: she would have to follow him in through that door and find out for herself.

And so, leaving her bike leaning against a tree, the girl walked up to the door the sad-looking man had walked in through, and as nobody stopped her and the door wasn't locked, she opened the door and went into the building.

But the moment she got inside it was all wrong, because she was in a dark and dingy corridor with bare concrete walls, and it was cold as well, a lot colder than it was outside. It didn't seem like a friendly place at all and she wondered why the sad-looking man would even want to come to a place like this.

The girl set off down the corridor, thinking that since there was nobody here, then maybe where she was was just the 'round the back' part of the building, and that if she just kept walking, soon she would come to somewhere where it was much nicer. And so she walked down the corridor and then when it went round a corner, she walked down another corridor that was exactly the same and it was still all damp and cold and not very bright.

But then the girl started to get a smell in her nose, and the smell was like farms and animals, an outdoor smell. And then she thought she heard a cow go moo—and then she heard it again and it was definitely a cow going moo, and that didn't seem right, because who would put cows inside a building instead of out in the fields where you're supposed to put cows? And the girl kept walking down the corridor and the farm smell got stronger and she could hear more cows going moo. And she came to where the corridor went round another corner and round that corner she saw that they *were* keeping cows inside the building, because there they were and they were being led out through these big doors like gates and into the corridor, and the people leading them were wearing these white clothes with helmets that looked like spacesuits, except that they were also wearing green wellies like farmer wore, and which didn't really go with the spacesuits. And these people in spacesuits had hold of these ropes that were attached to the cows and they were leading them down the corridor, down the corridor away from where the girl was standing.

The girl was having to change her ideas about what this big building was, and she was starting to think now that maybe the sad-looking man did just work on a farm after all—but whoever had heard of a farm that was all indoors like this one? The girl decided to follow the cows, thinking they might be going to where the sad-looking man was, and the cows, pulled along by the people in spacesuits, went round a corner and went down another corridor that was the same as all the other corridors, and the girl followed behind them and she suddenly had a thought: she remembered something they had said about in school, she remembered that there *were* farms where they kept all the cows inside and they were the farms where they milked the cows to get all the milk that filled up the bottles of milk that the milkman delivered to the houses every day; and they milked these cows indoors because it was easier to do it that way when you had a lot of cows and a lot of bottles that needed filling up with milk. Yes, so this must be a cow-milking farm and the sad-looking man was one of the cow-milkers and that meant he *did* keep his friends here because he was friends with all the cows!

And the girl was happy because it would be nice to see the cows being milked and maybe they would let her have a go, even though she wasn't wearing one of the spacesuits with green wellies that cow-milkers are supposed to wear.

But then the girl started to smell another smell on top of the cow-smell and it was a bad smell and it wasn't right at all; it was the like the smell you got when you were walking past a butcher's shop, only it was much worse than that, much worse and getting worser; and it got so bad it was starting to make the girl feel queasy. The cows were being led through a big door further down the corridor and it was from that door that the horrible butcher's shop smell was coming from. And there were sounds coming through the big door as well, sounds like sawing and chopping and hammering like you heard coming from a building site or a carpenter's yard.

And the girl started to feel scared. She didn't know why she felt scared, she just felt that something was not right, something about the smell and the noises just wasn't right. And it looked like the cows were feeling scared as well, because some of them were making noises and trying to walk backwards away from the big door so that the people in the spacesuits were having to really pull hard on the ropes attached to the cows and make them go in through the door even though they didn't want to. And when the last of the cows had been dragged through the door the girl followed them to see what was happening, even though part of her didn't want to because the butcher's shop smell was so strong it was making her feel sick and she was feeling more and more scared.

But the girl forced herself and she went in through the door and straight into a living nightmare that was worse than the worst bad dream she'd ever had.

It was a great big room, and here were lots of the people in spacesuits, and they were killing all the cows and cutting them up into pieces. The cows that had just come in were being shot in the head with a big gun; the gun would make a noise and the cow would just fall over on its side, and there were people tearing the skin off the cows and there were people cutting them up with saws and people who were hanging the bits of cow on hooks attached to chains that lifted them up in the air—and there was blood everywhere, blood all over the spacemen's spacesuits and their green wellies, blood all over the bits of cow and the cow skins hanging from the hooks, and the floor was just one big pool of blood and people with hoses were trying to wash the blood away but there was just too much of it.

And the girl started to scream; clawed hands clamped to the sides of her head, she started to scream, and she screamed and screamed and she kept on screaming, and the people in the spacesuits turned round and looked at her and the girl saw that one of them was the sad-looking man—only he wasn't looking sad right now, because instead he was looking completely horrified.

PART ONE
Chapter One
Introducing Rogue Males

The girl, a ten-year-old with dark brown twin-tails, polychromatic in t-shirt, ruffled skirt, striped stockings and shoes, stands before the climbing frame, into looking into the camera. Behind the girl and the geometric angles of the climbing frame, segments of fence, housetops and pastel grey sky can be seen. The girl has about her an air of professional composure which belies both her age and her attire. She looks serious, does this girl. She looks very serious. In fact, some might say that she looks *too* serious, and that a girl this young has no business to be looking this serious, and that really she ought to just leave being serious to people who are old enough to know what to do with it.

She begins to speak, and her polished and professional journalistic tone likewise belies her tweenie exterior.

'Hello, I'm Andalusia Seton, reporting from the town of Marchmont. Today we are going to be taking a look at the subject of rogue males...' She begins to walk, and the camera tracks her as, with pensive, measured steps she crosses the playground. 'Yes, rogue males... We have them in our town, you have them in your town, and they have them in every town.' She pauses, swings round to face the camera. 'But just what *are* rogue males?'

'Paedos!'

'Shut up, camerawoman!' snaps the girl, suddenly looking very angry and very unprofessional. 'The camerawoman's not supposed to say anything!'

Another pause.

'Rogue males,' she proceeds, resuming first her composure and then her slow walk, 'are the "outcasts of society,'" (audible quotation marks.) 'They are the grown-up men who live on their own and don't fit in with the normal people around them. And why don't they fit in? Because they're too strange, that's why. Rogue males are the men you see doing their food shopping on weekdays, because rogue males don't have jobs like most normal people do. Some of them are too stupid to have jobs, some of them are too lazy to have jobs, some of them are too smelly to have jobs, and some of them are too annoying to have jobs.' She comes to a halt in front of a seesaw, and again turns to face the camera. 'During the day, you see rogue males walking around the streets a lot, or sitting around on benches. Some of them won't talk to you when you talk to them, some of them will talk to you even if you don't want to talk to them, and some of them just go around talking to themselves. Rogue males haven't got wives or girlfriends—'

'What about the ones who are gay?'

'*They* haven't wives or girlfriends, either. And *shut up*, camerawoman! Rogue males are cut off from society because they're strange. And because they're cut off from society, they spend too much time on their own, and this makes them even more strange. Most rogue males are harmless, but some of them can be dangerous. For example, there are some rogue males who can turn into serial killers, but that mostly only happens in America, and there are some rogue males who can be sexual predators—'

'See? I said they were paedos!'

'*Bryony!* For the last time: will you SHUT UP!' Another pause and a deep breath for recovery of journalistic equilibrium. 'So, now we have a basic idea of what rogue males are; and in this video proj—in this *documentary*,' (carefully pronounced) 'we are going to be taking a closer look at some of the rogue males here in Marchmont. We shall be going out onto the streets and hopefully we will be able to catch sight of some of these rogue males, and have a chance of filming them in their natural habitat as they go about their daily routines.'

A pause. The girl relaxes her posture. 'Okay: cut! And in future, Bryony, keep your big mouth shut when we're recording!'

The Seton sisters. Andalusia Seton, our budding news reporter, being a ten-year-old is the eldest. Then there is Bryony, who's eight. The youngest, Carli, is just three.

An unusual name, Andalusia. But it wasn't just on a whim that her mother named her after this autonomous region of Spain: no, because it was there that she had met the girl's biological father. ('Mum named me Andalusia cuz that's where I was born!' 'Well, you weren't exactly *born* there...')

Most people just call her Andi.

Bryony Seton, tweenily dressed like her sister, wears a vest top, jeans and sandals, all brightly coloured. Her long hair, of the same dark brown shade as her sister's, is tied in ponytail. In spite of being two years younger, she's almost as tall as Andi and the two girls are often mistaken for being the same age. Bryony's features are sharper than Andi's and they possess a certain sardonic slyness. At least they do in moments like the present one when she's being herself. But there are other times when Bryony is not really being herself, and on those occasions, her features do not express very much at all.

Little Carli Seton, her hair in braids adorned with ribbons, wears a white frock with puffed sleeves, white socks and black buckle shoes. Now, judging by the fact that Carli is visibly at least fifty percent Afro-Caribbean, you might hazard a guess that Carli is adopted or that perhaps the three girls are just half-sisters—but you would be wrong on both counts. Their mum, Josephine Seton of this parish, gave birth to all three of the girls and she does not recognise the term *half*-sister. ('You all came out of my tummy, so you're all my daughters and you're each other's sisters. And if any teacher at school starts telling you you're only half-sisters, tell me about it and I'll bloody well tell *them* a thing or two!') A plain-spoken woman, is the Seton matriarch. The girls' biological fathers (they have one each) Jo Seton looks upon as merely sperm-donors, and all of them being out of the picture, she has raised her daughters to consider themselves as not having 'dads', as being essentially 'dadless.'

The three girls occupy a small play area, a gravelled enclosure with the usual gaudy swings, climbing frames, slides and springers. They currently have the place to themselves.

'So, what's the plan?' asks Bryony, sitting on the roundabout, with a video camera cradled in her hand, focussing on—although not recording—Andi, who is perched high on the jungle gym. Little Carli noisily amuses herself riding one of the springers.

'The plan,' replies Andi, 'is that first we record the intro that I've written, and then we go out and start looking for rogue males to film.'

'And what do we do when we find one?'

'We follow him and film him.'

'And what do we do if he sees us filming him and gets really angry with us?'

'Well, then we just run away, don't we?'

'Run away! Run away!' cries little Carli on her springer. (And no, she's not intentionally quoting Monty Python, she just has a tendency to repeat things other people say.)

Bryony ranges the video camera around the play area. 'We should go to the swimming pool…' she says.

'What for?' demands Andi. 'We won't find any rogue males at the swimming pool, stupid! Rogue males don't go swimming!'

'Yeah, but we could film in the changing rooms,' says Bryony, displaying a salacious toothy grin that ill-fits her tender years. 'Lots of naked women in the showers!' chuckling.

'Pervert!' cries Andi. ('Pervert! Pervert! Pervert!' comes her echo across the playground.) 'What you're thinking of is just what a rogue male would do! At least they would if they could get into the women's changing rooms.'

'They'd have to drag up to do that!' chuckles Bryony.

She walks up to the climbing frame and squatting down, aims the camera upwards at her sister.

Andi surveys her from her lofty eminence. 'What are you doing now?'

'Up-skirting you.'

'Well don't! That's illegal as well!' exclaims Andi. 'You always want to do illegal things, you do,' she says, climbing down from the climbing frame.

'I'm just getting used to using the camera,' explains Bryony.

'Well get used to using it doing things that aren't illegal,' instructs Andi.

'Like what?' asks Bryony.

Andi points across to the playground at Carli on the springer.

'What about Carli? Why don't you film her doing something?'

'Like what?'

'I don't know... dancing! Yeah, film her dancing!'

'Good idea! Hey, Carli!' calls out Bryony. 'Do you want to do your dance for the camera? You know: that dance you do to the Taylor Swift song!'

The little girl springs from the springer. 'Yay!' she exclaims, all enthusiasm. 'Film me dancing! Film me dancing!'

'Go on, then,' says Bryony. 'Do your dance.'

'I need the song first!' cries Carli. 'Can't dance without the song!'

'Hang on a minute,' says Andi. She gets out her

smartphone. 'I've got the song on my phone…'

Carli takes up position.

'Are you ready?' asks Andi.

She starts the song playing, and Carli begins her well-rehearsed dance routine. Bryony keeps the video camera trained on the girl, following her movements as she dances her dance.

The song ends, the dance with it.

'Cool! Nice one, Carli!' cheers Andi, clapping her hands.

'Yay!' Carli runs up to Bryony. 'Show me, show me! I wanna see *me* on the little screen!'

'See you on the little screen?' echoes Bryony, affecting puzzlement.

'My dance! Show it on the little screen!'

Now enlightenment is acted out. 'Ohhh! I get what you mean; but I can't do that, can I? I wasn't *recording* you; I was just looking at you through the viewfinder, so I can get used to using the camera!'

At this news Little Carli erupts like a small volcano, spewing tears and howls of rage.

'Oh, Bryony! You're *mean*,' declares Andi.

'You said you'd film me!' storms Carli. 'You promised you'd film me!'

'No, I *didn't* say I'd film!' retorts Bryony, truthfully enough (in words if not in spirit.)

'You did!'

'I didn't.'

'Did!'

'Didn't.'

'Did, did, did!'

'Didn't, didn't, didn't.'

'Pack it in, you two!' comes the voice of authority. 'We'll make a proper film of you dancing later, Carli; but right now we're supposed to be making a serious documentary!'

It's the first day of the Easter holidays, a sunny afternoon, and Andi's class at school have been given the assignment of making a video diary on a topic of their own choosing over the holidays. Now, it's a safe bet that most of the students' video diaries will be on the subject of such things as pet hamsters and the building of rock gardens—but not Andi. Andi has conceived a project that is on a much grander scale than those of her classmates: Andi has been inspired to embark on her grand documentary film entitled *Rogue Males*.

And in conceiving this grand design Andi has been motivated by much more than just the commendable desire to outdo her classmates: she has much loftier goals than just that. Because, as you will not be surprised to hear in the case of a girl so full of seriousness as this one, Andi already has her whole future life mapped out, and her ambition is to become a crusading television news reporter like her idol Jakarta Sunday (the one you always see dodging bullets on the BBC News), and Andi believes that this school holiday assignment will be the perfect opportunity for her to show the world what sort of stuff she's made of.

The class has been told to use their smartphones for making their video diaries, but this method just isn't going to be good enough for Andi and her grandiose scheme; she wants her film to look professional, and you can't look professional with a smartphone. Fortunately, her mum happens to possess a digital camcorder and, keen to encourage her daughter's career aspirations, she has granted her daughter the use of it during the holidays (with the proviso that if she breaks the thing, it's coming out of her allowance.)

And as Andi can't stand in front of the camera and behind it at the same time, she has enlisted the help of her sister Bryony as camerawoman. (And Carli is here because Mum's at work and they have to look after her.)

'Okay,' says Andi, 'let's start filming the intro. I'll stand over there by the climbing frame, and you start filming me, and I'm thinking… yeah, while I'm talking, I'll start walking along and you…'

Chapter Two
Dial L for Loser

'It's Mr Flipperty-Flop!'

So it is. It's Mr Flipperty-Flop, and Mr Flipperty-Flop is a Rogue Male.

Flipperty-flopping is how Mr Flipperty-Flop (three lines in and I'm already getting sick of typing those words) moves; Flipperty-flopping is the unique form of ambulation employed by Mr Flipperty-Flop. Flipperty-flopping is how Mr Flipperty-Flop walks; there are no other made-up words to describe it; a suitably silly name for a suitably silly walk.

Many people have tried to emulate Mr Flipperty-Flop's walk; in fact, only to see Mr Flipperty-Flop flipperty-flopping down the street is to become possessed of the urge to copy it; yes, many have tried to flipperty-flop like Mr Flipperty-Flop, but no-one has ever quite mastered the art. For one thing, in order to flipperty-flop with any authenticity, you need to be as fat as Mr Flipperty-Flop, and Mr Flipperty-Flop is very fat; so, if you don't have an excess of flabby stomach, if your stomach doesn't bounce up and down while you walk along, then you're not flipperty-flopping; you may think you are, but you're not.

But it's not just the stomach; you also have to walk with a very particular kind of spring in your stride; a spring that you wouldn't even have expected someone of Mr Flipperty-Flop's weight and dimensions to even be able to carry off. It couldn't be called a jaunty spring, this spring in Mr Flipperty-Flop's stride, because Mr Flipperty-Flop is not what you would call a jaunty fellow; but it is a spring nevertheless.

And it's not just that, either; because while you are walking with this spring in your step and your flabby stomach bouncing, at the same time you have to let your arms flap awkwardly at your sides like you don't really know what to do with them; and on top of that, you also have to have arms that are way too short for your body and make people who see you think of a penguin's flippers. Mr Flipperty-Flop's arms are too short for his body (or else his girth makes them appear so), but yours probably aren't, and this puts you at a further disadvantage when attempting to flipperty-flop.

In fact, I really don't advise you to try it at all—you'll only make a bloody fool of yourself.

'Start filming him!' urgently hisses Andi.

'Okay,' says Bryony, raising the camera. 'I've got him. It's recording.'

'Good! And have you got him in proper focus?'

'Yes, I've got him in proper focus! It does that on its own, doesn't it?'

'Okay. Let's follow him on this side of the road; this is going to be a tracking shot. I'll start doing the commentary.'

They proceed along the street, Bryony with the camera cradled in her hand, Andi walking beside her.

'This is Mr Flipperty-Flop,' begins Andi. 'We see him Flipperty-Flopping along the street. Notice Mr Flipperty-Flop's distinguishing features: he's very fat; he's humongously fat; he's so fat that he appears to be made completely out of blancmange. The only way Mr Flipperty-Flop can walk down the street is by flipperty-flopping; if Mr Flipperty-Flop tried to walk like a normal person, he would just fall down onto the ground and turn into a big wobbly blancmange with arms and legs pointing up in the air. As we can see—what's *she* doing?'

The reason for this self-interruption is clear: little Carli Seton, who, having been temporarily forgotten by the two elder sisters who are supposed to be keeping a close eye on her, has come up behind Mr Flipperty-Flop, and is now following in his footsteps and copying his walk. She's not doing it very well; her walk is more like that of a badly-drilled majorette than anything resembling a *bona fide* flipperty-flop. But the fact that she has ruined the shot is not the main cause for alarm here; the main cause for alarm is that to get to where she now is, Carli must have crossed the road entirely by herself and unsupervised by her sisters—if Mum finds out; she'll kill them!

And the proof of their culpable neglect has been captured on film; immortalised as digital information!

'Cut! Cut!' cries Andi.

They run across the road (which fortunately happens to be a quiet one); Mr Flipperty-Flop has just turned the corner at the end of the street and Carli is about to follow. Andi grabs her by the arm and drags her back.

'You naughty girl!' she thunders. 'You know you're not supposed to cross the road on your own! You're a very bad girl!' And to emphasise the extent of her sister's turpitude, she gives her a good shake.

Carli bursts into tears.

'I just want to be like Mr Flippery-Fop!' she sobs.

'Well, you're not supposed to be like him!' retorts Andi. ''Specially not when we're trying to make a documentary! You ruined the scene!'

Carli continues to cry, little fists vainly trying to staunch the flow from her leaking eyes.

'I'm sorry...!'

'It doesn't *matter*,' sighs Andi, giving her sister a hug. 'We'll just edit you out. But don't cross the road on your own again—and don't tell Mum you did it today!'

'What shall we do about Mr Flipperty-Flop?' asks Bryony.

'Catch up with him,' declares Andi. 'We can still get some more footage.'

The girls catch up with Mr Flipperty-Flop outside the One Stop round the corner. The shop is fronted by a forecourt boasting a couple of trees, a few benches, as well as bins for general waste, mixed recyclables and dog poop. Mr Flipperty-Flop's flipperty-flops to one of the benches and sits down.

The three girls make a beeline to one of the two trees. Hunkered down, Bryony, camera at the ready, pokes her head round one side of the tree, Andi pokes her head round the other side.

Andi resumes her commentary. 'Mr Flipperty-Flop has stopped to take a rest. He has to do this quite a lot because flipperty-flopping along uses up a lot of his energy. While he's not moving around, let's have a look at the plumage of Mr Flipperty-Flop. Like a lot of rogue males, Mr Flipperty-Flop doesn't have any fashion sense, and that's why he always wears these yucky stripey shirts that look like pyjamas. Mr Flipperty-Flop's shirts are so big, it takes a hundred people to sew them, and they can also be used as sails for sailing ships. Underneath the shirt are his trousers; his trousers are grey and have checks and they're very old because they were handed down to him from his great-great-great-*great* granddad. And as you can see, when he sits down, his trousers stop half way down to his ankles, so that we can see his icky brown socks and part of his blancmangy legs.'

A young man with a loud lumberjack shirt and very bad posture walks through the shot.

'Oooh, it's Monkey Boy!' exclaims Andi, watching him pass through the sliding doors into the shop.

Let's meet Monkey Boy.

Monkey Boy is also on Andalusia's list of rogue males, and in common with many of the people who can least afford to maintain such an expensive habit, he's a smoker; so he's come to the One Stop for his usual twenty B&H. But it's interesting that he should invariably choose to go to this particular shop to buy his cigarettes, because it is neither the closest outlet to his place of residence, nor is it the one that boasts the cheapest retail prices.

But there is a reason why Monkey Boy goes into this

shop, and a very cogent one. Monkey Boy goes into this shop because of Haseena. Haseena is the wife of the shop's owner, Mr Mohyedlin, and she sometimes serves at the checkout. Haseena is a Muslim lady, she wears a burka or hijab (Monkey Boy's a bit hazy about which is which), and Monkey Boy is in love with her. Monkey Boy himself is not a Muslim, he's a cynical atheist, but he doesn't consider religion (or lack of it) to be an obstacle where true love is concerned. There's also an age-difference, as Haseena must be at least ten years his senior (Monkey Boy is still in his early twenties), but he doesn't consider age difference an obstacle where true love is concerned, either. And as for her being a married woman, well that's the whole point, isn't it? She's all the more to be pitied because she's married to that surly git Mr Mohyedlin, who undoubtedly treats her like shit, because as Monkey Boy well knows, all these Muslim blokes treat their wives like shit, don't they?

There had been this one occasion when Monkey Boy had gone to his local surgery for a doctor's appointment, to find a Muslim woman (not Haseena) holding a baby and standing right in front of the inner entrance doors, obstructing the way. At first Monkey Boy had been annoyed, and thinking that the woman had chosen a very inconsiderate place to stand and wait, he was about to ask her if she would be good enough to move so that he could get in. But then, on the other side of the glass doors, he espied a man whom he rightly conjectured to be this woman's husband, standing at the end of the queue for the reception desk. And then he realised what must have just happened: the husband, making his wife walk the obligatory five paces behind him or however many it was, had gone and walked in through the surgery door and just let it swing shut right in his wife's face! And she, having her hands full with the baby she was carrying, was unable to open the door! So there she was, just standing there, and the bloody husband hadn't even noticed!

This incident had made a strong impression on Monkey

Boy, and by making use of that popular human pastime of taking an example and turning it into a generalisation, now firmly believes that all of these Islamic husbands treat their wives just as negligently as this one had on that one particular occasion. And therefore convinced that Haseena must be badly treated by her husband, and being in love with the woman, he wants to help her, he wants to save her. Not to actually make her desert her tyrannical and disrespectful husband and fly into his protecting embrace for good and all; no, Monkey Boy would never dream of taking such a liberty; but he would like to offer himself as a refuge, as a safe haven that Haseena can come to whenever she feels the need to escape from her husband—and to exact some harmless but well-deserved revenge on the guy by having lots of steamy and totally guilt-free sex with himself.

Such are Monkey Boy's noble and selfless intentions.

Monkey Boy's problem is how to make all this come about. For one thing, he only ever sees Haseena when she's serving in the shop, and even then her jealous husband's usually lurking around, which makes even striking up a conversation problematic, never mind actually arranging a rendezvous. And for another thing, striking up a conversation can be problematic anyway for Monkey Boy, because he is not all that good at striking up conversations, especially with women he fancies.

Of course, Haseena smiles at him and is very polite whenever she sees him, but then she smiles at and is very polite with all of the customers she serves. So, he doesn't really know how she feels about him, or how he can let her know how he feels about her. Monkey Boy is not much to look at. He's skinny, not very tall, and has tousled (i.e. unmanageable) hair, a very wide mouth and rather bulbous eyes underscored with permanent dark shadows that make him look like a junkie. On top of all that he also has a pair of very noticeable ears which, projecting almost at right-angles from the sides of his head, earn him his nickname.

And as if on purpose to emphasise the simian aspect to the utmost, Monkey Boy also sports a pair of full-length sideburns.

And another thing. Monkey Boy is not very good at smiling. He is aware that, to appear friendly and approachable, and to win people over, it helps things along if you smile at them, and that you smile back when they smile at you. Yes, he knows this; but smiling is something that's more easily said than done for Monkey Boy. You see, when he was younger, Monkey Boy was very shy around people, and his shyness would often manifest itself in the form of this involuntary embarrassed smile that would take up residence on his face whenever he wanted to say something to someone and was nervous about doing so. Now, 'the embarrassed smile,' although common enough amongst the bashful, is an often-misunderstood phenomenon. If a person you're talking to sees you smiling at them for no apparent reason they will often infer that the smile is at their expense; that there is something about their appearance or about whatever it is they are saying to you which you find quietly amusing. Monkey Boy, at length came to realise this fact, and he made the decision to try and cultivate a poker face and thereby get rid of that embarrassed smile of his. And over time he succeeded: he was able to overcome his embarrassed smile, and it would no longer come unbidden to his lips every time he wanted to talk to anyone—but either he succeeded too well, or the wind must have changed direction, because now he has become completely stuck with his poker face; his lineaments have frozen over and now he finds it hard to produce a smile at all, even when he wants to.

At times he wishes he could just get back that embarrassed smile of his younger days—at least it did good service as a greeting. He wants to be able to smile at Haseena. A single smile may not be enough to communicate to her all his honest feelings and altruistic intentions, but at least it would let her know that he's not a completely miserable git.

Today, upon entering the shop, he immediately sees that Haseena is standing at the cash register, as she often is of a weekday afternoon. On the debit side, however, her husband is also on the shopfloor; he espies that scowling, moustachioed face prowling the aisles.

The presence of Mohyedlin immediately puts Monkey Boy off his game and, approaching the counter, he completely forgets the warm, friendly smile of greeting with which he had intended to dazzle Haseena.

There she is: Haseena, her beautiful café au lait countenance and immaculate make-up, framed by that head-covering forming a tight circle from forehead to underjaw. In spite of her customer's doleful aspect, she smiles at him with a display of large, white teeth.

'Hello,' she says.

Ah.

Returning a greeting.

Even when he clears the first one, it's at this second hurdle that Monkey Boy often comes a cropper, and this is because Monkey Boy has not one but two enemies to contend with when it comes to social intercourse: there's not just his face, there's also his voice. Monkey Boy has, or thinks he has, which amounts to the same thing, absolutely no control over the modulation of his voice; and especially when it comes to delivering those common one-word answers like 'hello' and 'thanks': he just never knows exactly how his voice is going to sound until the word has already passed his lips and, beyond recall, has entered the world at large.

'Hello,' he blurts out. Failed! The word comes out cracked and wonky.

'How can I help you?'

'Twenty B&H, please.'

'Of course,' answers Haseena, turning to pull back the

screen door concealing the tobacco products. She doesn't really need to be told; Monkey Boy asks for the same thing every time he comes here. Looking round, Monkey Boys eyes encounter those of Mr Mohyedlin, glaring at him from over the top of a display of dog biscuits. Repelled by this contact, he quickly looks away.

Well, that's it. There's no way he can say anything else to Haseena; not today. He makes his contactless payment, and once more forgetting to smile, mumbles a thank-you and takes his leave.

Dejected, Monkey Boy lights a consolatory cigarette and then sets off homewards, unaware that his footsteps are being dogged (and filmed) by a trio of inquisitive girls.

'Here we have an example of a younger rogue male. His name is Monkey Boy, and he's at the age when most people are going to university or getting their first jobs, but Monkey Boy doesn't do either of those; he prefers to be a rogue male. Mum says he's neat, but he's not, because as you can see, he's very scruffy. Rogue males like Monkey Boy prefer to stay inside their burrows most of the time; that's why they always look nervous when you see them outside. They don't feel safe when they're out of the shelter of their burrows.'

A tabby-cat sits at the end of the driveway of a house. Espying it, Monkey Boy approaches it cautiously, greeting it in a coaxing voice.

'Here we see Monkey Boy trying to make friends with a cat. People like Monkey Boy are not very good at making friends with other people, so they try to be friends with cats instead. Will this cat be his friend?'

No. As if on purpose, the cat waits until Monkey Boy's hand is almost within petting distance, and then it hisses at him, turns and walks unhurriedly away, tail disdainfully raised in a blatant gesture of 'kiss my furry ass!'

'Oh, dear! It seems like this cat doesn't want to be friends with Monkey Boy...! Ah, but here's another one! Perhaps he'll be able to make friends with this cat...?'

No again. The cat ducks under a parked car.

'Oh, dear! Monkey Boy doesn't look like he's good at making friends with cats, as well as people. But he hasn't given up yet! Here's another cat, sitting on that garden wall! Will this cat want to be friends with Monkey Boy...? He approaches cautiously, avoiding direct eye-contact... And now, very slowly he reaches out his hand... The cat has seen him! Raising its head, it looks at the hand coming towards it... What will it do now? Will it let Monkey Boy stroke its fur...? He's almost there... almost...'

Yowling at him, the cat lashes out, scratching his hand.

'Ow! You bastard!'

The cat springs off the wall into the garden and the three sisters erupt into noisy mirth. Monkey Boy looks round, now sees his stalkers for the first time.

'What are you lot doing?' he demands.

'Filming you,' replies Andi, still giggling.

'Well, stop fucking filming me!' blazes Monkey Boy.

'Don't say swear words in front of our little sister!' snaps Andi.

A derisive snort from Monkey Boy. 'Oh, yeah: like your mum doesn't swear much!'

'Mum *doesn't* swear in front of Carli,' retorts Andi. 'Except when she forgets not to.'

'Well, whatever,' says Monkey Boy. 'Just stop pointing that bloody camera at me!'

'We were filming you with the cats,' explains Bryony. 'Cats don't like you, do they?'

'Not all cats!' flares up Monkey Boy, the accusation clearly having touched a sore-spot. 'There's plenty of cats on the estate I get on with! Plenty of 'em!'

'Show us then,' says Andi. 'We'll keep filming you and you can show us some of the cats who like you.'

'You *won't* keep filming me!' retorts Monkey Boy. 'I'm not some bloody clown who's here to entertain you! Clear off you little bleeps!'

So saying, Monkey Boy turns on his heel and stalks purposefully down the street—and as if on purpose to illustrate that he's nobody's clown, he steps on a garden rake.

Now, there are two things that can happen when you step on a rake and the pole springs up to the vertical: it can either hit you in the face or, if you're particularly unlucky and happen to be a man (or a pre-op transexual woman) it can hit you in the testicles.

Monkey Boy, being a man and not known for being especially blessed by lady luck, receives the impact firmly on the lower target.

He staggers, clutching his crotch, giving voice to the time-honoured cry of pain associated with blows to the testicles: that drawn-out cry somewhere between an 'ooh!' and an 'ahhh!'

Naturally, the three girls (heartless swine!) burst into gales of merriment.

'I hope you got that on film!' splutters Andi to Bryony.

'I did, I did!' confirms the latter.

And she's not the only one to have captured the moment. Two grey-haired senior citizens, a man and a woman, the former as tall and lanky as the latter is small and compact, appear from behind a parked car, the latter armed with a video camera.

'Congratulations!' cries the lanky man, all smiles of delight. 'You've just been pranked! Cuz we're the Prankies!'

The three sisters stop laughing.

'Oh, it's *them*,' says Andi, her tone derisive.

The Prankies are notorious in the neighbourhood—two senior citizens, Ted and Hilda by name, who to prove they haven't lost their youthful sense of fun, play practical jokes on people in the street, filming them for their YouTube channel. Jo Seton has a very low opinion of the Prankies, an opinion which has been passed on to her daughters.

'We may be senior citizens, but we're young at heart!' proceeds Ted Pranky. (Another one of their catchphrases.)

'You'll be fucking dead in a minute!' yells Monkey Boy.

Picking up the rake, he swings it at the Prankies, who retreat with cries of indignation and outraged protests at people's inability to take a harmless joke. Jumping onto an electric motorbike parked by the kerb, they accelerate down the street. And after them runs Monkey Boy, rake brandished like the staff of an enraged warrior monk in hot pursuit of the sacrilegious tourists who have just drawn a pair of glasses and a twirly moustache on the statue of Buddha.

'So!'

The exclamation comes from behind the Seton sisters. They turn round. A striking-looking Japanese girl, the same age as Andi, stands surveying them, hands-on-hips. Her thick black hair is cut in a side-parted bob, adorned with a colourful hairclip, framing a face whose expression in its seriousness content vies with Andalusia's, and in the haughtiness department beats her hands down. She wears a colourful tie-dye dress, a cardigan and chunky-soled sandals.

Behind the Japanese girl, two mousey-haired Caucasian girls, identical in clothing and appearance, and as gawkily unprepossessing as the other girl is flawlessly beautiful, stand one on her left, one on her right—and if they have the appearance of being the Japanese girl's lackeys, in this case as least, appearances do not deceive.

The Japanese girl's name is Rinda (actually Linda) Neves, and her minions are Sally and Clare Sawdust. Rinda is a classmate of Andalusia, while the Sawdust Sisters are in the same year but a different class. There are a lot of people who think that Rinda is only half Japanese, but these people are wrong because, although Rinda's mum is indeed married to a white Englishman, he is actually only Rinda's step-dad, Rinda being the product of her mother's previous marriage to a Japanese man. And thus it is from her step-dad that she has acquired her English surname, while her first name Rinda (actually Linda), is an Anglicisation of her Japanese given name Rin, 'r' and the 'l' being considered interchangeable in Japan.

'I saw what you were doing!' proceeds Rinda.

'And what did you see us doing?' asks Andi, unimpressed.

'You were filming the Prankies! Don't deny it! That is the subject of your video project, isn't it? You are making a film about the Prankies!'

'If you say so,' replies Andi airily.

'No, we're—!' begins Carli.

'Shush!' hisses Andi.

'And what's that?' demands Rinda, pointing to the video camera in Bryony's hand.

'It's a video camera,' replies Andi.

'Cheating!' Rinda hurls the word like a pronouncement.

'Cheating? Who's cheating?'

'You are! You are not supposed to be using a video camera!'

'Says who?'

'Our teacher, Miss O'Connor! She said we were to use our *smartphone* cameras!'

'Yeah, but she just said that cuz she knows we've all got smartphones. Not everyone's got a proper film camera, but our mum does have one, and she's letting us use it.'

'Cheating!' insists Rinda. 'Miss O'Connor did not say we could use video cameras for our assignment!'

'She didn't say we couldn't, either!' retorts Andi.

'Well, then *I* am going to use a video camera for *my* video project, also!' announces Rinda.

'Yeah? And where are you going to get one from?'

'My mother! She too has a video camera!'

'Well, use it then; what do I care?'

'And I'm going to make a film about the Prankies—and my film is going to be better than yours!'

'But we're not *doing* a film about—!'

Andi's 'shush!' comes too late this time: Rinda has heard and she is suspicious. She marches up to little Carli and towers over the girl.

'What was that? You're not making a film about the Prankies? Is that what you were going to say?'

'Don't tell her, Carli!' adjures Andi

'Not telling!' says Carli.

'What *are* you making a film about then?' demands Rinda.

'Not telling!'

'Tell me!'

'Not telling! Not telling!'

Frustrated, Rinda now turns her inquisition to a new target, and stands in front of Bryony.

'What is your sister's film about?' she demands.

Bryony doesn't reply. Her features immobile, she stares at the ground. She has pulled down the shutters.

'Well?' pursues Rinda. 'I order you to speak!'

'Leave her alone, you!' snaps Andi.

'Yeah, leave her alone!' echoes Carli.

You might not have guessed it from what you've seen of her up until now, but this sudden and impenetrable silence is quite normal for Bryony; because Bryony suffers from selective mutism. At home, and when just in the company of her sisters, she can express herself freely, as we have witnessed; but at school, or in other formal situations, down comes the shutter. Outside of her family, there are a select few with whom she will talk: a small group of friends at school and a few others beside; but for everyone else she is silent and withdrawn.

Monkey Boy, surprisingly enough, is one of that select few—Rinda Neves is not.

Failing to elicit a response from her, Rinda turns her back on the girl.

'It doesn't matter,' she says; 'because whatever *your* film is about,' fixing her eyes on Andi, '*my* film is going to be a lot better!'

And Rinda flounces off, her two minions falling into step behind her.

Chapter Three
Riot Mum!

Two boots, black, size seven, aggressive with chunky soles and polished toecaps, march purposefully down the street. Inside these size seven boots and providing their motive force, are two size seven feet. Attached to these size seven feet and providing *their* motive force are two shapely legs, cross-hatched with fishnets, the awning over their confluence a belted PVC skirt. Above the belted skirt a svelte torso with pierced navel bridging the interval between it and a black vest-top draped over hillocky breasts. From the shoulders of the torso swing two arms, heavily tattooed, while above them rises a slender neck, adorned with a buckled collar. The neck supports a head, a head surmounted with abundant hair, artificially sky-blue in pigment, lassoed in two fluffy bunches, and between the two bunches a face, amply pierced and painted, agreeable in feature, severe in expression.

Taken in the aggregate, the above components comprise one human female, her height a Caucasian average of five foot six inches, her age difficult to determine with any precision, but if the wrong side of thirty, the error must be of the smallest. Her dress, demeanour and accessories emphatically mark her out as a rock chick, a punk, a riot grrrl. You can almost hear the chainsaw power chords and angry, obscenity-laden vocals of the personal soundtrack that by all rights ought to accompany this woman wherever she goes.

And as she passes through the residential streets of Marchmont, walking with resolute footsteps, you can almost imagine the infants being swept from the pavements by alarmed mothers, and the hasty slamming of doors and window shutters.

And you would have to imagine all this, because nothing of the kind is actually happening. For one thing, this woman is no stranger from parts unknown who has just moseyed into town dragging a coffin behind her: she is a Marchmont resident and a familiar sight whose appearance passes without comment.

'You're a freak, darling!'

Mostly without comment, anyway.

A passing transit van, loutish workman leering from passenger window.

'I'm not your fucking darling, arsehole!' says the woman, raising a mid-digit, black enamelled at the retreating vehicle.

She marches on.

Wolf whistles from the gates of a park.

'How about a quick one behind the bushes, then?'

'Yeah, we'll pay you later!'

She turns to the speakers, a trio of grinning secondary-schoolboys.

'No thanks. I don't offer my services to little babies like you. Go home to your mummies.'

She marches on.

Rounding the corner, a raised voice, angry, threatening, directs the woman's attention across the street. A man, old, bald, but energetic, spitting threats of actual bodily harm at two scared boys. The Lagger, an ex-con and rogue male of notorious temper.

The road swiftly crossed, the woman intervenes, grabs the assailant collarwise, shaking him for good effect.

'You leave them alone, you old git! Don't you lay a finger

on them!'

'They was giving me lip!'

'I don't care what they were doing! Don't go picking on little kids!'

'Gerroff me, fuckin' bitch!'

The woman, complying violently, sends the Lagger stumbling.

'Bitch! Fuckin' whore! Fuckin' have you, I will!' (not in the Biblical sense.)

'Just piss off, you old fart!'

The woman stands guard over the two boys until the venerable flatulent, retreating with impotent threat and imprecation, has micturated out of eyeshot.

She marches on.

Round another corner, rendered blind by leafy quickset, she comes suddenly upon three girls—our heroines no less! in search of rogue males.

'Mum!' exclaimed in ecstatic triplicate.

'Hello, you little troublemakers!'

All smiles, the woman sweeps the girls in eager embrace.

'Come on, then! Let's get you home and Mummy'll make us some lovely din-dins!'

Yes, the big-booted, bad-ass riot grrrl to whom we have just been introduced is actually the mother of our three heroines. If the title of the chapter hadn't given the whole game away, some of you might even have been surprised.

Josephine Seton, Jo to her friends, has just finished her afternoon shift at the local supermarket that is her present place of employment. And if you're thinking that Jo's punk aesthetic might have hindered her from being accepted into such a mainstream establishment as a supermarket, you would be wrong on two counts. For one thing, while Jo is actually on the shopfloor, she wears the supermarket's regulation uniform, so aside from her blue hair and her piercings, she doesn't actually stand out that much. And secondly, and more importantly, her unorthodox appearance actually works in her favour in these days of inclusive employment practices, with subcultural groups now being officially recognised as a discriminated-against minorities.

So let us follow the family back to the Seton domicile, a small semi-detached house in a street of small semi-detached houses, built in the early eighties. The household consists of Jo Seton, her three daughters and a cat. It's a three-bedroom house, so Andi and Bryony share one large bedroom, whilst little Carli occupies the smallest one. The third bedroom is Jo's *sanctum sanctorum* and hard and as such is strictly off-limits to the girls; off-limits at all times, but off-limits most of all first thing in the morning—and not so much because she objects to the possibility of her offspring bursting noisily into her room to wake her up and remind her that it's time for breakfast, but more on account of the fact that she might not necessarily be *alone* in her bed first thing in the morning.

As an added security measure, on the wall of the bedroom hangs a framed chiaroscuro print of Myra Hindley, taken from her famous mugshot—and Myra is a very efficient watchdog.

And before you start ringing up social services, under the assumption that a mother who adorns her *boudoir* with the likeness of a notorious child-murderer has to be a very irresponsible mother, you would be shamefully mistaken, because, and in spite of a few undeniable eccentricities, Jo Seton is the best of mothers, and Setons are the happiest of families.

Dinner this evening is vegetarian—but then dinner at the Seton house is always vegetarian, and always has been, because Jo Seton happens to be a staunch vegetarian, and has been for a very long time. But she also happens to be a fully-trained vegetarian chef, so her dinners are always as tasty as they are healthy, and she never receives any complaints from her hungry offspring.

Jo Seton, as you will not be surprised to hear, is a woman of strong opinions, and one of those strong opinions is her belief that parents should not go around imposing their religious beliefs on their kids. This being the case, is it then right that Jo should be imposing her eating habits on *her* kids? Or, in doing this is she nothing more than a rank hypocrite? Not choosing to venture an opinion of my own on the subject, your impartial narrator can only say that Jo has no problem reconciling this apparent dichotomy with her own conscience, feels not one single pang of guilt on the subject, and if you were foolish enough to try and take her up on it, she would probably just start quoting the Smiths at you.

And so, Mother and daughters are enjoying their evening meal, seated at the dining table in the living- cum dining room of the Seton residence. The room, as you can see, is clean and tidy and this is because Jo, anarchist punk rocker though she may be, likes to keep a neat and tidy house. But in spite of the lack of disorder, clear evidence can be seen of this being a riot grrrl's living room: even before you've got to scrutinising the contents of the CD storage tower, conspicuous on the walls are framed posters of the bands Bikini Kill and the Red Aunts, two American girl bands from the nineties, and Jo's especial favourites. (Technically, the Red Aunts were never a part of the riot grrrl scene, but they were still a girl band and they made the right kind of noise.)

Jo has been asked by her daughters how Bikini Kill can be called a 'girl band' when one of the members is clearly a boy? And Jo has explained that a 'girl band' doesn't necessarily have to be an '*all*-girl band,' and it is acceptable to sometimes have a token male in your band, just to show that you've got at least *some* of the enemy under control and fully housetrained. (And in answer to their query as to what exactly is so red about the Red Aunts, she has had to explain that the band's name is actually an untranslatable pun.)

Mother and daughters sit in friendly converse as they enjoy their evening meal. Bryony has by now shaken off her earlier attack of mutism and contributes to the conversation; the only silent partner is Carli who, too young to multitask, gives her full attention to the business of transferring food from her plate to her mouth.

'They're really going at it next door,' remarks Bryony.

She refers to the sounds of juvenile histrionics coming from the all-too-thin wall that separates the Seton house from the adjacent property.

'And they were throwing stones at Courtney again today!' says Andi. 'We saw them!'

Jo frowns. 'Were they? Little sods!'

'You should tell their mum,' advises Andi, adopting the sage tone of an eldest daughter.

'They've already been told to leave Courtney alone, the little brats,' says Jo. 'If I catch them at it—'

Next door reside the James family, husband and wife and their two sons, Luke and Scott, both pupils at Andi and Bryony's school. The sound of the boys' tantrums has become a familiar background noise in the Seton house, so much so that it often goes unnoticed; but as Bryony has just remarked, the little horrors are in particularly fine form this evening, raging and stamping and shouting defiance at their long-suffering parents.

The Courtney just referred to is fifth member of the Seton household, a fluffy white cat with blue eyes and a pink nose, and the only nonvegetarian in the house. Courtney gets her name from Courtney Love, frontwoman of the nineties girl band Hole, and widow of the legendary Nirvana frontman Kurt Cobain. And does Courtney live up to her name? Well, she's vain, likes to preen herself, is intolerant of contradiction, insists on getting her own way and when angered she is quick to show her claws—but if that's all that's required then *all* cats might as well be called Courtney Love.

'Are Mr and Mrs James bad parents because they can't get them to behave properly?' asks Andi.

Jo, after swallowing a mouthful of cheese and leek kiev: 'No, I think they're just unlucky, really. Some kids can end up being unmanageable even if the mums and dads didn't really do anything wrong. So I suppose that makes me one of the lucky ones, doesn't it? Because I've got three very well-behaved little girls.' And then, surveying them narrowly: 'Well, *mostly* well-behaved.'

The girls chuckle at this.

Asks Andi: 'So Mum, you don't think even *you* could make Luke and Scott behave better?'

'Me? No, I'd soon sort out those little so-and-so's' declares Jo confidently.

'You should go round there and do it, then,' says Bryony. 'Then we could have some peace and quiet around here.'

'Yeah, but they're not my kids, are they? Mr and Mrs James wouldn't thank me for sticking my nose in.'

'They should call in Super Nanny!' says Andi.

'They should have done that years ago,' says Jo.

'Is it cuz they're boys that they're so bad?'

'Well, yeah… boys *can* be more of a handful than girls… But there are girls who can end up being pains in the ar- *bum* to their parents as well…'

'I bet *Rinda*'s a pain in the bum to her mum and dad!' declares Bryony venomously. Her encounter with the girl still rankles.

'Yeah, she acts like everyone's got to be her slaves!'

'Well, her mum's never complained about her to me,' says Jo. 'So maybe she's a good little girl when she's at home. What, did you run into her today?'

'Yeah, she saw us when we were out making our film,' says Andi. 'And now she's saying how she's going to use a video camera as well and make a film that's better than mine!'

Bryony, pulling up the corners of her eyes and sticking

out her overbite: 'Me Rinda Neves, and I show you who best at making film around here! Me make much better film than you, because me Japanese!'

Andi and Carli laugh.

'Bryony!' snaps Jo.

Andi and Carli stop laughing.

'That is *racist!*' continues Jo. 'Pack it in!'

Bryony looks down at her plate.

'But I was only—'

'You shouldn't do things like that! I've told you about that, haven't I? Making fun of somebody just because they're a bit different to you.'

'Yeah, but Rinda was being really mean to Bryony today,' speaks up Andi.

'Was she? What was she doing?'

'Oh, you know, being all bossy, trying to make her talk when she didn't want to…'

Jo sighs, fixing compassionate eyes on her plate-staring daughter. 'Look sweetie, I'm sorry about that, and you can take the piss out of Linda as much as you like, but not the way you were doing it just now.'

'Why not?' sulkily.

'Because, if a Japanese person saw you doing it, they'd think you were taking the piss out of *all* Japanese people, wouldn't they?'

'But I wasn't *doing it* in front of any Japanese people.'

'Yes, but that—' Jo breaks off, heaves another sigh. It occurs to her that there is an episode of Father Ted it would be very instructive for her daughter to watch this evening.

Chapter Four
Nocturnal Negotiations

'Ugh, another Christian! Why are the black women always Christians?'
Click.
'Oh, don't say you're looking for your partner in crime!'
Click.
'And don't say you're still not over the ending of Game of Thrones!'
Click.
' "Looking for a man who's got his shit together." Well, well; aren't we the picky one?'
Click.
'Yeurrgh! Tory! Fuck off!'
Click.
' "Looking for a real gentleman"? Yeah, news flash, love: only men who still call themselves "gentlemen" in this day and age are the fucking male supremacists!'
Click.
'No, you are not "curvy," you are "fat"!'
Click.
'Oh...! It's always the same: whenever there's two people in the main profile picture, it's always the one you don't want it to be!'
Click.
'No, I don't want to follow you on Instagram!'
Click.
'And I'm not going to be your passport into England!'
Click.
'And I'm not here to read your stupid self-published novel, either!'
Click.
'What the hell do you want kids for? They won't exactly thank you for bringing them into a doomed planet, will

they?'
Click.
'And what sane person prefers dogs to cats?'
Click.
'Oh, put 'em away, love!'
Click.
'Not with that hair!'
Click.
'Not that with that nose!'
Click.
'Not with those furs!'
Click.
'Oooh! She looks nice!'
Click.
'Arrgghhh! I don't believe it! I just clicked on pass! Oh, fuck, fuck, fuck!'

An uncomfortable room.

Uncomfortable for the two people standing in it; an uncomfortable silent moment after an agreement has been uncomfortably made. The two people in the uncomfortable room are a middle-aged man and a teenage girl. The man, bifocaled, whose length of face is enhanced by a baldness which likewise throws into relief a trouble-furrowed brow, has about him the aspect of a dedicated scholar for whom the troubles of the here and now are an unwelcome intrusion. The uncomfortable room is clearly his sanctum. Well-filled bookcases, a table piled with a jumble of papers and open books, a venerable map of the world framed upon the wall; a computer workstation the inevitable modern note.

The man's muted tints of the man's clothing blend with the surroundings. The girl's clothes, the fluffy white jacket, purple jeans and high-heeled sandals clash with the room, but not with the wearer: trim-figured, radiant good looks and long blonde hair, fashionably styled. And for her age this girl is no mean scholar herself, and popular at school as much for her academic record as her good looks. (Even eager-eyed adolescent boys are sapiosexual enough to despise a girl who's stupid.) We don't see her at her best right now, brows knit, half angry, half guilty.

The room's uncomfortable silence is now broken by the man.

'This can't go on, Milly,' he says, his voice pitched in an urgent whisper, fearful of being heard beyond the uncomfortable confines of the room. 'It's not fair; it's just not fair.'

The girl, Milly, scowls, her eyes shoot arrows into his. 'You can't say that,' replies she, the words confined in an overpacked *soto voce* in imminent threat of bursting open. 'You can't say what's fair and not fair. You've got no right to say things like that.'

'I *know* all that,' says the man. 'But it's becoming more and more difficult; and it would be just as bad for you as it would be for me if—'

The door opens.

'Oh, *there* you both are!' The woman standing on the threshold, of middle years, short and stout, with permed dark hair, directs a questioning smile at them. 'Why have you hidden yourselves in here?'

'Oh, I was just giving Milly some help with her history homework,' is the man's ready answer. He laughs. 'Only reason we ever see our niece these days!'

'Well, you are the expert, aren't you?' agrees Milly, laughing.

A family group: aunt and uncle and niece. Does the intruder into the uncomfortable room sense the prevailing discomfort, or is she oblivious? On the one hand it seems unlikely that anyone could lack the perspicuity to read a room as legible as this one, but on the other I have actually known people who have managed to make it all the way through *American Psycho* without realising that they were dealing with an unreliable narrator; so anything's possible.

'And what are you studying in history at the moment?' asks her aunt.

'Oh, it's the industrial revolution,' answers Milly, truthfully enough.

'Yes, I was just setting Milly straight about the corn laws,' confirms her uncle.

'Pretty boring stuff they're making you learn there, isn't it?'

'Tell me about it,' and 'Well, it was an important time in this country's history,' are the simultaneous replies.

'Well, I'd better be going now,' says Milly, snatching a glance at inner wrist. She moves towards the door.

'Going already?' says her aunt, standing aside for her. 'Don't you want a cup of tea?'

'No, I'm alright, ta. Better be getting home!' Out of the study, Milly crosses the hall to the front door, slowly followed by aunt and uncle. 'Well, see ya, then!'

Crunching down the drive, Milly turns back to the half-timbered demesne to see her aunt still standing in the illuminated rectangle of the doorway. She is not smiling and nor does she respond to Milly's half-hearted wave.

With uncomfortable feelings as to her aunt's room-reading literacy, Milly bends her steps homewards.

Who is this Milly Leeson, and why have we been introduced to her? She is clearly too old to be a classmate of even the eldest of the Seton sisters, and even more clearly, she is not one of our rogue males. Very true, but nevertheless there is a connection, because Milly happens to be the Setons' regular babysitter. A tenuous enough connection you may argue, but this story is basically telling itself, and Milly's participation is demanded.

Milly makes her way through the lamplit streets of Marchmont town centre, full of her own thoughts, so much so that she doesn't espy her schoolfriend Nicki until she literally bumps into the girl.

'Whoops! Sorry—oh, hi Nicki! What's up?'

'What do you mean what's up?' snaps Nicki. 'Who says anything's up? God, you're nosey!'

'Yeah, but I was just—'

'Oh, you were, were you? Well, who says I'm going anywhere? I was just walking down the street, wasn't I? Same as you. I can walk down the street if I want to, can't I? It's not your street, is it? You don't own it, do you? And I don't go around asking you where you're going, do I? No, cuz I'm not a nosey cow like you are. So why don't you just stop sticking your nose in where it's not wanted and mind your own bloody business? And *don't* follow me, either!'

And having just delivered this breathless tirade (the punctuation is mine, not hers), Nicki marches off, leaving Milly momentarily stunned.

And then, and perhaps inevitably all things considered, she starts to follow the other girl. If Nicki's outburst had been typical of the girl, Milly might not have given it much thought, but the outburst being decidedly *not* typical, Milly's curiosity has been piqued.

Nicki disappears round a corner, and Milly, hurrying to catch up, rounds the corner herself just in time to see Nicki climb into the passenger seat of a car drawn up at the kerb. The door slams and the car drives off.

The vehicle is not one that Milly recognises, but she *does* know what kind of car Nicki's mum and dad drive and that car was not it.

Milly bends her steps homewards once more and this time her thoughts are not of herself. Normally, the first thing she would have done on seeing what she'd just seen would have been to whip out her phone and text a few friends to tell them about it and trade juicy speculation as to who, what, where, etc—but on this occasion she decides, for now at least, to keep her information to herself.

She arrives home to a house much more modest than that of her aunt and uncle, one of a terrace. A further surprise awaits her as she lets herself in through the front door.

'Is that you, Milly? Can you come in here a minute, sweetie?'

Milly scowls. Her mum, calling her from the living room. Her mum calling her in a suspiciously friendly voice and with the even more suspicious use of the endearment 'sweetie.'

Wondering what bombshell lies in wait for her, Milly walks into the living room. Anticipating unwelcome news, she finds instead an unwelcome guest: as unexpected as he is unwelcome, a boy her own age, sits awkwardly in one of the armchairs, awkwardly holding a mug of tea on his clasped knees.

'Isn't this nice, dear?' says her mum. 'A friend from school here to see you.'

His name is Paul Straker and does indeed attend the same school as her; but a friend of Milly's he is most emphatically *not*, because, and in spite of having a name that would suit a television spy, and not actually being that bad-looking either, Paul is one of the loser fanboy crowd—and Milly would not be seen dead hanging out with any fanboy.

Paul has obviously been here for some time; long enough for her mum to make him tea and put him at his ease. Paul is one of those shy boys, bashful around girls, nervous with strangers.

'H-hello, Milly…!'

'Hey, Paul. What're you doing here?'

'He's come to see you, of course,' replies Mum. 'Sit down, dear. Paul's been telling me about this new sci-fi series on Prime—what's it called again?'

'*The Rings of Antares*,' says Paul.

'Never heard of it,' says Milly, reluctantly taking a seat.

'Oh, but it sounds really good,' says Mum. 'It's about a planet with all these ring things spinning round it—'

'Ringworlds,' supplies Paul.

'That's it. All these ringworlds. But only the rich people get to live up on the rings, and everyone else has to live down on the planet itself, which is this lawless toxic wasteland. And there's this bunch of rebels, aren't there?'

'Yes, they're called Steppenwolf, and they've got this base out in the wasteland and they're being hunted by mercenaries because the oligarchs up on the ringworlds have put a price on their heads—'

'I'm not really into science fiction,' cuts in Milly.

'Yes, but this series sounds very good, I think,' says Mum. 'Not like *Star Wars* or *Star Trek*,' and then, to Paul, in a mock-confidential tone: 'Milly's your typical teenage girl: it has to be horror: horror films, horror novels. Stephen King's her favourite. God, we were all reading him when back *I* was at school! Some things never change, do they?'

Paul turns to Milly, blurting out: 'You know, some of Stephen King's books are actually science fiction—!'

'Stephen King's horror,' says Milly flatly.

'Yeah, but some of his books, like *It*—'

'*It* is horror.'

'Yeah, but the monster in *It* is an alien! It came down from space, didn't it? So you could also say it's a science fiction nov—'

'Stephen King is *horror!*' repeats Milly.

'Well, I think Paul's got a point there, sweetie' says Mum. 'If there's an alien in the story then it qualifies as science fiction. And anyway, doesn't Stephen King himself not want his books being labelled horror these days?'

'Then Stephen King's a fucking idiot,' growls Milly.

Her Mum smiles wryly. 'Well, that's a nice way to talk about your favourite author, Miss Potty Mouth.'

'I'm just saying his books are *horror*.'

And so on...

The English language has many words to describe a bloody fool.

There's idiot, nincompoop, nimrod, ditz, dunderhead, dumbass, dunce, dummy, dolt, dimwit, imbecile, halfwit, arsewit, fuckwit, cretin, clown, clod, chump, chowderhead, buffoon, berk, jerk, jackass, goofball, goon, tit, twat, turkey; a whole lexicon of terms of abuse from synonyms to colloquialisms to proper nouns.

The Japanese language, on the other hand, being more succinct, has just the one, handy, one-size-fits-all word *baka*.

It is a word that frequently comes to the mind of Yukari Neves when thinking of her husband (because although being fluent in the English language, she still tends to think in her native Japanese.)

Yukari has come to the unavoidable conclusion that Peter Neves, the man she married, not *officially* for better or worse (it was a registry office ceremony), is *baka*; or, to use the English equivalent which most aptly expresses Yukari's feelings, a bloody fool.

One of the foolish things he does is that he always blurts out the first stupid thing that comes into his head, and it will invariably be something that's completely tactless towards whoever he happens to be talking to at the time. You have the people who find words with which to clothe their thoughts, and then you have the people who will just shove them out through the door stark naked...

Another foolish thing about Peter is his jokes: he's always making jokes at his own expense, jokes that have people laughing *at* him instead of *with* him. By making himself look stupid like this in company he embarrasses not only himself, but by association he embarrasses *her* as well!

And if that wasn't bad enough, in addition to his own material, he insists on spouting secondhand humour: quoting funny lines from things he's seen on TV; and as anyone on the receiving end of this kind of humour can tell you, jokes just somehow do not seem as funny when they come bracketed with quotation marks.

And so, Yukari has had to face facts, and to acknowledge, if only to her own private self, this undeniable truth: her husband is a bloody fool. Initially she had just thought that Peter was funny, and comparing him to her dour first husband left behind in Japan, she had liked the fact that he was funny. She had also liked the fact that he was good at making her daughter laugh as well, and it had been fine when it was just the three of them.

But just bring him out in public and put him in a room with a lot of other people and it's time to bring out the 'deeply embarrassed' emoji.

She looks sideways at him now, as he sits engrossed with the television programme they are watching, with that childlike expression of rapt attention she has come to know. He's a handsome enough man, with his clean-shaven boyish good looks, those ingenuous *gaijin* features…

Westerners always talk about the 'inscrutable' Oriental, but from Yukari's Asian perspective, it's the reverse that is the problem: that it's the *gaijin* who are just way too scrutable by half—*embarrassing* scrutable. In Yukari's estimation, hearts should *not* be worn on sleeves, or at least if worn at all, should only be brought out on special occasions and when appropriate.

Well, for better or worse… And it's not like she would leave him… You don't leave someone just because they're a bloody fool… Leaving him would leave him high and dry. He's basically a child and the mother in her feels a sense of responsibility towards him.

Which brings Yukari second problem in her life at the moment; which problem, being ambulatory, chooses this moment to walk into the room, placing itself between *The Rings of Antares* and the couple on the sofa.

Her daughter Rin.

'Where is the video camera, Mum?' she asks without preamble. 'I can't find it.'

'What do you want the video camera for?' inquires Yukari.

'I need it for the film I've got to make for my homework

project,' replies Rinda.

The resemblance between mother and daughter grows more distinct as Rinda advances in years. Her face more oval in shape than her daughter's, the lineaments that are only softly sketched on Rinda's countenance are, on the mother's fully defined; gentle features that have about them a somewhat careworn look, while discernible amongst her long raven tresses, loosely tied at the nape, shines an occasional comet tail of silver.

'You can use the camera in your phone for that,' says Yukari. 'You don't need the video camera for that.'

'But I *want* to use the video camera, Mum!' with a verbal stamp of the foot. 'You can make a better film with a video camera. This is very important.'

'No. You'll only drop the camera and break it. Just use your smartphone. That's what everybody else is doing.'

'That is *not* what everybody else is doing!' with another verbal stamp. 'I saw Andalusia Seton today, and *she* was using a video camera to make her film. *Her* mum let her use hers.'

'I don't care what Andalusia's mother allowed her daughter to do. I am not letting you use my video camera. You'll drop it and break it.'

'Oh, let her use it!' breaks in Peter the peacemaker. 'You won't drop it, will you, sweetie?'

'No, I won't drop it, Daddy!' says Rinda eagerly. 'I will be very, very careful with it!'

'There! You see!' says Peter, turning his (now infuriatingly) ingenuous face to Yukari. 'She won't drop it! And she'll be able to make a better film with the camera than just using her phone!'

'No,' says Yukari firmly. 'It's my video camera and I don't want Linda using it.'

'Well, in that case,' whipping out his smartphone, 'how about I buy you a brand-new video camera of your own, hey sweetie? It can be an early birthday present from me to you!'

'It was her birthday two months ago!' snaps Yukari.

'Alright then, a *late* birthday present.'

'Oh, yes please, Daddy! Do buy me a video camera and then I won't have to use Mum's!'

'One video camera coming up! Let's see...' scrolling down the page. 'Here we go... recommended products... Ah, this one's on offer...! And *yes*, we've still got time for next day delivery...! There! All done! It's on its way!'

Rinda leaps into her step-father's lap, throwing her arms around him and kissing him noisily. 'Oh, thank you, Daddy! Thank you, thank you, thank you!'

And, hugging his step-daughter, Peter grins at Yukari with the complacent and praise-seeking grin of someone who believes he has successfully resolved a situation to the satisfaction of everyone concerned.

Baka!

Chapter Five
Estate of Decay

'Good morning. Today we're reporting live from the Belton Estate—'

'It's not really *live*, is it?'

'Of course it's live! We're here and it's right now, aren't we?'

'Yeah, but by the time people get to see this it won't be right now, it'll be the week after next. So it won't be live then, will it?'

'Hm... Yes, I suppose you've got a point there... Okay, let's start again. Cut!'

'Good morning. Today we're reporting from the Belton Estate, here in Marchmont. The Belton Estate is a big estate of council houses and council flats that was first built a long time ago in the 1970s—'

'Even before Mum was born!'

'Even before—will you shut up! The camerawoman isn't supposed to speak! Where was I...? Oh, yes: built a long time ago in the 1970s, but they didn't build it very well, and that's why you always see lots of workmen here putting scaffolding around the houses to stop them from falling down. This is probably because they used the same cement that they used to build all those schools that are starting to fall down. The houses and flats on the estate are built in big squares with grass in the middle, like this one we are walking through now, and as you can see, they all look exactly the same: the same yellow bricks for the walls, the same grey tiles for the roofs, the same shaped windows and the same colour front doors. Between these big squares of houses that all look the same, there are smaller squares of houses with smaller bits of grass that also all look the same, and the squares are all attached to each other by these passageways, and sometimes the passageways lead to little roads that are all connected to each other and a lot of them end in dead ends—so this means it can be very easy to get lost on the Belton Estate if you don't know your way around.

'The Belton Estate is most famous for hosting the famous Belton Estate Riots, which happened in the 1990s. Because of the Belton Estate Riots, Marchmont actually got onto the national television news, so that's something we can all be proud of. But we're not here to celebrate that today! No, because the Belton Estate is also the place where a lot of rogue males live, and it's a nice sunny morning, so conditions are perfect for us to observe some rogue males in their natural habitat.'

'And even better, we don't have to look after Carli today!'

'And even better, we don't—*shut up*, camerawoman!'

'What if we don't find any?' inquires Bryony.

'We *will* find some,' is the confident reply. 'Rogue males

always come out during the day. They do their shopping during the day, don't they? And even when they don't need to go to the shops, they do things like walking around and sitting on benches and things.'

At present there are no signs of rogue male activity or any activity at all. The two girls make their way from silent court to silent court, two brightly-coloured spots against the monotonous urban landscape. Andi is sporting a crop top and denim skirt, while Bryony, who doesn't like skirts, wears flared jeans and a pink t-shirt emblazoned with the winking face of a cartoon girl.

Andi's news reporting instincts are all fired up today. She's going to make a super-fantastic video documentary and when they see it at school it's going to blow everyone away! Everyone will say that Andi's a born reporter! And then, when she's a grown-up, she's going to be a roving news reporter like her idol Jakarta Sunday, and go reporting around the world.

Andi prides herself on always watching the evening news with Mum. Her sisters don't, because Carli's too young for the news to be suitable viewing material and Bryony just thinks it's boring. For that matter, most girls of Andi's age still think that the news is boring, but Andi is precocious, and this diet of current affairs she has imbibed probably accounts for that abundance of seriousness of which she is possessed.

True, there have occurred a few misconceptions along the way, about which her mum has had to step in and set her straight: for instance, there was that misunderstanding as to the meaning of the word femicide, and that it is in fact *not* a gas that only kills women; then there was that other one regarding precisely which species of primate takes part in guerilla warfare….

Mum is always especially interested in the stories about women around the world because, says Mum, a lot more bad things happen to the women than happen to the men. And

Jakarta Sunday thinks this as well, which is why she always goes to those places where bad things are happening to women, so she can tell the world about them.

But to become a globe-trotting news reporter you have to work your way up. You have to be national before you can be international, and you have to be local before you can be national.

'Bzzzzzzzz... Bzzzzzzzz...'

'Shh! Listen!' says Andi, stopping in her tracks.

'Bzzzzzzzz... Bzzzzzzzz...'

'What? It's just someone using a hedge trimmer.'

'It's *not* a hedge trimmer!'

'Bzzzzzzzz... Bzzzzzzzz...'

'What is it, then?'

'It's Antenna Head, that's what it is! Come on!'

They track the sound to an adjacent court. A man, wearing a filthy white lab coat, is making his way along the footpath ahead of them, moving with jerky, mechanical steps while all the time emitting that 'Bzzzzzzzz... Bzzzzzzzz...' sound between his teeth. On the man's head is a red baseball cap and from the summit of the baseball cap rises an antenna which looks like a smaller version of a traditional rooftop television aerial. The antenna remains surprisingly rigid as the man robot-walks along; a fact which has given rise to the suspicion that the shaft of the aerial actually pierces not only its wearer's baseball cap but also his skull, thereby directly interfacing with his brain.

'See, it's him! I knew it!' stage-whispers Andi. 'Come on: you start filming and I'll do the commentary.'

Stealthily, they creep up behind Antenna Head, Bryony with camera raised. But in spite of their caution, their quarry suddenly stops in his tracks, his body becoming rigid, like an animal that has scented danger. And now he spins round, transfixing the two girls with the enhanced gaze of a pair of magnifying goggles. The buzzing lenses rotate, extending and retracting as they focus on their target.

'What are you two doing?' demands Antenna Head.

Caught in the act by the subject they are filming! What was it Andi had said they should do in this event? Yes: run away! And her first instinct is to do just that—but then her reporter's instincts kick in and come up with a better plan: interview the bastard!

'Ah, good morning!' she says. 'We're making a video documentary about rogue—about interesting people who live around here, and we think you're very interesting, Antenna Head. So, we were wondering if we could do a brief interview with you, for our documentary…?'

'What's this documentary for?' asks Antenna Head suspiciously. 'I mean, who's going to see it?'

'My class at school.'

'School? Oh, I see. For educational purposes. Hmm. Yes, I don't mind doing an interview if it's for educational purposes. Go ahead: what do you want to ask me about?'

'Well, my first question is why do you have that antenna on your head?'

'For picking up signals, of course! Why else would anyone have an antenna on their head? Next question!'

'What kind of signals does your antenna pick up?'

'All of them! This antenna of mine can pick up everything! Audio, visual, analogue, digital: everything! They're all around us, you know! Everywhere!' spreading his arms wide. 'The air's full of them! Saturated! All these signals flying around! Most people can't see them, but I can! I can see them!' tapping his goggles. 'And I can hear them, as well! I can hear the sound of them buzzing in my ears! Buzzing, buzzing, all the time! Bzzzzzzzz… Bzzzzzzz…'

'That's because you keep saying "buzz buzz" all the time,' mutters Bryony.

Antenna Head ignores this. 'It's the memes, you see? They're the ones behind it all!' he declares. 'The memes are the ones behind all the signals! And do you know what memes are? Of course you don't! People are always spelling memes with an e these days, but it should be spelt with an i! An i! The same spelling as mimes! But just because people used to keep mispronouncing memes as mimes, they had to start spelling it phonetically with an e! But it should be an i! An i, I tell you!'

(What Antenna Head has just said about the spelling of meme is actually true, but for clarity's sake your narrator is going to stick to the popular spelling.)

'What are memes, then?' inquires Andi. 'Are they like aliens or something?'

'Aliens! Ha! Aliens, she says…! Well, yes, now that you mention it, they might be aliens…' For a moment he pauses, digesting the idea. But then: 'But that's not the point, is it? Instead of asking what the memes *are*, you should be asking what they're up to!'

'What are the memes up to?'

'Excellent question! So, you want to know what they're up to, do you? You want to know what the memes are up to… Well, I'll tell you what they're up to! They want to turn us all into a singularity! That's they're plan! A singularity! The whole world! The entire human race! That's the goal they've been working towards; ever since the day Marconi invented radio! He was the one who did it! He was the one who opened the door and let them in! It was Marconi! The fool! The meddling, irresponsible fool!'

Antenna Head clutches the sides of his head. 'Argh! The Buzzing in my ears! Always this buzzing in my ears!' He lurches towards the girls. 'Can you hear it? Can you hear the buzzing? You've got to warn them! All the children in your school! Warn them about the memes and the signals and the information overload! You've got to warn them! Before it's too late! Before it's too late and we all get turned into a singularity!'

'Well, yes, we'll certainly remember to do that,' Andi assures him, backing away. 'And—oh dear!—we seem to have run out of time! Well, thank you for taking the time to speak to us this morning, Antenna Head!'

And with this Andi and Bryony turn and beat a hasty retreat, stopping only when they have put a safe distance between themselves and Antenna Head.

'Whew!' says Andi, catching her breath. And then: 'Well, I think that went *very* well! That was a good idea of mine, doing an interview. I wonder why I didn't think of it before, really... Interviewing the rogue males, as well as just following them around.'

'I don't think Mum would like us going up and talking to them,' says Bryony. 'Some of them she didn't even want us going near at all, remember.'

This is true. When Andi had conceived her brilliant plan, she had drawn up a list of all the notable rogue males she could think of, and Jo had immediately snatched the list out of her daughter's hand and going through it, had put a line through the name of every rogue male she didn't want the girls going anywhere near.

'We won't interview *all* of them,' says Andi. 'Just some of the less weird ones who it's easy to talk to.'

'But Antenna Head *is* one of the weird ones!' replies Bryony.

'Well, I had to talk to him, didn't I?' retorts Andi. 'Cuz he caught us following him!'

'We could've just run away from him,' argues Bryony.

'Well, we did both, didn't we?' responds Andi reasonably enough. 'We talked to him and then we ran away.'

'So, what other rogue males do you want to do interviews with...? Hang on a minute... Where are we?' looking round her.

'What do you mean "where are we"?' snaps Andi. 'We're back where we started, aren't we? This is Ambermere Court, where we first started filming.'

'Yeah, that's what I thought, except that we're not where we started. Look at that mattress.'

She points to an old double bed mattress propped up

against a dead wall. The Belton Estate is a notorious hotbed for fly-tipping. As the town council charges a fee for taking away unwanted furniture, most of the residents prefer to just dump it around the estate and leave it to the council to come and take it away at its own expense.

'*That* wasn't there before,' declares Bryony.

'Then someone's just put it there,' argues Andi. 'Look, we've come back the same way we went when we first heard Antenna Head buzzing, didn't we? So we're back in Ambermere Court, aren't we?'

Bryony is unconvinced. 'I don't know... I don't think this is where we were before...'

'How can you tell? All these squares look the same, don't they? Look: we came from there, didn't we?' pointing to the other end of the court. 'And through there is the main road. Come on!'

They cross the court and follow the passageway between the apartment buildings, which brings them out onto— another court.

'See?' says Bryony, at once annoyed and triumphant. 'That wasn't Ambermere Court! I told you we weren't where we were before!'

'Then *this* is Ambermere Court!' insists Andi. 'We just somehow came back one court further on from where we started, that's all!'

'But this doesn't look like Ambermere Court, either,' counter-insists Bryony. 'I haven't seen *that* before,' pointing to a fly-tipped wardrobe standing on the grass.

'Then someone probably just put it there,' says Andi once again. 'And anyhow, it doesn't matter where we are: we don't want to go home yet, do we? We're meant to be exploring; looking for rogue males. And we can't get lost, can we? Not when we've got our phones with us. Come on: let's go back this way; we want to go further into the estate, not out of it; that's where we'll find more rogue males.'

Leaving the court with the wardrobe, they return to the

court with the mattress. Andi surveys the scene. 'We came down *there* when we were running away from Antenna Head,' pointing to one alley; 'so let's go down *there*,' pointing to another.

The alley is a narrow one between two high walls; and just as they reach the entrance, a gaunt apparition appears. Squealing, Andi and Bryony leap backwards, hugging the wall and each other.

The apparition stops and looks at them. A pale shadow of man, dressed in a threadbare black suit, his posture is slack and round-shouldered. His thinning hair is lank and lifeless; grey smudges underscore the deep-set woebegone eyes; and the expression, the expression carved upon those lean and haggard features is one of such bleak and hopeless misery, that compared to it Monkey Boy's poker face looks positively affable. What loose skin there is upon the cadaverous face all seems to be drawn towards the permanently downturned corners of the doleful mouth, as though impelled by an irresistible force.

Such is the apparition confronting the girls, and its name is Mr Deep Sigh.

For a moment he just stands there looking bleakly at the two girls, while they stand against the wall, quaking with fear, eyes tightly closed; and then, turning away, he lets forth a dejected sigh, a sound of weary despair ejected from the very depths of the man's soul; and then, the shoulders sinking back to their usual slumped position, Mr Deep Sigh proceeds slowly and wearily across the court.

The girls now relax and Andi moves to follow him, but Bryony holds her back.

'Don't follow him!' she hisses. 'We'll catch depression!'

'Not if we keep at a safe distance!' hisses back Andi.

'But he looked at us! We might be infected already!'

'We closed our eyes, didn't we? And anyway, news reporters have to face all kinds of dangers like this if they want to report the truth—and the same goes for the camerawomen, so get your poop together and start filming!'

Excrement assembled, Bryony starts recording. Matching his pace, the girls follow in Mr Deep Sigh's doleful footsteps, and Andi commences her commentary.

'We are now following Mr Deep Sigh. You have to be very careful when you're filming Mr Deep Sigh because Mr Deep Sigh has depression, and depression is very contagious, so it's important not to get too close to Mr Deep Sigh, and you should never make eye-contact with him. Because if you do you might catch depression, and if you catch depression, you'll turn into another Mr Deep Sigh. First, you start to feel really sad and then your face gets longer and longer so that you can't smile anymore. And then your shoulders go all saggy and you start to walk really slowly. And then a cloud comes along and it stays right over your head and it follows you around wherever you go, and every two minutes or so you have to stop and let out a deep sigh.'

(Obligingly, Mr Deep Sigh pauses in his steps at this moment and does just that.)

'Unfortunately, there's no cure for depression, so if you catch it, you have to stay depressed forever. Because it's so contagious, lots of people with depression are quarantined in places called funny farms. They're called funny farms because the doctors and nurses there tell jokes and slip on banana peels all the time to try and cure the patients' depression, but so far none of these experimental treatments have worked. Because there are so many people with depression, the funny farms get filled up very quickly, so some of the patients have to live in the community. So remember: if a person like Mr Deep Sigh lives near you, to avoid catching depression you should always keep at a safe distance and avoid direct eye contact.'

'This has been a public service announcement from the Rogue Males Broadcasting Company.'

'Cut and *shut up, Bryony*!' snaps Andi. 'One more

comment from you while we're filming and I'm going to have your name removed from the credits!'

'Oh! Is the film going to have credits, then?'

'Well, no…' admits Andi. 'I don't know how to do credits…'

'So!' exclaims a voice.

'Oh crap!' exclaims Bryony. 'It's her!'

'Her' being Rinda Neves, who, along with her unpaid hirelings Clare and Sally Sawdust, has appeared at the far side of the court.

'I have found you!' she cries, pointing a triumphant finger.

'Run for it!' yells Andi.

And the two girls run for it, and, an imperious cry of 'stop!' yielding no results, Rinda and the Sawdust Sisters give chase.

Andi and Bryony run from Ambermere Court onto Ravenswyke Court, then weave a zigzag path through Dolphin Court, Witchend Court, Nettleford Court, Redshank Court, Snowfell Court, Buzzard Court and thence to Tuscany Court. The pursuing contingent, after having tracked their quarry from Ambermere Court to Ravenswyke Court, and thence to Dolphin Court and Witchend Court, here, instead of swinging a left into Nettleford Court, make the tactical error of going straight on into Sallowby Court, and then proceeding pell-mell through Grasshopper Court, Sea Witch Court, Alpine Rose Court, Buckingham Court, Amorys Court, Villa Rosa Court, White Gates Court, and, by the time they reach Saucers Over the Moor Court, are obliged to stop and face the fact that they have completely lost the scent.

'Fools!' snarls Rinda, turning on the Sawdust Sisters. A good leader always knows when to put the blame on her subordinates, and the culprits, aware of the magnitude of their crime, hang their tousled heads in silent shame.

And Rinda was already in a bad mood this morning. Her

new video camera, ordered online for her last night by her dear step-father, is going to be late. Although arriving today as promised, it is not scheduled for delivery until this evening! This evening! Prior to this, deliveries to the Neves's from Amazon Prime have been known to arrive as early as lunchtime; so why does it have to be *today* of all days that the stupid driver somehow can't get to their house until this evening? It's infuriating! Intolerable!

'We must find Andi Seton!' Rinda tells her minions irefully. 'I am *going* to find out what she is making her film about, and *then* I'm going to make a better one! So, you two had better do your jobs and help me find them again! Because if you do not, you shall *not* be getting those ice creams I promised you! Instead, I shall buy all three for myself, and your punishment will be to watch me eat them!'

(With such fiendish ingenuity at her fingertips, it really is a shame that Rinda is too young to have fought for her country in the Second World War.)

Meanwhile, back in Tuscany Court, Andi and Bryony have had the good fortune to discover another rogue male.

'Behind me you can see Straightman-Funnyman. Straightman-Funnyman is an unusual person because he is actually two people in one. Sometimes he's Straightman and sometimes he's Funnyman, but he's never both of them at the same time. When he's Straightman he talks in a normal voice and he's boring and stupid; but when he's Funnyman he talks in a screechy voice like a parrot and he says lots of funny things that make people laugh. He's coming this way now, so let's go and talk to him and see who he is today.'

The man approaching the girl is small in stature, with a very large head, completely bald on top, a band of grey at the back and sides. His face holds a vacant, rather bemused expression.

Andi walks up to him.

'Hello! We're making a film and I was wondering if we

could have a quick word with you?'

Straightman-Funnyman glances nervously at the camera. 'What's this? Making a film? What sort of film's that?' he asks, in a voice harmonious with his clueless expression.

Andi turns to the camera. 'Ah! This is his normal voice, which means Straightman-Funnyman is Straightman today.' Turning back to the subject: 'So tell us, what are you doing today, Straightman?'

'Just been to the doctors.'

'You've been to the doctors! Really? Are you feeling poorly, then?'

'Yeah. I'm always poorly.'

'And what are you poorly with, Straightman?'

'Lots of things, really. I got these haemorrhoids—'

'*So!*'

Yes, it's Rinda Neves and company, who, entirely by luck and without even a passing nod to judgement, have relocated their quarry.

'Run for it!' yells Andi.

They run for it.

Straightman-Funnyman stands bewildered as one set of girls runs away from him while another set of girls runs towards him.

'Wait a minute!' says Rinda, halting the pursuit. She walks up to Straightman-Funnyman. 'What were you talking about just now?' she demands. 'Those girls were interviewing you, weren't they? What were you talking about?'

'I was telling them about my haemorrhoids…'

'Your haemorrhoids? Why were you telling them about your haemorrhoids?'

'Well, they was asking me what I'm poorly with—'

'Asking you what you're poorly with!' Rinda pounces on the words. 'That's it!' turning to Sally and Clare: 'They must be making a film about people's illnesses! Yes! First they were filming Mr Deep Sigh, and now they were asking *him* about his haemorrhoids! You!' turning back to Straightman-Funnyman: 'I wish to see you again tomorrow, when I have my video camera, and then you can tell *me* all about your haemorrhoids! Just me, understand? If anybody else tries to ask you about them, especially those two girls who were here just now: *do not tell them anything.* Understand? You are forbidden to say a word about your haemorrhoids to anyone except me! Right?'

'Alright…' says Straightman-Funnyman, confused but acquiescent. 'Don't tell anyone except you…'

Andi and Bryony, unaware that they are not being pursued, run on until, turning a blind corner, they almost run into someone coming the other way—that someone being the angry ex-con known as the Lagger. You will remember their mum had an altercation with him yesterday.

And speaking of whom, when Jo Seton had vetted Andi's 'to do' list of rogue males, the first name to be struck off said list was that of the Lagger, because Jo Seton doesn't want her daughters going anywhere near the man. There are some who claim the Lagger was inside for paedophile offences, but people invariably say that about mysterious ex-cons who suddenly appear in the neighbourhood, and Jo herself is doubtful, thinking he seems more the violent armed robbery type. But paedophile or not, the Lagger is not child-friendly.

'Watch where yer going!' he snarls. 'Nearly knocked me over, you did! You got no respect for yer elders and betters, you kids!'

'Sorry, we didn't see you…!' begins Andi.

'Hang on a minute, I know you two!' says the Lagger, glaring at the two girls. 'You're Jo Seton's brats, aren't yer? Aren't yer?'

'Jo Seton?' says Andi. 'No, that's not our mum's name!'

'Don't bloody lie to me!' snarls the Lagger, looming over Andi, veins standing out on his bald head. 'I know you're that punk bitch's brats! She bloody knocked me down yesterday, she did! Right onter the pavement! Like I'm gunna take that crap from her! Who does she think she is, eh?' He breaks off, switching his ireful gaze to Bryony. 'Here, what you doing with that camera?'

'We're not doing anything—!' begins Andi.

'Gimme that camera! I'm not having you filming me! Give it 'ere!'

The Lagger lunges at them, and Andi doesn't even have to shout 'Run for it!' this time.

'Now where are we?'

The court in which they find themselves is a small one, made to appear even more so by the looming presence of a venerable beech tree planted in the centre of the grass plot, whose gnarled branches reach out to graze the gutters and upper windows of the terrace houses. The houses themselves have a neglected appearance, the brief front gardens overgrown, the paintwork on doors and window frames blistered and peeling. The windows, veiled with net curtains, are like so many sightless eyes. Nothing stirs, not a sound can be heard.

'No-one's been here for a million years,' says Bryony, voicing how they both feel.

'I wonder why they put this tree here,' says Andi. 'It's too big for the square; if it gets any bigger it's going to go through the windows of the houses.'

'We are *totally* lost,' says Bryony.

'We are *not* totally lost!' snaps Andi. 'We *can't* get lost, can we? Not when we've got our phones with us. Go on: check your phone: find out whereabouts we are.'

'Why don't you check your phone?' counters Bryony.

'No,' firmly; '*you* can check *your* phone! *You're* the one who thinks we're lost.'

'I can't check my phone,' confesses Bryony. 'I haven't got it with me. It's at home, recharging.'

Andi impales her with accusing eyes. 'Why didn't you

recharge it last night?' she demands.

'Because I forgot to.'

'Forgot? You're really stupid, you know that?'

'Well, it doesn't matter, does it? We can just use yours, can't we?'

'Yes...'

'Well go on, then: have a look. Find out where we are.'

'I can't,' mumbling. 'Mine's at home recharging as well.'

'And you call me stupid?' flaring up.

'Well, it wouldn't matter that I hadn't brought my phone if you'd brought yours!'

'And it wouldn't matter that I hadn't brought my phone if *you'd* brought *yours*.'

Silence.

And then: 'We're totally lost, aren't we?' says Bryony.

Chapter Six
Estate of Decay (Continued)

'We are *so* totally lost.'

The road, a busy main road, is unfamiliar to Andi and Bryony. The view across the street of a group of square buildings that look like offices, is also unfamiliar to them.

Wandering through the endless courts of the Belton Estate, they had come upon an access road, and they had followed it, hoping it would take them to the main road; they had followed it to a cul-de-sac; whereupon they had retraced their steps and followed it to another cul-de-sac; they had retraced their steps once again, taken a different turning, and followed the road to the perimeter of the estate where it joins this main road.

A main road; but not the one they are looking for; not the friendly, familiar main road that will take them back home.

'Would you stop saying that?' demands Andi irritably.

'Well, we *are* lost,' insists Bryony, waving a hand at the

unfamiliar prospect. 'We must've walked all the way to the next town.'

'Don't be stupid. The Belton Estate doesn't *go* all the way to the next town; we're still in Marchmont. It's just that this is a bit of Marchmont we've never been to before.'

'So we're lost then, aren't we? Lost is when you don't know where you are, and we don't know where we are, so we're lost.'

'Alright, so we're lost!' snaps Andi. 'But we're not going to be lost *forever*, are we? Marchmont's not *that* big; so sooner or later we're going to get back to somewhere we know.'

'And how do we get back to somewhere we know? Do we go right or left?'

'We don't do either. We turn around and go back the way we came. We've come the wrong way, haven't we? So this must be the other side of the estate from the side we know. So, all we've got to do is go back the way we came, and keep walking in a straight line and then we'll come to *our* side of the estate, right?'

And so, they turn and retrace their steps.

Half an hour later and they find themselves back at the same junction with the same unfamiliar main road, and facing them the same unfamiliar collection of office buildings.

'Now what?' groans Bryony. 'We're never gunna get out of here, and I'm *starving*.'

'We *are* going to get out of here,' retorts Andi. 'We've just gone in a circle, that's all.'

'So, what do we do now?'

'We go back again. We tried walking in a straight line and we ended up going in a circle; so this time all we've got to do is try going round in a circle, and that way we should end up walking in a straight line right to the other side of the estate!'

'If we had our phones, we could call Mum up to come

and get us.'

'If we had our phones, we wouldn't be lost in the first place, would we? Duh!'

'Well, I can't help it! It's cuz I'm hungry!'

'Stop thinking about your stomach!' snaps Andi.

Her own stomach chooses this moment to make a loud noise.

They turn and retrace their steps.

Some workmen, aloft upon the scaffolding are performing maintenance work on one of the blocks of flats.

'We must be getting somewhere,' declares Andi. 'We haven't been here before.'

'How do you know we haven't? We've passed lots of buildings where they've got scaffolding up.'

'Yeah, but none of them had workmen working on them, did they?'

'That might just mean the workmen just weren't here before,' argues Bryony. 'Anyway, go'n ask them the way out of here.'

'I'm not going up to some workmen!' exclaims Andi, appalled at the idea.

'Well, *I* can't do it, can I?' retorts Bryony.

'But neither can I. They'll say dirty things to me.'

'No, they won't. They only start doing that to you when you're at secondary school.'

'It doesn't matter if I'm not at secondary school,' drawing herself up to her full height: 'I'm still a woman!'

Bryony rolls her eyes. 'Oh, just cuz your periods have started...!'

'Well, that's what Mum said, didn't she? When my first one started, that's what she said! She said: "You're a woman now"!'

'She was just joking when she said that. And anyway, it doesn't matter if your periods have started, cuz you still don't *look* like you're secondary school, so the workmen won't say dirty things to you.'

'They *will*,' insists Andi. 'They'll *know*. Men can always tell!'

'*How* can men tell? You think they can smell your whiffy period blood or something?'

'Just you wait till *yours* start!' says Andi venomously.

'Look, just go and ask them how we get out of here. *Please!* Then we can get something to eat…!'

'Oh, alright then,' sighs Andi.

Affecting insouciance, she approaches the foot of the scaffolding. The workmen, engaged in lively conversation, have not noticed her. Andi is just in the act of opening her mouth to voice the words 'excuse me!' when two of the workmen, finding themselves suddenly of divergent opinions with respect to some weighty issue or other, start loudly throwing f-bombs at each other. Andi closes her mouth and walks straight back to her sister.

'Let's ask someone else.'

The next person they see is a teenage girl, busy on her smartphone.

'She looks like she's askable,' says Bryony.

'Yeah, and I think I know her…' says Andi. 'She's one of Milly's friends; I'm sure she is. I forget her name… Hey!'

The name Andi has forgotten is Nicki; the very same Nicki Milly bumped into on her way home the night before.

'Remember us?' says Andi brightly.

'No…' eyeing them narrowly.

'We're friends of Milly! We just wanted to ask you—'

'Oh, your friends of Milly's, are you? And you wanted to ask me *what*, eh? Wanted to ask me *what*? I bet she sent you, didn't she? Yeah, that's right! Wants to know what I was doing last night, does she? Nosey cow! Well, who says I was doing anything? Who says I was doing anything? And even if I was doing something, it's got nothing to do with her, has it? So you can just go and tell that nosey cow to mind her own fucking business!'

The girl marches off.

'And don't follow me, neither!'

The sisters watch her retreating form in puzzled silence.

'And all that was about *what*, exactly?' wonders Bryony.

'God knows,' says Andi. 'Come on. We'll ask someone else.'

'There's someone,' says Bryony, pointing.

'Where—? Oh yeah, it's Straightman-Funnyman! Come on!'

Joyful, they run towards him, calling out. Straightman-Funnyman might be a bit dim, but at least he knows his way around the estate: they'll soon be home free!

'Hello! It's us again! Can you tell us—?'

''Ello, girlies!' squawks Straightman-Funnyman, in a voice like a Pythonesque housewife, his face transformed to that of a demented Punchinello.

Straightman-Funnyman has turned into Funnyman.

'What you two do been doin', then? You been chasin' Aunt Fanny round the gasworks? You been pokin' the porkpie? You been shakin' hands with the president?'

'No,' says Andi. 'We just wanted to—'

'You been pointin' Percy at the porcelain? You been spearin' the bearded clam? You been droppin' some kids off at the pool?'

'Please, can you tell us—?'

'You been spankin' the monkeys? You been ridin' the matrimony pony? You been ticklin' Timmy's tonsils?'

'No, we haven't done any of those things. We just—'

'You been takin' the dog for a walk? You been slappin' Sammy senseless? You been plantin' a King Edwards?'

'Let's go,' says Andi.

The girls depart, sent on their way by a fanfare of further interrogatories as to their recent activities.

'When he's Funnyman he's more weird than funny,' is Bryony's opinion.

'Well, never mind,' says Andi. 'Third time lucky, eh?'

In making this calculation, Andi must be discounting the workmen, presumably because she never got as far as speaking to them; but either way she's wrong, because the next person they run into, and just as abruptly as on the last occasion, is the least askable person of them all: the Lagger.

'Found yer!' he snarls. 'Now you gimme that camera! You ain't makin' no film of me, you little sluts!'

Exit, with precipitation.

They stop to catch their breath. What with walking, running and not eating, the girls on the brink of collapse. But when Andi looks up from her oxygen-retrieval a vision greets her eyes: to wit a signboard bearing the legend ONE STOP.

She blinks. The vision is still there.

'Look!' she exclaims. 'Do you see what I see?'

Bryony looks. 'It's a One Stop shop!'

'You mean you can actually see it?'

'Course I can see it!'

'Then it's not a mirage!'

Personally, I don't know enough about mirages to say whether or not the same mirage can be witnessed by more than one person simultaneously; but whatever the case, it seems that Andi is right in her estimate of this particular vision, because when, with a cry of 'Food!' the girls make a beeline for the hallowed portals, they do not shimmer out of existence, nor, when the automatic doors slide open to admit them, do they come into sudden and violent contact with a brick wall.

'A One Stop shop right in the middle of the Belton Estate!' marvels Andi as, moments later they emerge arms laden with soft drinks, bags of crisps and other comestibles. 'And we never even knew about it!'

Bryony's response is lost in a mouthful of chocolate bar.

'You not what I don't get?' continues Andi. 'If there's a One Stop shop right here on the estate, then why does

Monkey Boy go all the way to the one on Angel Street to buy his fags?'

Because the One Stop shop on the estate doesn't have a Haseena working at the cash register. We know this, but Andi doesn't.

And speaking of Monkey Boy, he has just stepped outside to stretch his legs; and for Monkey Boy, taking a stroll through the estate also means looking out for cats, because as you may recall, after the Haseenas of this world, Monkey Boy's other main interest is cats. Knowing the whereabouts of nearly all the local feline population, he always plans his constitutionals to take in those places where he is most likely to bump into some of them.

The first cat Monkey Boy sees is a tortoiseshell that resides in Redshank Square. The cat is sitting to attention in the middle of the grass plot, minding its own business. Staying on the footpath, Monkey Boy hunkers down and endeavours to attract the cat's attention. He clicks his tongue, he whistles, he pats his knees, he calls out to it in soft and dulcet tones. The cat, making no move to approach him, turns its head to stare intently first in one direction, then another, and then another; and in fact proceeds to systematically stare intently in every single direction except that of the young man who is so vigorously striving to attract its attention.

The Victorians, who were very good at it, had a name for this activity: they called it 'cutting a fellow dead.'

To describe the extent of Monkey Boy's wounded feelings at being snubbed by this cat would be to make him appear even more ridiculous than he already does, so I shall forgo doing this.

Especially as he is about to be humiliated in a much more public way.

He proceeds on his way, perking up again when he espies, not cats, but even more exciting, a trio of burka-clad Muslim women. He decides to follow them. (And the fact that he doesn't even think there's anything wrong in his doing this just goes to show that Monkey Boy has within him all the makings of a very good stalker. We can only hope that he finds himself a steady girlfriend before he gets much older.)

Maybe one of them is Haseena, he thinks. He has often wondered if Haseena lives here on the estate, which as a sizeable portion of Marchmont's Islamic population do happen to reside here, seems not improbable. He has long dreamed of discovering Haseena's place of abode and of her catching sight of him one day as he is 'just happening to pass by' when she is home alone, and how she would open the front door and silently beckon him inside with an inviting smile on her hijab-framed face. Maybe these three women, when they get to wherever they're going, will do the same. Being blessed with eyes in the back of their hijabs they will have seen him following them, and being suitably flattered will all three of them silently beckon him to follow them into the house…

Preoccupied with extravagant daydreams, heady with incense, of languorous dancing, discarded veils (seven of them), bells and cymbals tinkling on fingers and toes, Monkey Boy fails to hear his name being called out repeatedly from somewhere behind him.

The caller out is Andi. Failing to get Monkey Boy to respond to his name, he tries 'Oi, cloth ears!' with no better result.

'Come on!' she says to her sister. 'Let's catch up with him!'

The girls are very glad to see Monkey Boy, a remarkable state of affairs, because not many people are ever glad to see Monkey Boy. But for Andi and Bryony, right now Monkey Boy is salvation; Monkey Boy is someone they can talk to and from whom they might actually get a straight answer. And then they can finally get out of this place!

Picture the scene: Andi and Bryony run to catch up with

Monkey Boy. Ahead of Monkey Boy are the three Muslim women. Unaware of Monkey Boy's special interests, the girls have no idea that he is actually following the Muslim women; to them, Monkey Boy and the Muslim women appear simply to be walking in the same direction. At the end of the court the path disappears into a passageway set into the row of flats. The passageway leads to the next court, and the entrance to it is surrounded by scaffolding. The three women pass under the scaffolding and into the passageway. Monkey Boy, close behind them, approaches the passageway, and then without warning a bucket, brimful of water, falls from the highest level of the scaffolding, and with commendable precision disgorges its contents over Monkey Boy, before landing upturned on his head.

The Muslim ladies turn round and laugh. Andi and Bryony laugh. The tortoiseshell cat, had it been witness to the event, would have laughed as well.

'A bucket hat!' howls Bryony, pointing.

Monkey Boy removes the bucket from his drenched head. 'What the fucking hell—?' he splutters.

Two people now spring from the shadows beneath the scaffolding, a lanky old man and a tiny old woman, the latter armed with a video camera: Ted and Hilda Pranky.

'Congratulations! You've just been pranked!' says Ted. 'Cuz we're the Prankies! We may be senior citizens, but we're young at heart!'

'*You* again?' roars Monkey Boy. 'You—! You—!'

Words failing him, Monkey Boy falls back on actions, these being of fuller voice. He picks up the bucket and hurls it at Ted Pranky's face. His aim is true.

While Hilda Pranky screams with outrage, Andi and Bryony scream with laughter, deeming the response to be even funnier than the original prank. With Monkey Boy showing strong signs of following up his opening salvo, the Prankies, one with bloody nose, beat a hasty retreat, and only the presence of the still-watching Muslim ladies deters

Monkey Boy from giving chase. Instead, he turns and starts making his drenched and humiliated way home.

Andi and Bryony fall in with his squelching footsteps.

'Monkey Boy...?' ventures Andi.

No response.

'Monkey Boy...?' repeats Andi, more firmly.

This time Monkey Boy looks round.

'Piss off,' he says.

'We only want to *ask* you something!' says Andi.

'Well, tough,' walking stolidly on.

'Why are you being like that?' asks Andi.

'Like what?'

'All stroppy with us.'

'Why am I being stroppy? Why am I being stroppy? Ooh, now let me see... Maybe it's because I've just had the whole world laughing at me for getting a bucket of water dropped on my fucking head! Maybe it's that!'

'But *we* didn't do it!' protests Andi.

'You still bloody laughed at me!'

'Yeah, but then we laughed even more when you threw the bucket at Ted, so that sort of evens it out, doesn't it?'

Monkey Boy snorts. 'Does it?'

'Yes!' insists Andi. 'Look; we only want to know how to get out.'

'Get out? Get out of what?'

'This estate! We've been here *hours*, and we can't get out!'

'What do you mean you can't get out? This is a housing estate, not a bloody Escher picture!'

Had Andi and Bryony known who Escher was, they would have argued that this particular estate is *very much* like one of his pictures!

'Look, can you please just tell us the way out?' begs Andi.

'Find it yourself,' is the sulky reply.

They come to the front door of Monkey Boy's ground

floor flat. He opens the door and steps into the hallway, Andi and Bryony following. The hallway has three doors, the door on the right leading to the bedroom, the door on the left leading to the living room, the door in the middle leading to the bathroom.

Monkey Boy opens the latter door and only then does he turn around and see that the two girls have followed him into the flat.

'What are you doing here?' he flares up. 'I didn't say you could come in! Piss off out of my house, you little sods!'

'But we still need to know how to get off this estate!' pleads Andi.

'Use your bloody phones!'

'We haven't *got* our phones!'

'Then ask someone else! Just clear off!'

'But we—!'

'Look,' says Monkey Boy firmly; 'I am in a *very* bad mood, and I cannot be dealing with you little brats. So, I am now going to go into this bathroom to dry myself off, and by the time I come out I want you two to be out that bloody door, over the green hills and away. *Comprendez*?'

And without waiting for an answer, he walks into the bathroom and slams the door.

'And I want to hear you leaving!' comes his voice.

'Alright,' calls back Andi. Winking at her sister, she walks up to the front door, says in a very loud voice: 'Come on then, Bryony; let's go!' takes hold of the door and closes it firmly.

Conjuring her sister to silence with a raised finger to the lips, Andi nods her head to the living room door. They creep quietly through it. Monkey Boy's living room is furnished with a mismatched armchair and sofa, a coffee table, a bookcase and a cabinet with an LCD television, which between them take up most of the available space. The air, heavy with dust reeks of tobacco and male body odour.

'Why are we doing this?' whispers Bryony, mouth to her

sister's ear.

'We still need him to tell us the way out of here,' replies Andi, using the same method. 'By the time he's dried himself and got changed and everything, he'll be in a better mood, won't he?'

'He won't be when he sees we're still here,' opines Bryony.

Andi thinks about this, then she points to the doorway of the adjoining kitchenette. 'We can make him a cup of tea. That'll put him in a good mood.'

'No! Let's hide instead!'

Bryony grins, but Andi looks puzzled. 'What for?'

'Cuz then he won't know we're here and we can film him,' whispers Bryony.

'Why do we want to do that?'

'It'd be for the documentary, wouldn't it? Filming a rogue male in his lair.'

Filming a rogue male in his lair...! Andi likes the sound of that. Her ace reporter instincts, temporarily in abeyance, now they return. Yes! To capture actual footage of a rogue male in his actual den: opportunities like this don't come along every day: and when they do, they have to be seized!

First to find a vantagepoint from which to film the subject, one from which they will not be observed. Behind the armchair is selected as the best place of concealment the room affords, by virtue of being the only place of concealment. The chair is positioned at an angle in a corner of the room, leaving behind it more than enough room to conceal two tweenaged girls.

The girls get into position. They hear the bathroom door open and Monkey Boy crossing the hall to his bedroom. Moments later he walks into the living room, hair stuck up in the air from a vigorous towelling, dressed only in a pair of boxer shorts. The two concealed intruders have to compress their lips tightly to prevent explosions of laughter. Blissfully unaware that he is being surreptitiously observed (and filmed), Monkey Boy drops heavily onto the sofa, muttering to himself.

Having scratched an armpit and rooted around his left nostril with an index finger, Monkey Boy picks up a small tin from the coffee table, opens it, and takes out what looks like the paraphernalia for rolling a handmade cigarette. At first Andi is puzzled, having always known Monkey Boy to smoke readymade cigarettes; but then, she reflects, maybe he only smokes the readymade cigarettes when he's outdoors, and at home he smokes the handmade kind to save money.

A reasonable deduction on Andi's part—but nonetheless wrong.

Having rolled his cigarette, which looks a funny one to Andi, all twisted at one end and much thicker at the other, Monkey Boy lights it with his pocket lighter, and sitting back on the sofa, takes a long drag. He exhales slowly and the fumes of the cigarette soon permeate the air.

Funny, thinks Andi, nostrils twitching; it doesn't smell like a normal cigarette…

About a minute later and Monkey Boy's front door opens, ejecting first a thick plume of smoke, and then Andi and Bryony, marching single-file with glazed eyes and big, stupid smiles on their faces.

The door slams shut behind them and the two girls proceed on their merry way, oblivious of the stupefied Rinda Neves and Sawdust Sisters whom they walk right past. And then—and I really don't know how to explain this, I just present the facts as they are—in spite of marching along with what seems a complete disregard for their surroundings, Andi and Bryony march their way straight out of the Belton Estate and all the way home.

Chapter Seven
Mum's Dating Disasters: Number One Million and Seven in an Ongoing Series

Sitting in the pub with a vodka and tonic waiting for your blind date to arrive.

You just never know what you're going to get.

There was this one bloke, and she'd met him at the same pub she's sitting in now, and at first he'd seemed like a totally normal guy, good-looking, good conversation, no awkward silences. She'd felt really good, really happy, thinking this was going to be a blind date that turned out well. But then, out of the blue, the guy had just whipped out this box of very weird-looking sex aids that he'd just bought from the local sex shop on his way to the pub.

He'd never got the opportunity to try out his new toys; not with her, anyway. Not on a first date, thank you very much. The kind of guy who thinks it's alright to bring that kind of thing along to a first date… Once again, no thank you.

Jo looks at her watch. Just coming up to eight o'clock. She has arrived early, because she always likes to be the one who arrives first; a habit that's become a ritual with her, and like most rituals it's silly and meaningless but somehow comforting…

She'd caught sight of one of the Chuckle Brothers groping Yukari's backside this afternoon. Yukari, being Yukari, hadn't turned round and told him to fuck off like Jo would have done; she hadn't reacted at all, or rather, her reaction had been to do nothing, to pretend it hadn't happened… Trouble with doing that is that there are a lot of men around who are either stupid or conceited enough to believe a lack of reaction somehow implies acquiescence. Yeah, you really liked having your arse groped, but being a lady, you prefer not to verbally express your pleasure.

Yukari hadn't reacted to her groping, but Jo had. She hadn't caused a scene, figuring Yukari might not appreciate that, but she'd stared hard at Mr Chuckle, stared at him and made it very clear that she'd seen what he'd just done and what she thought of him for doing it.

It had been good to see the little turd squirm.

Do guys actually imagine that their pawing a woman's arse-cheeks and or her fanny is going to be favourably received? ('Ooh, you naughty boy! Your place or mine?') Do they honestly think she'll take it as a compliment? ('He's groping my bum! How sweet of him!') A lot of the time it seems like they just do it on automatic pilot: for a man, to see is to touch.

The Chuckle Brothers are so-called (behind their backs) by Jo and the other girls at the supermarket on account of their resemblance to the famous children's entertainers. (Mind you, there's only one of them left now! 'To me…! To me…! To me…!') The Chuckle Brothers are middle management, the visible face of authority on the shopfloor. (The actual manager, this entrepreneur in a smart suit, hardly ever graces them with his presence.) Jo knows only too painfully well how it all must come across to the customers at the shop: them, a gaggle of females, shelf-stackers and sales assistants, being bossed around by a couple of men— and a couple of men who are complete fucking clowns at that. Christ, it's embarrassing!

The Mirthful Brethren had both (one at time; not together) tried it on with Jo, back when she'd first started working there. Jo knows that because of the way she looks a lot of men like to think she must be 'easy,' a sexed-up rock chick with a nice loose set of morals; and the Chuckle Brothers had been no exception. Yes, they'd both tried it on with her—and neither of them have ever repeated the mistake.

Jo likes Yukari and at work together they're best friends; but Yukari's never shown any interest in meeting up with Jo outside of work... Perhaps it's differing interests: Yukari's into classical music, so maybe she thinks she'd be too much of a fish out of water amongst Jo's circle of friends... But Jo wouldn't have dragged her off to a rock concert, anyway. What she'd really like would be for just the two of them to get together and just have a cosy girls night out; kick back, get hammered, open their hearts to each other...

How does Yukari get along with that husband of hers...? Peter Neves... God, she went to school with that guy; she's known him most her life... A bit of tit, really. A clown; one of those overgrown boys, needs his nose wiped for him... You meet plenty of that type on the blind-dating circuit... How did Yukari end up with Peter Neves? Jo's just never really seen Yukari and Peter together, not enough to get a sense of how they really get along... Mind you, you never *can* really tell how a husband and wife get along; not unless you were somehow able to see them when nobody else was around.

She wonders if Yukari has told her husband about the groping incident.

Yukari Neves, our recent grope-victim (and no, she *hasn't* told her husband), is a woman of many pastimes. Her hobbies include opera and ballet, hiking, photography, urban exploration, piano playing, yachting and flower arrangement (the latter being a fine-art in Japan.) Her latest addition to the list is pottery, in which she is taking a course of evening classes. Her class is this evening, and she is in her bedroom applying her makeup prior to setting off. She hears the knock at the front door. She knows what it will be: that video camera her husband has (so idiotically) bought for her daughter. Her reflection in the mirror scowls back at her as she listens to the sounds of jubilation coming from both husband and daughter below.

Children. Two children. Her daughter and her overgrown boy of a husband.

Makeup complete, she goes downstairs to the living room. Here she finds her ecstatic husband in possession of the video camera, flitting round Rinda and filming her as she strikes a series of exaggerated model poses.

Yukari's frown deepens.

Peter ceases his gyrations. 'The camera's arrived!' he announces.

'I can see that.'

'Isn't it great, Mummy?' says Rinda. 'My very own film camera!'

'Let me see it.' Yukari holds out her hand. Peter surrenders the camera to her. She inspects it and then she glares at her husband. 'It's the same!'

'What?'

'The camera: it's the *same!*'

Yukari turns, goes back upstairs, and comes back with her own video camera. She holds it out to her husband.

'Look: it's the same! You bought her the same camera as my own!'

'Oh...' says Peter, comparing the two devices. 'Yes, they do look... Well, it doesn't matter, does it? I mean, you wouldn't let Linda use yours, so now she's got her own! Doesn't really matter if it's the same model as yours or if it's a different one, does it?'

'Yes, it does matter,' insists Yukari. 'It's a waste of money.'

'Well, no... no, it's not, is it? Linda needed a camera and you didn't want her using yours, so I bought her her own one and now everyone's happy!'

'She didn't need to have a camera at all. She could have just used the camera in her smartphone for her school project; that's what they were told to do.'

'No, I couldn't just use my phone, Mummy,' protests

Rinda mildly. 'I need to be able to make a film that's better than Andalusia's, and if she is using a video camera then so also must I.'

'Yes, she's right, darling, she—No, wait! Wait just one doggone minute! They're *not* the same, you know!' triumphantly displaying the side panels of the two devices. 'Look at the model numbers: they're different! See: yours is a Super-HDVD-950, and *this one* is a Super-HDVD-950X! It's a different model!'

His enthusiasm is not shared by Yukari.

'Yes, but they're both still exactly the same!' she insists. 'Aside from that X in the serial number, they are still exactly the same!'

'No, Mummy,' argues Rinda. 'The different numbers mean mine is a newer model, so my camera will be better than yours.'

'Yes!' agrees Peter. 'She's right! They might both *look* the same, but this one probably has some more advanced features or something!'

Yukari looks at her watch. 'I have no time for this; I need to be going. I'll be back at ten o'clock.'

Out in the hallway Yukari dons her coat and her shoes, picks up her handbag, and then she exits the house, closing the front door with emphasis.

Baka!

Jo goes to the bar to buy herself another vodka and tonic. It's just gone eight and her date is officially late. Well, she's had dates who turned up late before and they've always had good reasons for being late. But then you'd expect them to, wouldn't you? If there's one occasion when you wouldn't want to make a bad impression by being late, that occasion would be a blind date!

Contactlessly paying for her drink, Jo returns to her table.

It's pretty quiet in this pub tonight. A middle-aged couple talking quietly. A trio of beefy-looking women with sports bags; rugby players, maybe. And a couple of rogue males. The pub-going rogue male is a solitary drinker; he is the man, middle-aged to elderly, who arrives at the pub on his own, sits drinking his drinks on his own, and then goes home again on his own. The two here tonight are both nondescript examples of the genus, nothing her daughter Andi would be interested in.

Andalusia. So-called because sperm-donor was a Spaniard. Jo had been doing the usual gap-year backpacking with friends across Europe thing, when she'd met the guy. They'd only had sex that one night. But then, when she'd got home and found out she was pregnant, she'd decided to have the baby—and this in spite of being firmly in the pro-abortion camp!

Bryony is her only daughter to have been the product of a more long-term relationship, a steady boyfriend she had lived with for a while. Mind you, 'steady' wasn't the best word to describe that particular walking car-crash. He'd been one of the overgrown boy variety, but he had problems and these problems had caused him to lash out like a child at times, and when the child doing the lashing out has the body of a grown man, it can hurt more. On top of that, she's pretty sure the guy must have had some sort of autistic condition—and that this has been transmitted to Bryony.

And as for her latest, little Carli, she was also the result of a one-night stand. She'd just been so surprised to actually see a black man at a rock music gig!

Andalusia, Bryony and Carli. A, B and C. *'I'm going through the alphabet!'* she'd jokingly said to her daughters.

But she doesn't have any plans to add a 'D' to the collection. She isn't playing the dating game to find another sperm donor. She isn't looking for a husband either. An independent woman who knows her own mind, she is quite capable of raising her three precious girls without any male assistance. She's just looking for company, a connection, and yes, the sex. Something that's hopefully more than just a one-night stand, but nothing with 'commitments.' Right now, she likes her independence too much for that.

But as far as dating goes, Jo has been cursed with bad luck of late. None of her blind dates have turned out well. Not a single one has been anywhere near good enough to take home with her. Tonight's date, in spite of the tardiness, she feels more hopeful about. They're into the same kind of music for one thing. Yes, she knows common interests aren't guaranteed to seal a relationship, but they are a conversational icebreaker. And when it comes to a 'scene' like the alternative rock circuit, you get that feeling of like-mindedness, of compatible views, compatible temperament.

Not that it always turns out that way. There is one dating disaster Jo can never recall without a shudder. Yes, the guy had been a self-confessed alternative rock fan—but what he had neglected to mention until their actual meeting was that his favourite band was the Fall. And when a fan of the Fall gets to talking on his pet subject, his conversation, unless you happen to be a fan of the band yourself, very quickly becomes unbearable. And that night, after enduring an hour and a half of her date monologuing on the subject of the Fall, Jo had found herself starting to think how nice it would be to go and hire herself out as a suicide bomber.

She checks her phone. Ten past eight. Carrie should have been put to bed by now if Milly's doing her job properly, and she has no reason to doubt this because she hears nothing but good reports about Milly from her daughters. And Milly's into indie music, which is always a good sign as far as Jo's concerned. Her daughters of course listen to all that pop rubbish that's in the download charts, but Jo has never tried to impose her own musical preferences on her girls, preferring instead to leave it to time for them to cultivate a better taste in music; and Jo's own history provides an encouraging example, because even *she* used to listen to that shit until she was fourteen!

Over at Seton House, Milly Leeson has indeed been doing her job properly and Carrie has been satisfactorily put to bed. She now sits chatting with her other two charges as they watch a film on Netflix, herself in an armchair, the two sisters on the floor. Courtney Love is also present, but being curled up asleep on the sofa takes no part in the conversation. (And as for the film, she's seen it before.)

Andi and Bryony get along famously with Milly, so much so that Milly ranks amongst that exclusive minority of people that Bryony will actually talk to.

'We saw one of your friends today,' says Andi.

'What friend was that?'

'One of your friends from school; can't remember her name. She's got this big frizzy hair. It was on the estate, and we only wanted to ask her for directions, but she went all bitchy on us, didn't she?' looking to her sister for confirmation.

Bryony launches into an impersonation: 'What do you two want? Why are you asking me questions? I bet Milly Leeson sent you, didn't she? Nosey cow! She always wants to know what I'm doing! She should mind her own business, she should! Bleh, bleh, bleh, bleh, bleh!'

'Oh, that's Nicki,' declares Milly, smiling grimly.

'What, have you fallen out with her or something?' asks Andi.

'Basically. She's up to something she doesn't want me to know about and she thinks I'm sticking my nose in. Like I could give a toss what she's doing.'

'What *is* she doing?'

Milly shrugs. 'I reckon she's just got herself a new boyfriend.'

'And why doesn't she want you to know about that?'

'Well, I reckon it's cuz he's a man.'

Andi is confused. 'Well, he would be a man if he's her boyfriend, wouldn't he?'

'Yeah, but I mean a *man* man; you know, a grown-up

man, an adult.'

'She's going out with a grownup? That's against the law, isn't it?'

'Pretty much. If he's older than you, people say it's grooming.'

'Why do they call it that?' asks Bryony. 'Mum calls it grooming when we have to brush Courtney's fur!'

'Yeah, that's a different kind of grooming, not sex grooming,' Milly informs her. 'Sex grooming is when an adult gets hold of someone younger and he like teaches them how to do sex stuff.'

'I thought people your age already knew about sex stuff!'

'Well, yeah, some of us do. But an adult, who's been around longer, they'll know lots more stuff about sex than most of us still at school know. And they teach you how to do all that stuff just so's you can do it with them, and it's like they're taking advantage of you cuz they're older and they know more than you do.'

Bryony grins from ear to ear. 'So, what would *you* do if some man came along and tried to groom you?' she asks Milly eagerly.

Milly shrugs. 'A bit late to worry about that.'

'A bit late?' echoes Andi. 'Why's that?'

'Oh, nothing. I just meant I already know most of it.' And, with a subject-changing 'So!' inquires: 'Who's your mum's blind date tonight? Know what he's like?'

'Yes, Mum showed us his picture,' says Andi. 'He looks really nice.'

'Well, that's a start! Maybe he'll be the one that works out for her.'

'We'll know that if she brings him back home with her!' grins Bryony. 'We'll get woken up by all the noise!'

'Bryony!' remonstrates Andi. 'Don't say things like that!'

'Oh, I don't mind,' says Milly. 'Has it been a while since she's brought one home, has it?'

'Yes, Mum's been having a lot of bad luck recently,' confirms Andi.

'Dating disasters!' chuckles Bryony.

'What about your mum, Milly? Is she doing dating now she's single again?'

Milly pulls a face. 'I don't know and I don't care.'

'How come?'

'Oh, we don't get on that well, me and Mum.'

'That's funny. We always get on with our Mum, don't we, Bryony?'

'Yeah!'

'Yeah, but your Mum's cool; mine's *not*. It's like we're rivals or something...'

Dating disasters, muses Jo as she downs her fifth vodka and tonic, usually tend to fall into one of several basic categories:

There's the blind date who turns out to be a creepy pervert, the blind date who turns out to be an unsalvageable nonentity, the blind date who turns out to have way too many annoying personal habits, the blind date who turns out to be a junkie, and the blind date who turns out to be insufferably full of himself...

But for Jo, tonight's dating disaster does not fall into any of the above familiar categories, at least not in so far as she is aware—because tonight is a first; tonight, her blind date has failed to show up at all.

Chapter Eight
The Twenty-Five Pound Note

A desert valley. The girl reporter, wearing a military helmet and flak jacket, crouches behind the boulders as bullets ricochet around her. She addresses the camera.

'This is ace reporter Andalusia Seton reporting from Mexico, where women everywhere are being attacked by the drugs gangs because as part of the ongoing War on Women. Today, I'm here with the *El Lesbos* girl-gang, taking cover behind these rocks as we get shot at by the gangsters, who are positioned behind the cactuses on the other side of the valley.'

The camera pulls back from the reporter to show a group of tough-looking teenage girls, all wearing reversed baseball caps, squatting beside her. Some of the girls have handguns and are firing off shots at their assailants.

Andalusia addresses the gang leader: 'So Conchita, explain to our viewers at home: why is the drugs gang shooting at you?'

'Eez because they don' like uz because we are weemin an' we are lezbian, si?' replies Conchita. 'An' eez also because we don' let them take our mules to smuggle their drugs across zee border.'

'So there you have it,' says ace reporter Andalusia Seton, turning back to the camera. 'Misogyny and homophobia. It's all part of the War on Women which is happening here in Mexico and lots of other places as well. Oh, wait! The shooting's stopped! Has the drugs gang finally given up?'

The camera turns to look across the valley. At first there is no movement from behind the row of cactuses, but then a cloud of white smoke appears. Growing in size, it starts to drift across the valley.

'This is bad!' cries Andalusia. 'They've released the femicide! That deadly gas that only kills women! We've got to get out of here!'

The cloud of gas advances toward them, but then a truck suddenly appears, honking its bullhorn. It pulls up in front of the boulders and the woman driver leans out of the cab window.

'Get in zee back, ladies! I'll get you out of here!'

'Hooray! It's one of Mexico's female truck drivers, here to save us in the nick of time!'

They all pile into the back of the lorry. Inside it is a fully equipped playroom. The doors slam shut and the lorry drives off. And now the Mexican girls all burst into laughter. Pointing at Andalusia, they roll around on the floor, laughing helplessly.

'What's so funny?' demands ace reporter Andalusia Seton hotly.

'You theenk femeecide eez a gas!' laughs Conchita. 'Eez funny! You so stupeed!'

Gales of laughter.

'I know it's not a gas! I know it's not a gas!'

'I know it's not a gas!'

Andi wakes up. She sees Bryony, perched on the ladder of the bunkbed, forearms resting on the guardrail.

'God, you're not still on about that, are you?'

'Not still on about what?' asks Andi, confused. She's already forgotten her dream.

'You were going on about femicide gas,' says Bryony. 'But never mind that: just get your lazy bum out of bed and downstairs. Mum's doing an early shift today, remember? So it's your job to make breakfast.'

'Breakfast! Breakfast!' comes Carli's voice from below.

***

Rinda sits on her bed buckling her shoes when her step-dad Peter, dressed for the office, walks into the room. A flower-patterned dress, a fluffy angora cardigan, schoolgirl buckled shoes and white knee-socks. The clothes Rinda is wearing today are destined to become famous.

'So you're heading out soon, then?' he says, surveying the bedroom.

'Yes, Daddy,' replies Rinda. 'I'm meeting up with Sally and Clare.'

Peter pulls a face. 'Those two. Why do you always hang around with them?'

'I like them,' replies Rinda simply. 'They obey my

orders.'

Peter can find no argument to this. After all, what more can you ask of any friend worthy of the name?

'They are going to assist me in making my film today,' proceeds Rinda, standing up; 'and my film is going to be a lot better than Andi Seton's!'

'Yeah, where's the video camera...?' inquires Peter casually, giving the room another onceover. 'I don't see it here...'

'That's because I've already taken it downstairs,' says Rinda. 'It's in the front room.'

'Oh, right,' says Peter. 'In the front room, is it? Well, I'll leave you to it...'

He backs out through the doorway, makes his way downstairs into the living room. He sees the video camera sitting on a side table next to one of the armchairs. He heads towards it, but then a small blur of frenetic energy sweeps past him and snatches up the camera.

'I don't think so, Daddy!' Rinda grins triumphantly. 'This is *my* camera and you are not having it!'

'I know it's your camera, sweetie,' says Peter. He moves towards her coaxingly, placatingly, arm outstretched palm-upwardly. 'I just need to check something...'

'No!' evading his grasp. 'It is mine! Mine, mine, mine!'

'Honey bunch, just for a second...'

'No, Daddy! You have to catch me if you want it!'

Giddy with mischief and sparkling spring-water joy, Rinda darts giggle-squealing around the room, light and nimble, easily evading her step-dad's clumsy, lunging pursuit.

Frustrated in his efforts to catch the girl, Peter tries adopting the stern voice of parental authority. 'Now that's enough, Rinda. You know you're not allowed to run in the house. What would your mother say?'

'Nothing! Mother is not here!' retorts Rinda, jack-in-the-boxing from behind an armchair. 'You have to catch me!'

'Rinda!' now with anger unassumed. 'Just stop running and give me that camera! There's something I've got to... I won't let you go out today, if you don't give it to me!'

Rinda's only response is to laugh and make a beeline for the hallway. And then she is out through the front door and running down the driveway. Peter runs after her, but he is shoeless, an amused neighbour is watching, and he is compelled to give up the chase. Rinda escapes down the street.

Andi is pumped up and ready for her third day's filming.

'Everyone ready?' she calls out, emerging minty-fresh from the bathroom.

A heavy and unexpected silence is the only response.

'I said: is everyone ready?' louder this time, emphasising the words for extra clarity.

Silence.

'Well, don't sound too excited!' says Andi. She marches up to her bedroom door, pushes it open. 'I said, don't sound—!'

The room is empty. She checks Carli's room. Also empty.

'Where are you? It's time to go out!'

She goes downstairs. No-one in the living room. No-one in the kitchen, either.

'Is this hide and seek?' she demands, standing hands on hips in the middle of the kitchen. 'Cuz we haven't got time for hide and seek! We can play hide and seek later! So, just stop messing around and come out!'

She waits. Nothing happens. The house remains silent.

'Look, I'm not going to come looking for you, you know! D'you hear? I'm not going to come looking for you!''

She goes looking for them. She looks in every conceivable place, inside the house and out. Every place but one.

'You better not be in Mum's room! Mum'll kill you if she finds out you've been in there!'

She goes back upstairs and very slowly opens the door of the forbidden room. Myra Hindley stares down at her from the wall.

'Are you two hiding in here?' she stage-whispers. 'I'll tell Mum you've been in here...!'

Andi performs a rapid search of all likely hiding places. Her sisters are not here.

She returns to her bedroom and checks her phone. No messages. Back downstairs she looks to see if a note has been left for her. No note.

They've deserted her.

They've gone off somewhere without telling her and left her to do all her filming on her own, the little bleeps! Well, fine then! Who needs them, anyway! She only let Bryony be camerawoman in the first place because she couldn't film herself while she was doing the introductions. Well, the introductions are done now, so who needs her? Yes, she can do all the filming herself now!

Right then! And as they didn't leave a message for her, she's not going to leave one for them, either. Time to set off.

But when she returns to the bedroom, Andi discovers that her absconding sisters have absconded with the video camera.

'Where we going?'

'For the millionth time, we are going to *the swimming pool*.'

'We haven't got our swimming things!'

'I *know* we haven't got our swimming things, because *we are not going swimming*.'

Hand in hand, Bryony and Carli make their way into town, Carli carrying a satchel over her shoulder.

'Why are we going to the swimming pool if we're not going swimming?'

'Because, we're going there to do some *filming*,' explains Bryony, summoning all the patience she can muster. 'That's why we've got the video camera with us. We're doing some filming at the swimming pool.'

'Filming people swimming?'

'Yes, filming people swimming... and getting ready for swimming... and that sort of thing... It's for Andi's video project.'

Yes, this is Bryony's masterplan: with video camera concealed in her satchel, her aim is to capture some candid footage of the women's changing rooms at the swimming pool. An endeavour which has bugger all to do with rogue males—unless you count the tenuous connection of it being something many a rogue male would give his right arm to be able to do.

But then, Bryony has just been telling her little sister a fib: her masterplan is in no way intended for the benefit of her sister's documentary. No, Bryony is in this entirely for herself. She's implementing this masterplan primarily for her own pleasure, although she also has the vague secondary idea of making some money from the fruits of her filming by putting it up on YouTube.

The masterplan has been simmering in Bryony's mind for several days now, and today she decided to put it into action, and she has seized the moment, careless of the fact she is leaving her unfortunate elder sister high and dry in the process. A very unreliable sidekick is our Bryony, all things considered. One can't help but imagine that if Andi needed to set up a mantrap in order to overcome some adversary, and she instructed Bryony to keep a firm hold on the rope holding up the anvil, the moment Andi was standing directly underneath said anvil, Bryony would let go of the rope and have a good snigger at the results.

The reason Bryony has dragged Carli along with her is as camouflage. Her idea is that, accompanied by a small child, she won't look so suspicious when she's walking around the changing rooms pointing her satchel at people.

'So, have you got that?' says Bryony. 'We're going to the

swimming pool to do some filming!'

'Yay! We're going to the swimming pool!' cheers Carli. And then: 'We haven't got our swimming things!'

Bryony is beginning to wonder if this camouflage idea is going to be worth the effort.

'Look, just—' She breaks off. 'What's *he* doing?'

Further down the street, a man crouched at the kerbside beside a parked car, seems to be tugging at something, something that's stuck either to the road surface or the wheel of the car. Whatever it is, it's apparently stuck fast because the man now gives up tugging and walks off down the street, casting frequent looks behind him. As the two girls continue to watch, a second pedestrian passes the first man, and drawing level with the parked car pulls up short, his attention caught by the same mysterious object. Whatever it is, is clearly a tempting prize, because the second man now hunkers down and starts tugging at it. But his efforts meet with no more success than those of his predecessor.

'What's he doing?' asks Carli.

'Dunno,' says Bryony. 'Let's go'n see.'

Espying the two approaching girls, the man springs to his feet and resumes his passage along the pavement. Hands in pockets, whistling insouciantly, he passes the two girls, avoiding eye contact.

Bryony and Carli now hurry up to the parked car and there they see the prize that has tempted these passersby. Projecting half its length from beneath the front wheel of the car, is a crisp Bank of England note, one which promises to pay the bearer the sum of fifty pounds.

Bryony's face lights up. 'Fifty pounds!' she gasps, dropping to her knees beside the prize. Bryony has never seen a fifty-pound note before.

'Fifty pounds! Fifty pounds!' echoes Carli, infected by her sister's enthusiasm.

'Yeah, and finders-keepers, so it's ours!' declares Bryony.

She takes hold of the note, only to make the same discovery as her predecessors, that extracting a polymer banknote from beneath the wheel of a one-and-a-half-ton motor car is not as easy as it might appear at first glance.

'It won't come out!' She tugs furiously at the note. She tugs it to the left, she tugs it to the right, she tugs quickly, she tugs slowly; but the note will not budge.

Bryony pauses for reflection. Clearly she is doing something wrong. Those other two men were doing something wrong as well, but Bryony, she's smarter than those stupid grownups. She knows she will hit upon the solution if she just gives it some thought...

'Hmm... Maybe, if I get hold of the front of the car and lift it up a bit, then you can pull the note out...'

The experiment is a failure. Bryony pulls with all her might, but Carli is unable to slide the note out from under the wheel.

Bryony adjusts her thinking cap.

'Hmm... Oh, I know! If we just tear off the half of the note that's sticking out, that's still twenty-five pounds, isn't it?'

Of course! Those stupid grownups must have been complete idiots not to have realised this! Bryony Seton strikes again!

She takes hold of the innermost edge of the note and tears it straight across. Success! Triumphant, she holds aloft the torn note, and Carli claps her little hands with glee.

'Oi! What have you done?'

They look up. Filling the upstairs window of the house behind them are the mortified faces of the Prankies, Ted and Hilda. A video camera is positioned on the windowsill, aimed down at the street.

'That's ours!' cries Ted.

Theirs? This twenty-five-pound note, theirs? What are they talking about, the old farts? Haven't they heard of finders-keepers, one of the oldest laws of the land, and right up there with that one about eyes and teeth?

'Give it back, you vandals!'

Clearly they haven't.

Bryony, eschewing verbal debate as to legal niceties in favour of tactical withdrawal, cries: 'Run for it!' and the girls scarper down the street, heedless of the oaths, objurgations and shaken fists aimed at them from the upstairs window.

The swimming baths are part of the Marchmont Sports Centre, located here in the centre of town. The centre boasts a refreshment hall which is also open to non-gym users by means of a separate entrance. Bryony, averse to the idea of buying a ticket when she has no intention of using the facilities, walks in via this entrance, and then, with sister in tow, and utilising a knowledge of the building's layout gleaned from school trips, finds her way to the swimming pool changing rooms.

She pauses outside the door to adjust the camera and satchel for filming.

She turns to Carli.

'Now listen,' she says, adopting her most serious and grown-up tone. 'When we go in there, you just stay next to me, *and don't say a word*. We're making a film, remember? If you talk, you'll ruin the film, so, keep your mouth shut, okay? *Keep your mouth shut*. Got it?'

'Yes!' affirms Carli cheerfully.

'So, what have you got to do, then?'

'Keep your mouth shut!'

'No, keep *your* mouth shut!'

'Keep my mouth shut!'

'Right! Now, come on.'

The two girls enter the changing rooms and stroll around, as though surveying the premises to find the most desirable location for changing into their swimming things. There are disappointingly few patrons, and at first there seem to be none who measure up to Bryony's exacting standards of female pulchritude, being either too old, too ugly or too fat.

But then, they come to a cubicle where a woman with long dark hair is in the process of undressing herself. Her face, briefly seen in profile, is elegantly beautiful.

Jackpot! This is more like it! Fit body, good-looking and not too old!

Bryony positions herself in front of the cubicle, camera aimed and recording, while her oblivious star performer, back turned, continues to undress. That older-than-her-years salacious grin spreads itself over Bryony's face as she watches the woman divest herself of first skirt, then blouse, then tights, and then bra and knickers, performing the operation with the effortless grace of someone who's clearly done it before.

Nice bum! thinks Bryony. Now, just turn round so we can get some shots of your front bits. That's it...

The woman turns round, and catching sight of the two children her face lights up.

'Oh hello, Bryony! Hi there, Carli!'

Bryony's dirty grin freezes into a sickly rictus. It's Janet, one of Mum's friends!

'Keep your mouth shut!' snaps Carli, pointing an accusing finger. 'We're making a film!'

'Making a film?' Janet looks confused. 'Where's Andi, then? Isn't she with you?'

'Yes, I'm here!'

And it *is* Andi!

Smiling broadly, she walks up to her petrified sister and throws a companionable arm around her shoulders. 'Bryony! Now, why did you rush off without me like that?' To Janet: 'Silly thing: she's got her dates mixed up! It's *tomorrow* we're going swimming, not today!' To Bryony: 'You really are forgetful, aren't you? We've got something else we need to do today, remember? So, come on! You two, Carli!'

And tightening her grip on Bryony's shoulders, Andi guides her out of the changing rooms, Carli following in their wake.

'How did you know we'd be at the swimming pool?'

'Because I know how your filthy mind works, that's why! God! You should've been born a boy, you should! You sure you don't want to put your name down for gender reassignment?'

The three girls stand outside the main entrance of the sports centre, Bryony with the air of a defendant in the dock and Andi with that of the prosecuting council.

'You are *so* stupid, you know that?' proceeds Andi. 'What would you have done if you'd got caught? They'd have probably called the police in! And even if they hadn't done *that*, they'd still have told Mum! And *then* what would have happened?'

'Mum would have a go at me, and probably ground me for the rest of the holidays,' answers Bryony.

'Well yeah, she would—but I don't care about *that!* That would just serve you right. What *I* do care about is that she'd have never let any of us use the video camera again! And *that* would've ruined my documentary!'

Silence.

'Well? What have you got to say for yourself?'

'Sorry,' mumbles Bryony contritely, apparently to her shoes.

'Good! Now, let's jus—'

'Oh!' says Bryony, perking up. 'We found some money!'

'Eh? You found some money?'

'Yeah! Twenty-five pounds!' Eagerly extracting her wallet, Bryony fishes out the torn fifty-pound note and presents it to her sister.

As a placatory offering, this one falls flat on its face. Andi is signally unimpressed. 'This is half of a fifty-pound note,' she says, holding it between index finger and thumb.

'Yeah! So it's worth twenty-five pounds, right?' eagerly.

'Wrong!' snaps Andi. 'It's not worth *anything!* God, you're a duh-brain, aren't you?'

'Are you sure...?' questions Bryony, her tone urging caution.

'Sure that you're a duh-brain? Yes!' firmly.

'I mean about the note...'

'Yes, I am sure. Look: if I walk into a shop with a five-pound note and I buy something that costs two-pound fifty, the shop person isn't going to just tear the note in half and give half of it back to me, are they? *This*,' brandishing the torn banknote, 'isn't worth anything. Not without the other half!'

And so saying, Andi tears the note into shreds. (They really don't make those polymer banknotes like they used to.)

A cry of despair rends the air.

The Prankies are tearing down the street towards the girls as fast as their electric motorcycle can propel them. Ted, riding pillion, waves aloft, now rather forlornly, a small square of paper; and if you look closely, you can see that it bears a printed image of Her late Majesty the Queen.

Chapter Nine
Fatal Afternoon

Like Jo Seton, Yukari Neves has worked a morning shift today, and knocking off at lunchtime she returns home. She finds the house quiet—which can only mean her daughter is out. She is in the kitchen making herself a sandwich for her lunch when the phone in the hallway starts ringing.

The caller is her husband. 'Hello...? Yes, I just got back... Linda? No, she's not here... No, I don't know when she will be back. When she gets hungry, I suppose... No, I do not know why she's not answering her mobile. She's probably too busy playing with the new camera you bought her. What do you need to speak to her about so urgently anyway…? Well, if it's not important then surely it can wait till you get home this afternoon… Yes… Yes, goodbye…'

Yukari replaces the receiver and returns to the kitchen.

Her lunch ready, she takes it into the living room, seats herself on the sofa. Picking up the television remote, she sees a video camera lying on the table. Linda hasn't taken her new camera out with her…? It hardly seems possible… All that fuss and she's already lost interest… Wait, no! No, it's her own camera, of course! Yes, she'd forgotten to take it back upstairs when she came back from class last night…

The camera focuses on the man rummaging through the bins in the yard, zooming in until he fills the frame, blurred at first, and then swimming into automatic focus. The man's appearance is that of a stereotypical bucolic tramp: a wild, thickety beard, unkempt hair, monk-tonsured, the visible skin of face, neck and hands embrowned as much with ingrained dirt as exposure to the elements. His clothes, old and much-repaired echo the drab colours of waterlogged countryside under a leaden sky: a leafy-coloured shooting jacket, frayed and patched at the elbows, dun-coloured trousers tucked into a pair of ancient turndown wellington boots. A length of old rope tied around his middle serves as a belt.

'This is Andalusia Seton, coming to you today from the yard behind Billton's Hardware Store on Main Street, here in the centre of Marchmont. I'm having to talk very quietly because we don't want to startle this rare Rogue Male we have just tracked down. You can see him now: he is none other than the elusive Raggedy Man. And how did we manage to track down this rare creature? Well, this is because Raggedy Man gives off a very strong scent and you can smell him from a very long way off. Lots of people mistake the smell of raggedy Man for the smell of a rubbish tip. We were lucky enough to pick up this scent and we followed it down an alley into this yard. We've taken cover behind these crates so that Raggedy Man won't see that we're filming him, because if he sees us he'll run away back to his lair, and nobody really knows where Raggedy Man's lair *is*. Some people say that Raggedy Man lives in a big mansion that's all falling to pieces. But how could Raggedy Man afford to have a big house like that when he doesn't have a job? Well, that's because there's another rumour about Raggedy Man that says that even though he looks like a tramp—'

'And smells like one.'

'And smells like—shut up, Bryony!—that even though he looks like a tramp, he's really a millionaire, but that he's one of those misers who hides all his money away instead of just spending it like normal people. But where does Raggedy Man keep his millions of pounds of money? Some people say he's got it all buried in a treasure chest in the garden of his mansion—but Mum says that no-one has that much money in notes these days and says it's probably just in a bank account.

'Raggedy Man doesn't come out very much, and when he does come out, he likes to go scavenging. And as you can see, this is what he's doing right now. He's searching through all the rubbish behind the hardware shop, and if he finds anything he likes, he will take it home with him.

'What will Raggedy Man find today…? Look: he's just found one of those wobbly strips of metal they use to do up boxes with! And now he's carefully examining it… You can see the thoughtful look on his face… Is this wobbly metal strip good enough for him to take home with him…? Decisions… Decisions… Oh, he's just thrown it away! No, the wobbly metal strip is *not* good enough for Raggedy Man to take home with him! Poor wobbly metal strip! Poor abandoned wobbly metal strip! Thrown away like a piece of rubbish!'

The sound of tittering.

'Shhh, Bryony—! Argh! He's seen us!'

Raggedy Man has stopped rummaging and looks towards the camera. The frame goes suddenly dark.

'Shhhh! Keep still!'

Darkness and vague shapes, the rustling of clothes.

'Did he see us?'

'I don't know!'

...

'What's he doing now?'

'Not sure! Shall I have a look?'

'Yes.'

The camera tilts upwards: a low-angle shot, backdrop of sky—and Raggedy Man looming over the crates, staring wild-eyed into the lens!

Screams, image jerking violently, sound of running feet.

'Whew!' says Andi, when they emerge onto Main Street.

'It's alright; he's not coming after us,' reports Bryony, looking back towards the alley.

'Probably gone back to his scavenging,' says Andi. 'Come on, then. We've got enough footage of him.'

'Uh-oh! Here comes Rinda!' reports Bryony.

'Where?'

'Over there!'

'Quick: don't let her see us!'

The girls duck down behind a pair of bins. Across the street, Rinda Neves and the Sawdust Sisters walk along the pavement. Andi peers at them from between the two bins.

'She's got a video camera!' she gasps. 'Where'd she get that from?'

'It's her mum's. She said she was going to borrow it, remember?' says Bryony.

'Oh yeah, the little copy-cat... Wait a minute: did she have it with her yesterday? I don't remember seeing it then...'

'Yeah, but we didn't really see her much, did we? We were always running away from her. You want to follow her now?'

'No, thanks. If she's going that way, we'll go the other way.'

Don't Muslim women 'taken in adultery' get stoned to death? Monkey Boy has a woolly idea that this is the traditional punishment meted out for offences of this nature in the Islamic world.

A disturbing possibility, if true: because right now Monkey Boy is on his way to his favourite One Stop Shop to buy his ciggies, and if Haseena is working at the checkout—well, who knows what that might lead to, and God (or Allah) knows he doesn't want to drop the poor woman in it!

But no, that sort of thing might fly in places like Afghanistan, but in these sceptred isles of freedom and democracy the criminal code frowns on stoning people to death, regardless of the gravity of the offence.

He enters the shop. Yes, there she is! There's Haseena at the till, and no sign of that bastard husband of hers!

A clear field of attack!

He walks up to the counter. Haseena greats him with that dazzling smile of hers—and Monkey Boy actually remembers to smile back at her! Yes, just for once that poker face of his decides to take a lunch break and he smiles at his inamorata, and he can feel that it's a genuine smile, warm and sincere; not one of those strained and sickly smiles like the ones defiling his dating site profile page.

'Hello!' says Haseena.

'Hello!' replies Monkey Boy.

Without even thinking about it, he's cleared the second hurdle. That 'hello' has got to be the best one 'hellos' he's delivered in years. Clear as a bell, and simply oozing charm and affability!

'And what can I get for you today?' asks Haseena, still smiling.

Monkey Boy is on the verge of giving his usual response of 'Twenty B&H, please,' when inspiration hits him.

'Have a guess!' he says, grinning.

The bait is taken. Haseena affects a pensive expression, eyes raised, tapping her underlip. 'Now let me see...' The dazzling orbs turn to face him. 'Could it be... Twenty B&H?'

'Correct!' grins Monkey Boy.

Laughing, Haseena turns to the screen door concealing the tobacco products.

You know: just for a change...

Should he add that?

You know: just for a change...

Would it sound good...?

You know: just for a change...

But by now Haseena has turned back to the counter with his cigarettes and the moment for adding those words has passed beyond recall.

Oh, well! thinks Monkey Boy, quickly shoring up his good mood. Probably just as well: if he'd said it and then he hadn't got a reaction from her, he'd have felt a right prawn, wouldn't he? Yes, best not to get overconfident and get in over your head. Just take these things one step at a time...

And having paid for his cigarettes and delivered a 'goodbye!' as affable and intelligible as his 'hello!' Monkey Boy exits the shop, feeling as pleased with himself as he has felt in a long time.

Yes, he has definitely made progress today! There had been a connection there; a palpable rapport. No doubt about it...

We shall just leave Monkey Boy to enjoy his brief stroll in fool's paradise—because things are only going to be going rapidly downhill for him from hereon in.

'Wants to interview me? what's she talkin' about interviewin' me thinks she the police or somethin' well I ain't talkin' to the police an' 'elpin them wi' their inquiries cuz I ain't done nothin' they ain't get nothin' one me an' anyhow she ain't the police she's just a kid wi' one o' them camera things and the other one wi' the big hooter an' the goofy teeth she's just standin' there laughin' at me laughin' in my face no respect kids these days they ain't got no respect for their elders an' betters—'

'Please just ignore my sister, External Monologue; she's stupid and just laughs all the time. And I'm not with the police, either. You see, I just want to interview for this video project I'm doing for school. It's a film about all the really interesting people who live in Marchmont, and I'd like to ask you about the interesting way you always keep thinking your thoughts out loud all the time.'

'Thinkin' out loud? what's she on about thinkin' out loud can't think out loud can *talk* out loud can't *think* out loud an' anyhow what I'm thinkin' is none of her business people's thoughts is private they is you can't just go askin' people what they're thinkin' about that's invasion of privacy that is don't catch me goin' around askin' other people what they're thinkin' about no respect no respect at all these days they want to know this an' they want to know that an everyone keeps stickin' their noses in other people's business the kids an' the police 'specially well I ain't tellin no-one what I'm thinkin' my thoughts is my business an no-one else's an' I ain't done nothin' wrong an people pointin' cameras at you an' askin' you all these questions I'm gettin' out of here I am I ain't standin' 'ere bein' filmed an people askin' my questions I'm goin' an' they better not follow me neither cuz that's stalkin' that is an' I ain't never stalked anyone no matter what anyone says so they can all shove it an' just leave a bloke alone what ain't doin' nothin' wrong…'

'And that was External Monologue, the only person who talks to you even when he's refusing to talk to you.'

The girls proceed on their way through the maze of residential streets, in search of further subjects to film. They are approaching an intersection when:

'Raggedy Man!' hisses Bryony.

The girls flatten themselves against the wall and watch as Raggedy Man makes his away along the path across the intersection, walking with the rapid loping stride typical of him.

When he has passed:

'Come on: let's follow him!' says Andi.

'What for?' protests Bryony. 'You said you'd already got enough film of him.'

'Yes, but I want to see where he's going,' says Andi.

'Why?'

'What if he's going home?'

'What if he is?'

'Well? Don't you want to find out if it's true what they say about him? About how he's really a millionaire and lives in a big mansion? If we follow him, we can find out!'

The sisters dart across the road and begin tailing Raggedy Man, who is already some distance ahead of them. Suddenly he turns off the pavement and disappears from sight.

'Where's he gone?' wonders Andi.

The girls hurry to spot where he disappeared and discover the entrance to a narrow footpath confined by tall fencing.

Andi sniffs the air.

'Yes, this is where he went!' she says. 'Come on!'

They hurry down the path, and find themselves at the entrance to a row of allotments. Ahead of them they see Raggedy Man; he strides along the path bisecting the plots of cultivated ground.

'Here's your millionaire's mansion,' sneers Bryony. 'He just lives in one of these sheds!'

A reasonable assumption and, judging by appearances at

least, Raggedy Man would look right at home dossing down in one of these rickety toolsheds; but apparently this not the case because, Raggedy Man traverses the allotments from one end to the other without stopping. Which just goes to show that you shouldn't go around judging by appearances.

The girls hurry across the allotments in pursuit of their quarry. Beyond them, the path narrows again, following its zigzagging course between tall fences. By now the girls are well outside their usual stomping grounds, and they have no idea where the path might be taking them. Keeping Raggedy Man in sight, they presently emerge into open country, where the path proceeds, skirting orchards and pastures.

'How far's he going?' demands Bryony. 'We're gunna end up getting totally lost like yesterday!'

'We can't get totally lost like yesterday cuz we've got our phones with us today,' Andi reminds her. 'So stop whining.'

Finally, after traversing a stretch of scrubby wasteland, they emerge onto a country road. The road is bordered by trees, and there is no traffic. Not a house can be seen in either direction. Raggedy Man has crossed the road and makes his way along the verge in the direction leading away from Marchmont.

'Oh, God,' groans Bryony. 'How much further?'

'Come on!' urges Andi. 'I've got a feeling we're nearly there.'

And it looks like Andi is correct in her intuition, because round the next bend, a tall brick wall runs alongside the road. Further on there is a pillared gateway. The gates are open and Raggedy Man turns off the road and passes between them without pausing in his stride. Andi and Bryony run to up to the gateway. They see Raggedy Man advancing along a treelined avenue, visible at the end of which is a large old house. The gates are rusty, the grounds overgrown and the house gloomy and tumbledown.

'So, it's true then!' gasps Andi. 'Raggedy Man really *is* a millionaire, and this is his house, just like the stories say!'

Raggedy Man, now reaching the house, climbs the steps to the porch, opens the one leaf of the front door and disappears inside.

'What now?' asks Bryony. 'You want to follow him...?' Her tone suggests she's not in love with the idea.

'Well, it's private property, isn't it...?' says Andi, equally unsmitten. She looks at her watch. 'We should probably be getting back now...'

'Yeah, we should...'

'...But at least we know where he lives!'

Bryony agrees that this is useful information and the two girls turn and retrace their steps back along the road.

'Raggedy Towers!' suddenly exclaims Andi. 'That's a good name for Raggedy Man's house, don't you think? Raggedy Towers!'

'Yeah: Raggedy Towers!' enthuses Bryony. The house in question seems much less scary now that they're walking away from it.

A car, the first they have seen on this quiet road, passes them, and much to the girls' surprise, they see it turn in through the gateway of Raggedy Towers.

Now everyone knows that rogue males are not supposed to entertain visitors. Entertaining visitors is a social activity and rogue males are not social animals: so who could be calling on the Raggedy Man?

As the girls retrace their steps, we will retrace ours as well and catch up with Rinda Neves and the Sawdust Sisters—and if you've been wondering where they were heading when Andi and Bryony saw them walking along Main Street, then you really haven't been paying attention. They were heading for the Belton Estate, of course. Where else? Rinda, now possessed of her very own video camera is ready to start production on her documentary: which means she has a date with Straightman-Funnyman and his haemorrhoids.

'What do I care about Straightman-Funnyman?' says Rinda.

Or maybe she doesn't. (Even us omniscient narrators can get it wrong sometimes. We're only human, you know.)

'But I thought you wanted to ask him about his haemorrhoids,' ventures Clare Sawdust.

'And why would I be interested in Straightman-Funnyman's haemorrhoids?' retorts Rinda contemptuously.

This brings up an interesting dilemma: if you wish to express your supreme indifference to a person's haemorrhoids, what do you tell them they can do with them? You can't consign them to the usual destination: they're already there!

'We're doing a film about people's illnesses, aren't we?' says Clare.

'Wrong!' says Rina; and then, just to clarify the point: 'Wrong, wrong, wrong, wrong, wrong!'

'But that's what the Seton girls are doing…'

'That is *not* what the Seton girls are doing!' fires back Rinda. 'Only a stupid person like you would think such a thing. That was just a trick to deceive us. They wanted us to *think* they were making a film about people's illnesses to conceal their real purpose—but they have not fooled *me!*'

'What is it they're doing a film about, then?' asks Clare.

'Yeah, what is it?' echoes Sally.

'Silence!' commands Rinda. 'Follow me and I will show you.'

Obediently mute, the Sawdust Sisters follow their leader across the estate. Presently they arrive at a particular row of flats in a particular court, which they survey from the cover of an adjacent alleyway.

'*That* is our destination,' declares Rinda, pointing at one of the doors.

'But that's just Monkey Boy's place,' says Clare, confused.

'Exactly!' triumphantly.

'But... what for...?'

'Fool! Have you forgotten what we saw yesterday? Andalusia and her sister coming out of that apartment? So: what do you think they'd been doing in there?'

'Paedo stuff!' says Sally, grinning with splayed teeth. Clare chuckles her agreement.

'Wrong!' replies Rinda. 'Virgins like them know nothing about sex.' (Is she just referring to Andi and Bryony here? Or does her statement include Monkey Boy as well?) 'They were in there making their film!'

'They're making a film about Monkey Boy...?' Clare sounds doubtful.

'Yes! Think about it: what were they doing that day we first saw them filming? They were filming Monkey Boy being pranked by the Prankies, yes? *You two* thought this must mean they were making a film about the Prankies.' (Actually, it was Rinda who had made this assumption, but Sally and Clare know better than to contradict their leader.) 'But they were not, because in fact it was Monkey Boy they were filming, not the Prankies! *He* is the subject of their film!'

'But why would they want to be doing a film about Monkey Boy?' Clare wants to know. 'What's so special about him?'

'Yeah, he's just a boring loser,' adds Sally.

'No, he just *looks like* he's a boring loser,' contends Rinda. 'But secretly he must be doing something very interesting, and Andalusia Seton has found this out about it and she is making a film about it.'

'What could he be doing that's interesting?' wonders Clare. 'It can't be that he's got an interesting job, cuz he hasn't got *any* job.'

'Yes, but he's doing something there in his flat, something interesting.'

'Like what?'

'That's what I am going to find out. Perhaps he's an

inventor or an artist. There are lots of interesting things you can do at home. Now, pay attention: my plan is to conceal myself in his flat and find out what he is doing. And you two shall assist me.'

'How do we do that?'

'By following my instructions. In a minute, I want the both of you to go up to Monkey Boy's door and ring the doorbell; and then you run straight back here before he has time to answer the door.'

'But how—?'

'Silence! I haven't finished yet. You will do this repeatedly, and sooner or later Monkey Boy will realise someone is tricking him, and the next time you go back to ring the doorbell he will be lying in wait behind the door, and he will open it as soon as you press the bell and catch you in the act. When that happens, you must both run off, but *that* way, across the court; not back here, because I will be waiting here, and when he chases after you, I'll be able to sneak into the house and conceal myself.'

'Yeah, but what if he doesn't come after us?' asks Clare. 'He might just swear at us and then go back inside.'

'Then you must *make him* come after you! Taunt him! Mock him! Monkey Boy has a short temper so he is bound to come after you.'

Whether this scheme of Rinda's would have paid off or not will sadly never be known, because Monkey Boy himself now steps in and renders the whole plan redundant.

He appears through the front door carrying a bag of (we trust) non-compostable and non-recyclable rubbish, and he goes round the corner to dispose of this in the communal bin, leaving the front door wide open.

Rinda seizes the moment. Briefly instructing her minions to stay put and keep watch, she makes a dash for the front door and slips inside and into the front room. Here she discovers many signs of slovenliness and disorder, but no evidence of any interesting hobbies: no easel with a masterpiece-in-progress, no workbench laden with scientific gadgetry. A powered-up laptop sits on the cluttered coffee table, but displays nothing more interesting than a background picture of some rock band. The curtains are drawn, the air stuffy and carcinogenic.

The sound of Monkey Boy's return sends Rinda scuttling for the nearest cover, this being the same armchair behind which Andi and Bryony had concealed themselves behind the day before.

Projecting the business-end of her video camera round the side of the chair, Rinda observes Monkey Boy as he re-enters the room. Standing in the doorway, he pauses there, scratching his head. Judging from his expression, he is evidently deep in thought. Whatever the subject of these cogitations, they clearly now resolve themselves into a firm course of action. Moving like a man with a purpose, Monkey Boy crosses the room to the kitchenette, from which he returns bearing a kitchen roll. Dropping onto the sofa, he tears off a couple of sheets from the roll and then picks up his laptop from the coffee table.

And while what follows could be described as a hobby of sorts, it is a hobby that is common to the point of ubiquity, requires little or nothing in the way of talent and ingenuity, and that cannot be said to be of any real benefit to society as a whole.

'What the fuck—?'

The exclamation, loud and angry, reaches the ears of Sally and Clare through the curtained but open window of the flat. It is quickly followed by a peal of girlish laughter.

'You? Come here you little—!'

The sound of violent movement, displaced furniture, girlish laughter and mannish anger, and then the front door opens and Rinda Neves erupts into the sunlight like a cork from a champagne bottle, eyes sparkling, giggling gleefully.

'Run!' she yells, flying straight past nonplussed Sally and

Clare.

Monkey Boy appears in the doorway, a picture of mingled outrage and consternation. 'Gimme that fucking camera!'

Sally and Clare catch up with their leader in her hilarious headlong retreat, and Monkey Boy gives chase (at the same time making the discovery that it's not that easy to do up your flies while running at the same time.)

'Get back here!' he roars.

'Can't catch me!' throws back taunting Rinda.

'Look, I am *serious!*' roars Monkey Boy.

From the look on his face this is self-evident—but unfortunately, Rinda does not share his sense of gravity, and she responds only with mocking laughter.

The chase proceeds from court to court across the estate, Monkey Boy single-mindedly determined to get his hands on the girl and her video camera. So intent on his pursuit is Monkey Boy that for once in his life he isn't keeping a weather eye open for cats—which is a shame really, because if he had been he might have seen the one that tripped him up before it was too late.

Did the cat do it on purpose?

Did the cat, even at risk of injury to itself, deliberately step out in front of Monkey Boy in order to impede his progress, disrupt his balance and send him flat on his face? I just don't know. (As we've already established, omniscient third-person narrators can't be expected to know everything) All I can state are the facts, and it is a fact that the cat, in direct contradiction of established feline behaviour (i.e., that cats usually retreat from, rather than approach, running human beings) steps out in front of Monkey Boy, and it is likewise a fact that Monkey Boy and this particular cat (in common with every other cat in the neighbourhood) have never been on good terms—so there you have your motive.

And so, whatever its reason, the cat steps in front of Monkey Boy, Monkey Boy sees it at the last minute and, in an effort to avoid treading on or kicking the animal, swerves, loses his balance and takes a nosedive into the asphalt.

But is this the end of the chase? Not on your nelly. In spite of pain in his knees and grazes on his hands, Monkey Boy's determination is undiminished. He scrambles to his feet. The fleeing girls have made it to the next court, but are still in sight through the passageway between the buildings. Monkey Boy resumes his pursuit, running fast. He sees the girls stop, look back, and then, seeing they are still pursued, start running again. Monkey Boy puts on a spurt; he closes the distance, reaches the entrance to the passageway—and runs into an invisible concrete wall.

At least that's what he feels like. The next thing he knows he is flat on his back and when his vision clears, he's staring up at a placid blue sky.

For a moment he just lies there, stunned as much with incomprehension as by the physical shock of the impact. He staggers dizzily to his feet. The girls have disappeared. Cautiously, he approaches the passageway entrance with hands, the palms extended. They meet a solid surface. He touches it. He taps it. Perspex! Someone has gone and put a huge sheet of Perspex over the passage entrance! Why the hell would anyone do something like that?

'Congratulations! You've just been pranked!'

Monkey Boy turns. It is Ted and Hilda Pranky, the latter with camera trained on him.

'Yes, we're the Prankies! We may be senior—oh, it's you…'

Monkey Boy flies at him.

In the end Hilda has to jump on Monkey Boy's back and start hitting him over the head with her camera to stop him from throttling her associate to death.

Rinda and the Sawdust Sisters stop running.

'Looks like we lost him,' observes Clare. To Rinda: 'What happened in there? What were you doing with him?'

Rinda shakes her head, laughing breathlessly, helplessly. 'He was, he was—!' (giggle) 'He was—!' (splutter) 'Look, I got—I got it on camera!' (giggle) 'Look, I'll show you—!'

She raises the camera and suddenly her mirth evaporates. She stares at the device.

'What's wrong?' asks Clare. 'Is it broken?'

'It's the wrong one…'

Rinda turns and runs. Sally and Clare call out after her but their calls are unanswered. Bewildered, they watch the Japanese girl as she runs until she is out of sight.

They don't know it yet, but these two girls have just earned themselves the distinction of being the last people known to have seen Rinda Neves before she disappeared.

PART TWO
Chapter Ten
The Disappearance of Rinda Neves

The girl, microphone in hand, stands before the camera, behind her can be seen a skyline of towers and minarets.

'This is ace reporter Andalusia Seton reporting live from Baghdad, the capital of Iran, the country where schoolgirls are getting shot at on their way to school. And why are these schoolgirls being shot at? It's because these brave girls have started a revolution, saying they don't want to have to wear their hijabs to school. A hijab is the Islamic headdress, which a lot of people think is called a burka, but those people are wrong because a burka is a whole dress; when it's just the headdress, it's a hijab.'

'*I* knew that!'

'Shut up, camerawoman. I'm now going to talk to some of these brave schoolgirls who are with me now.' The camera pulls back to show a group of teenage girls in school uniform standing beside the reporter.

'So tell us, why is it that you don't want to wear your hijabs to school?' asks Andalusia, pointing her microphone at the nearest girl.

'Because we want to be free to show off our hair like the girls in New York!' says the girl. 'We don't want old men with beards telling us what to do! Down with the clerics!'

'Down with the clerics!' chant the other girls.

'So, explain to our viewers: why are you hiding behind this wall?' asks Andalusia.

'Because we have to get to school, but if we go out into the street, the soldiers on the roofs will start shooting at us. But if we don't go to school, we'll get arrested for playing hooky.'

Andalusia turns back to the camera. 'Yes, this is the dilemma these girls are faced with. And now we're going to join these girls as they make a run for it through the streets to get to school and brave the same dangers as them!'

'Yeah, except that we've got bullet-proof vests,' says a voice.

'Shut up, camerawoman! Right: let's go.' Turning to the schoolgirls: 'You go first, so we can follow and film you getting shot at.'

The schoolgirls break cover and start running down the street, followed by Andalusia and her camerawoman. The rooftop snipers open fire and bullets rain down on them. Fortunately the snipers are very bad shots, and nobody gets hit.

A woman in a black burka appears, beckoning from an alleyway. 'Over here! Over here!'

'Over there!' cries Andalusia.

They run to the alley and join the woman, who is wearing a comical Angelina Jolie mask over her face. 'Ah!' says Andalusia Seton, ace reporter, recognising the comical Angelina Jolie mask. 'You're Fatemah Khishvand, aren't you? The woman who did that comedy Angelina Jolie impersonation on YouTube and who got arrested and put in prison for having a sense of humour, which is against the law for women in Iran!'

'This is so. But now I am free because the real Angelina Jolie came to visit me in prison and helped me to escape!'

'That was nice of her! How did she help you to escape?'

'Well, I hit her over the head with my chamber pot, and while she was unconscious I swapped clothes with her and put on this mask, so the guards thought I was the real Angelina Jolie and they let me out of the prison!'

Andalusia Seton, ace reporter, turns to the camera. 'Yes viewers, Angelina Jolie has bravely swapped places with Fatemah to help her escape from prison!' Turning back to

Fatemah: 'And now you're going to help all these girls get safely to school, aren't you?'

'This is so. I have brought a box full of Angelina Jolie masks for everyone to wear and then we will all look like Angelina Jolie.'

'And then the snipers won't shoot because they'd think we were all Angelina Jolie and they won't want to shoot a Hollywood star because that would cause an international incident! Isn't that right?'

'This is so.'

'Right! Let's all put on our Angelina Jolie masks!' Everybody puts on their Angelina Jolie masks. 'Right! Let's go! To the airport!'

'The airport? I thought we were going to school?'

'Shut up, camerawoman!'

They start running and sure enough the confused snipers hold their fire. They run through the streets and make it to Baghdad airport and out onto the dusty desert runway where a plane has just landed and is taxying in. The door opens and the passengers, who are all hijab-wearing schoolgirls, start coming down the stairs, waving at the girls on the ground.

'*Bonjour!*' '*Bonjour!*' '*Bonjour!*' '*Bonjour!*'

'Bonjour, indeed!' says Andalusia Seton, ace reporter. 'Thanks to my new school exchange programme, these schoolgirls from France, who aren't allowed to wear their hijabs at school, can now go to school in Iran and wear their hijabs, and the Iranian schoolgirls can go Paris and go to school there where they won't have to wear theirs!' and turning to the nearest Iranian schoolgirl: 'So, how do you feel about this exchange programme?'

'*C'est bon! C'est bon!*' says the Iranian schoolgirl.

Turning back to the camera: '*C'est bon*, indeed!' And so, once again the day is saved thanks to Andalusia Seton, ace reporter!'

'This wasn't your idea, you copycat! It was Angelina Jolie's!'

'Shut up, camerawoman!'

***

Andi and Bryony are sitting on their bedroom floor playing a boardgame when Milly Leeson arrives with the news.

The room looks pretty much like you'd expect a tweeny bedroom to look. Not excessively pink and fluffy (both girls have a tomboyish streak) but still cute and friendly. There are soft toys in abundance, sitting on every available shelf and flat surface; a dressing table with heart-shaped mirror, littered with colourful accessories; posters of popstars adorning the walls... There is just one discordant note, one incongruity that would immediately draw the attention of any newcomer: amongst the posters of the usual suspects like Taylor Swift and Billie Ellish, is a very different poster. It depicts a copper-skinned woman wearing a military helmet and a flak-jacket; behind her can be seen a burning car on a jungle road. The subject of this poster, although young and good-looking, is clearly no popstar. She is none other than Jakarta Sunday, third culture kid, roving BBC news reporter, and Andi Seton's idol and inspiration. And a popular figure though she is, Jakarta Sunday posters are not actually mass-produced: Andi's mum had this one specially made for her.

A tap on the door and Milly walks into the room.

Greetings are exchanged.

'I thought I'd come and tell you the news,' says the babysitter, seating herself on the bottom bunk of the bed where Courtney Love lies curled up. 'That Japanese girl Linda Neves: she's in your class, isn't she?'

Andi confirms this.

'Well, she's disappeared.'

'Rinda's disappeared?' exclaims Andi—and if her dice cup doesn't fall from nerveless fingers, it is only because she doesn't happen to be holding it.

Both girls stare wide-eyed at Milly, who, pleased with the reaction to her announcement, starts making a fuss of

Courtney Love, who has climbed onto her lap.

'She's disappeared? When? How?'

'Yesterday afternoon, they're saying,' replies Milly. 'She went out in the morning and she never came home.'

'But we saw Rinda yesterday! We saw her on Main Street with Sally and Clare!'

'Yeah? What time was it?'

'It was just after lunchtime. About one o'clock, wasn't it...?' turning to Bryony for confirmation. 'But what's happened to her? When did it happen? How did she disappear? Have they called the police?'

'One question at a time, please! Yes, the cops have been called, but as for when and how she disappeared, they're still trying to figure that one out. Word is the last people to see her were the two friends she was with. Who did you say they were?'

'Clare and Sally Sawdust.'

'Oh, the trailer-trash twins. Well, they were with her on the Belton Estate, and Linda left them to go home and that's the last anyone saw of her. She never made it home.'

'But what happened to her? Don't they know?'

'Well, they don't *know*; not yet; but it's pretty obvious what's happened, isn't it? Abduction: someone's grabbed her.'

'She might not have been kidnapped,' argues Andi. 'She might have run away from home, mightn't she?'

'In the middle of the day while she was out playing with her friends? Come off it. She was grabbed. Only explanation.'

'Oh...' says Andi. 'I hope they find her in time...'

'"In time"?' echoes Milly scornfully. 'Forget it. She's been missing a whole day now; it'll already be too late. Just face it: your class at school is gunna be one student short next term.'

'You don't know that!' protests Andi.

'Come on, Andi; you watch the news, don't you? When

a girl your age or my age disappears, they pretty much always turn up dead, except for when they don't turn up at all; and when that happens that only means the killer's done a better job of getting rid of the body.'

'So you think Rinda's really been… killed…?'

'Bound to be. Someone grabbed her and dragged her off in a car or into their house or into some bushes; and when they'd finished doing whatever they wanted to do with her, they killed her.'

'Is that what the police think, then?'

'Well, it's not what they're *saying*. They're saying it's early days, that there's still hope, and all that crap. They have to say that; they have to go through the motions. But really, they'll know she's only going to turn up dead.'

'But who could have done it?' wonders Andi.

Milly shrugs. 'Could be anyone. Could be one of your rogue males who did it.'

'But not all the rogue males are dangerous!' argues Andi.

'Yeah, well sometimes you don't know which are the dangerous ones until it's too late. It could be any of 'em. They're all weirdos, aren't they?'

'Someone must've seen Rinda getting kidnapped,' muses Andi. 'I mean, it happened right in the middle of the day, didn't it? Somebody must've seen something!'

'You'd be surprised what people don't see,' replies Milly. 'You often hear about kids getting grabbed off the street in broad daylight. It happens. And if the cops pick up any clues, all it does is help them find the body.'

'Rinda might not be dead!' insists Andi. 'You're just guessing!'

'Alright then, she *might* still be alive,' says Milly. 'But if she is, she won't exactly be having a good time, will she? She'd be better off if she *was* dead! And anyway, what are you so upset about? You didn't even like the girl, did you?'

'Yeah, but I still wouldn't want her to be murdered!' retorts Andi.

'*I* would,' says Bryony firmly. 'It'd serve her right.'

Bryony is not as forgiving as her sister; she has a tendency to nurture grievances, and she hasn't forgiven Rinda for that grilling she suffered at her hands the other day.

There's an atmosphere of suppressed excitement on the streets of Marchmont. Milly feels it as she makes her way home. People are standing on doorsteps and on the pavements in gossiping groups. She sees police officers going from door to door, questioning residents. Local television news teams have appeared on the scene, and there are rumours that reporters from the national dailies are already sniffing around. If this keeps up, Marchmont could be finding itself achieving poll-position on the national news. Just think: an honour that has not accorded to the town since the Belton Estate Riots!

Milly had intended to call round her uncle's house today to pick up that money he's promised her, but she is deterred by the idea that it might seem heartless to be doing something like that on a day like this.

Even blackmailers can have a concern for appearances.

So instead, she makes her way home and, arriving on her street, sees Paul Straker walking down the path towards her.

Milly scowls. He's been calling round for her again. There's somebody here who can't take a hint.

Seeing her, Paul's face becomes a picture of embarrassment, and this only serves to annoy Milly even more, because in Milly's considered opinion, shyness in boys is seriously *not* cute.

Controlling her feelings, she puts a smile on her face and greets him with a friendly 'Hey, Paul!'

'Hello!' replies Paul, blushing all over. 'I… I was… I was just…'

'Calling round for me, right?'

'Yes… Your mum… she… answered…'

'Yeah, I was out. Heard about that girl going missing?'

'Yes, it's... I heard about it... I... hope they find her...'

'Yeah, me too. Look, thing is, Paul: I don't fancy you. You're a nice boy and all that, but you're not really my type. So you really need to start looking for someone else, okay? But I'm not mad at you, okay? I don't hate you or anything, but I just don't fancy going out with you. But there's plenty more fish in the sea, right? You'll find someone! Okay, then?'

'Okay, then,' says Paul, nodding his agreement. 'Well, I'll see you, then...'

'Right! Well, see ya...!'

Paul walks off, leaving Milly feeling vaguely annoyed. Not quite the response she'd been expecting. She'd expected him to look more upset by his dismissal, thought he might even start blubbering... She'd been all ready to throw her arms around him and cheer him up with a consolatory hug— but after that half-arsed 'okay, then!' reaction, he didn't bloody deserve a hug!

He'd almost looked like he was relieved or something...

Dismissing Paul with a shrug, Milly walks on.

'Mum, do you think it'll be on the main news?'

'Depends really. They might run the story tonight, or it might not be till tomorrow morning. It all depends on what else is going on. It might just get a brief mention.'

It is early evening, and the Seton clan are sitting in the living room.

'They won't make it the main headline story, then?' pursues Andi.

'Doubt it,' says Mum. 'Still too early for that. Mind you, you never know; sometimes these things catch on. Especially if it's a slow news day.'

'What's slow news?'

'It's when there isn't much happening in the news, so a story that wouldn't normally be the top story ends up being the top story. There's a famous example of that: it was… when was it…?' counting on her fingers. 'Christ, it must've been when I was the same age as you, Andi! Yeah, it must've been. There were these two girls Holly and Jessica who disappeared—and *they* were both ten, as well, come to think of it—and because it was a slow news day, the story caught on: it was the main story on the national news, it was all over the papers; the whole country was talking about it, wondering what had happened to Holly and Jessica.'

'And what *had* happened to them?'

'They were dead,' is the grim reply. 'They'd been murdered. They caught the guy who did it, though; he was right under their noses the whole time: this local man called Ian Huntley.'

'Was he a rogue male?' asks Andi.

'Well, yeah, I suppose he was really, though you might not have had him on your list, Andi, because he had a job and he wasn't a loner; he had a girlfriend he lived with, Maxine Carr. They arrested her, as well.'

'Ooh, was she like Myra Hindley, then? Did they both do the murders?'

'No, she wasn't involved in the murders; she wasn't even there the day it happened; she was off visiting relatives, I think. That didn't stop people calling her a Myra Hindley, though.'

'But Mum, why did they arrest her, if she didn't help with the murders?'

'Well, she did try to cover up for the guy when she found out what he'd done; an "accessory after the event," they call it. But no, she wasn't really a bad person: she was just stupid, poor cow.'

'And did they both get put in prison? That doesn't seem fair, if only the man did the murders!'

'She wasn't in for long. A year, was it…? Can't remember now… But *him* they threw the book at. He'll be in prison for life.'

'Why did he kill those girls?'

'Because he was a sexual predator, sweetheart. The girls knew Maxine Carr, and they went to her and Huntley's house to see her that day, but *she* wasn't there, and *he* was. God knows what he did to those girls; I doubt we'll ever know the full story, except that a bath came into it... But whatever he did, in the end he killed them, probably just to stop them from telling on him. And that, my darlings, is the motive for a lot of these murders of women and girls you hear about; they start off as sexual assaults, but then the guy ends up killing the girl afterwards just to stop her from talking.'

'And is that what's happened to Rinda, Mum? Has the man who kidnapped her killed her just to stop her from telling on him?'

'We don't know that Linda's been *killed*, sweetie!' protests Jo. 'We don't even know for sure she's been kidnapped. You shouldn't write her off just yet.'

'But Milly says she *is* dead! Milly says that when girls our age go missing, it always means someone's killed them!'

'Milly says that, does she? Well, that's just her cynical teenager's way of looking at things. Girls who go missing don't always get killed.'

'But Milly says even if Rinda *is* still alive, she'd be better off dead, because of all the horrible things that'll be happening to her!'

'I'm going to have to have a word with that young woman about infecting you with her pessimistic outlook on life,' declares Jo. 'Well yes, if Linda has been abducted—and we don't know for sure that she has—she'll be going through a very bad time, but even so, she isn't "better off dead" as our Millicent so compassionately puts it. No-one's ever better off dead.' She pauses. 'As a rule, anyway. And if Linda can get rescued in time, or if she escapes from whoever's abducted her, she's still got the rest of her life ahead of her; and there'll be people who can help her—help her to deal with what she's been through. And like I said, we don't even know if she *has* been abducted yet. There are other possibilities, you know.'

'Yeah, but Milly says—'

'Never mind what Milly says!' snaps Jo.

'Mum?' says Andi. 'If they don't find Rinda straight away and this story goes on for long enough, do you think maybe Jakarta Sunday will come here to report on it? It'd be great if she did, cuz then I'd get to meet her!'

'Don't get your hopes up, lovey,' says Jo. 'Jakarta doesn't really cover domestic stories like this one, does she? And anyway, isn't she still in Africa?'

'Oh yeah,' says Andi. 'Yes, she is, isn't she…'

Chapter Eleven
Trailer Park of Error

Emerging from the jungle, the armed gorillas are coming down the hillside towards the village. Ace reporter Andalusia Seton knows that they really ought to be armed *guerillas*, but this time they are actually gorillas, actual hairy ape gorillas, except that these ones are walking on their back legs and carrying automatic rifles. Now this is funny, because Andi always thought she'd been wrong about guerillas being gorillas, just like she'd been wrong about femicide gas—but now it turns out she wasn't wrong after all!

She'll have to tell Mum about this.

But not right now, because right now she's got some ace reporting to do! The gorillas are going to attack the village and there are only women and children living in the village, and the women and children don't even have any guns to fight back with!

She addresses the camera. 'This is ace reporter Andalusia

Seton, reporting from war-torn Africa—'

'You can't just say "reporting from Africa!"'

'Shut up, camerawoman!'

'But you can't! Africa's lots of countries, not just one country!'

'I know it is, but I can't remember the names of all of them, can I? Now, shut up! We'll take it from the top: this is ace reporter Andalusia Seton reporting from—'

'Excuse me, but I'm doing this story.'

Andi looks round. It's ace BBC reporter Jakarta Sunday, Andi's idol! Like Andi she's wearing a military helmet and bulletproof vest.

'You're doing this story? So am I!'

'No, Andalusia, you're not,' says Jakarta.

'Ooh! You know who I am!'

'Of course I know who you are. You know who I am, don't you? You're Andalusia Seton, my biggest fan, and you're in the wrong place; you shouldn't be here.'

'Shouldn't I? Where should I be, then?'

'You should be back home, looking for Rinda Neves. That's where you should be. It's a reporter's job to uncover the truth and save people who are in trouble!'

'But who's going to save all the villagers from the gorillas?'

'Just leave that to me. Now, get going, Andalusia! You've got to solve the mystery and find Rinda Neves!'

'You're right! I've got to solve the mystery and find Rinda Neves!'

Andi wakes up with a start, sitting bolt upright in bed.

'I've got to solve the mystery and find Rinda Neves!'

***

The exterior of the Marchmont Mobile Home Park does not look pretty. The park is enclosed by a corrugated iron fence, and corrugated iron fences never do look pretty, especially when they're old and rusty and they've never seen a lick of paint. The barbed wire running along the top doesn't help much, either. But in its defence, the appearance of the trailer park is at least harmonious with its surroundings: this straggling street of tumbledown houses and bungalows half-buried in weed-tangled gardens.

Andi, Bryony and Carli stand across the road from the entrance to the park, a pair of dilapidated wire mesh gates standing wide open.

Morning has brought no new developments in the Rinda Neves case; no witnesses have come forward and the police have still yet to strike a single lead. The incident has now earned itself a place on the national news headlines, although regrettably being kept from poll position by a war in the middle east which has very inconsiderately chosen this moment to escalate into what looks like the tentative early stages of World War Three. The story has also made it into the daily newspapers, the same school photograph of Rinda being reproduced in all of them.

Andi has remembered her dream of the night before and seeing it as a message and a sign she is resolved to act upon it. And so, she is no longer a documentary filmmaker; she is now an investigative reporter, and every atom of that precocious abundant seriousness of which we have had cause to mention already has been brought to bear on this endeavour. She is going to solve the mystery. She is going to track down the culprit in this kidnapping case and rescue the victim—and if she can capture these events on film, so much the better.

The first port of call on this exercise in investigative reportage is the mobile home park. Andi wants to interview the Sawdust Sisters, the last people to see Rinda. She wants to hear their story firsthand; and especially she wants to know if they noticed any of the estate's rogue males around at the time Rinda disappeared. Milly's suggestion that a rogue male could be the culprit has struck home with Andi.

The Marchmont Mobile Home Park is located out on the edge of town and enjoys an even worse reputation than the Belton Estate. Andi had always planned on visiting the park anyway on account of it being home to a number of rogue males, and Mum is okay with them going there. (Actually, Mum is *not* entirely okay with them going there, but she has granted them permission anyway, deciding that to refuse would smack more of prejudice than caution.)

Through the open gates they see a dusty gravel apron which apparently does service as a car park, and at the end of which stands a recycling slash fly-tipping centre, the plastic bins projecting their slotted heads above the accumulation of rubbish piled up around them. Beyond the bins can be seen the first of the serried ranks of the mobile homes; a conglomeration of caravans and trailers old and new, of all shapes and sizes, jumbled together in uncomfortable proximity, with a forest of antennas and satellite dishes rising from their roofs. In one sense the word 'park' is a misnomer, there not being a single blade of grass to be seen in the Marchmont Mobile Home Park; just a lot of dust and gravel and rusting corrugated iron. A hut with a reception window stands on the right just inside the gates.

'How are we going to find where the Sawdust Sisters live in all that lot?' wonders Bryony aloud.

'Easy,' responds Andi. 'We just ask at that reception place. They'll tell us what number their caravan is.'

'Caravans don't have numbers!' expostulates Bryony. 'Only houses have numbers!'

'Of course caravans have numbers!' insists Andi. 'Otherwise how would the postman know where to deliver the letters to?'

Bryony thinks about this. 'The postmen don't deliver letters to caravans,' she decides.

'Of course they do! And what about things like Amazon? How would they know where to deliver parcels to if the caravans didn't have numbers?'

No hesitation this time. 'Amazon don't deliver to caravans.'

'That's stupid! If that was true, people living in caravans wouldn't be able to do online shopping!'

'They *can* buy things online; they just don't get home delivery. They have to go to one of those collection places. The same with letters through the post: they have to pick them up from the post office.'

'Are you sure about that?'

'Yes, I am,' says Bryony.

'Well, let's just ask at the reception place anyway,' says Andi.

They cross the road and pass through the gates. They walk hand-in-hand, Carli between her older sisters. (They have strict instructions from Mum not to let her wander off while they're in the trailer park.)

They approach the hut. Through the unglazed reception window, they see a fat man reclining in a chair reading a newspaper. On the wall behind him are rows of numbered mailboxes.

'Hello?' says Andi.

The man lowers his newspaper. 'Morning, love. What can I do for you?'

'We want to see Clare and Sally Sawdust,' explains Andi. 'They live in one of the mobile homes here.'

'Sure. Just go on in.'

The man raises his newspaper.

'But we don't know where to find them!' says Andi. 'We don't know which one's their caravan.'

'Just give 'em a buzz, then,' says the man, unconcerned. 'Then they can come and meet you.'

'How do we buzz them?' asks Andi.

'On your *phone*, love; your mobile phone,' raising his newspaper again.

'But we don't know their phone numbers, either!'

The paper is lowered again, sounding irritated this time. 'Didn't they know what time you were coming? They should've come out to meet you.'

'They *don't* know that we're coming,' says Andi. 'We don't know their phone numbers or their email addresses, so we couldn't talk to them to arrange anything.'

'Good pals of yours then, these girls?' says the man.

'What are those little doors with numbers behind you?' inquires Andi, ignoring the sarcasm.

'Them? They're the mailboxes, aren't they?'

'Mailboxes! You mean mailboxes for the people in the caravans?'

'Well, they wouldn't be for anyone else, would they?'

'And is the one for each caravan?'

'That's right. Everyone's got one.'

'So they *do* have numbers!' looking at Bryony triumphantly. 'Just like I said!' Turning back to the caretaker: 'Can you tell us what number the Sawdust family's mailbox is?'

'Well, yeah...' looking round, scanning the name cards on the mailboxes. 'Sawdusts' is this one, number nineteen; though I don't see what good knowing that's gunna do you...'

'Simple! We'll just go along all the caravans until we get to the one with number nineteen on the door!'

'The *caravans* ain't numbered, love,' smiles the caretaker. 'The *mailboxes* is numbered, but the caravans ain't.'

'Well, that doesn't matter, does it? We just have to count each caravan as we go along, and when we get to the nineteenth one, that'll be the Sawdusts' one, won't it?'

The caretaker shakes his head. 'No, it won't. That's what I'm trying to tell you: these mailboxes is just given out any old how; they're not in any order.'

'Oh... Then, can you just tell us how to find the Sawdusts' caravan? We've *got* to speak to Sally and Clare;

it's really important.'

'Yeah, I reckon I can point you in the right direction. Lemme see… Sawdust, Sawdust… Yeah, I got it: it's third row in, fourth one on along… Or is it fifth one…? Well, anyhow, it's third row in; if you can't find it just ask someone.'

Thanking the caretaker, the girls set off across the carpark.

Bryony roars with laughter. 'What a duh-brain!' she crows. 'I told you, didn't I? I told you that caravans don't have numbers!'

'Told you! Told you!' chants Carli.

'Well, you were still wrong about the postman not coming here,' mutters Andi.

They come to the first row of caravans. The row of immobile mobile homes, with their backs churlishly turned to the visitors, spans the entire width of the park, from one corrugated iron fence to the other.

'Well, this is the first row,' says Andi. 'The man said Sally and Clare's caravan was on the third row, so we need to get to the third row.'

The mobile homes being parked too close together to allow passage between them, the girls proceed to the end of the row. Attaining the other side of it, they now discover that the first row of caravans stands face-to-face with the second row with a strip of hardpacked gravel between them, forming a street of mobile homes. And a rather rundown-looking street it has to be confessed; a shanty-town of mismatched mobile homes, the smaller ones dwarfed by the larger, presenting their grimy facades to one another. One or two residents can be seen, sitting on their doorsteps, smoking or busy with their smartphones. The only splashes of colour are provided by the clothing hung out on drying racks outside some of the caravans.

'Well, these are the first and second rows,' says Andi; 'so we need to go on to the next one. Come on.'

The third row of mobile homes faces the fourth row, forming a second avenue parallel to the first. (This pattern is evidently repeated for the entire length of the trailer park.) The girls won't be needing to ask directions of anybody to find the Sawdust residence: they espy the curly heads of Clare and Sally at once. The siblings, dressed alike as usual, sit perched on the steps of their mobile home (and it's the *sixth* one along!) engrossed in their smartphones.

Becoming aware of the approaching Seton trio, they look up from their phone screens, their matching faces assuming matching expressions of annoyance.

Clare: 'What are you lot doing here?'

'We've come here to see you,' answers Andi. 'We want to talk to you.'

Clare: 'Talk to us about what? No, let me guess: it's about Rinda, right? Well, we ain't got nothing to tell you, so piss off.'

Sally: 'Yeah, piss off.'

'Look, we came here because we want to help. We just want to know where abouts you were when you last saw Rinda.'

Clare: 'Do you now? Well, we ain't telling you.'

'It was on the Belton Estate, wasn't it? That's where you were when Rinda disappeared?'

Clare: 'Might've been, might not've been.'

'It *was* on the Belton Estate. Even the news says that; but where abouts on the estate were you?'

Clare: 'Wouldn't you like to know?'

'Look, we're not asking cuz we're nosy; we want to try and help! Where abouts on the estate were you?'

Clare: 'That's for us to know and you to find out.'

'Just *tell* us, will you?'

Clare: 'Shan't.'

Sally: 'So there.'

'Why not? I bet you told the police when they asked you!'

Clare: 'That's different: we had to tell the old bill, didn't we? But we don't have to tell you. So piss off.'

Sally: 'Yeah, piss off.'

'Look, we're trying to *help*, you stupid pinheads! Don't you want to save Rinda?'

Sally and Clare laugh at this.

Clare: 'Save her? Save Rinda? How can we save Rinda? She's dead, isn't she?'

Sally: 'Dead in a ditch somewhere.'

'You don't know that she's dead!'

Clare: 'Yes, we do!'

Sally: 'So there!'

'How?'

Clare: 'Cuz that's what everyone says: Mum and Dad; everyone. When a girl goes missing like that it means she's been killed by some paedo serial killer.'

'That's just normalising it!' accuses Andi. 'You shouldn't go around normalising things just because they happen all the time! Rinda might be still alive! She might have been grabbed by someone on the estate, and he might be keeping her prisoner! And if we can find out who it was who grabbed her, we can rescue her!'

More laughter.

Clare: 'Too late for that! She'll be chopped up in little pieces by now!'

Sally: 'Thrown out with the rubbish.'

'What's wrong with you two? She was your friend, wasn't she?'

Clare: 'Yeah, but she wasn't *your* friend, was she? She hated your guts. So why do you care what's happened to her?'

'We may have had our differences,' is the airy reply, 'but I'd still help her if I can. And anyway, our mum's friends with her mum.'

Clare: 'Well, that's tough, ain't it? Cuz we ain't telling you anything.'

Sally: 'So there.'

Andi stamps her foot. 'What is *wrong* with you pinheads? That's what you are: pinheads!'

Clare: 'Takes one to know one.'

Sally: 'Yeah, takes one to know one, pinheads!'

Clare: 'Yeah, and didn't there used to be three of you?'

'Three of us—?' Andi breaks off. She looks down at her side. She looks at Bryony. Bryony looks at her.

'Where's Carli?' asks Andi, keeping her voice nice and pleasant.

'She's—' begins Bryony.

Andi and Bryony look helplessly up and down the street of mobile homes. Of their little sister there is no sign.

Chapter Twelve
Trailer Park of Error (Continued)

'Carli! Carli! Can you hear me?'

Andi runs along the dusty caravan streets in zig-zagging course, up one street and down the next, calling out to her errant sister, alternately coaxing the girl with the prospect of ice cream and threatening her with her mother's wrath (although, as Andi well knows, *she* is the one who's going to be on the receiving end of that maternal wrath if they've gone and lost Carli!)

Stupid Bryony! Why did she have to go and let go of Carli's hand and let her wander off like that? True, Andi herself had let go of Carli's other hand, but she'd been the one talking to the Trailer Trash Sisters, hadn't she? And you need both hands for talking to people: everybody knows that! But Bryony had just been standing there and listening—and you don't need both hands for standing there and listening.

And as for Sally and Clare Sawdust: they *must* have seen Carli wander off; they *must* have seen which way she went! They denied it, the cows, but they *must* have! They'd seen

Carli wander off, and then they'd deliberately waited until she was gone out of sight before letting them know about it! That's what they'd done! Stupid Trailer Trash Sisters! (And it is compelling evidence of just how overwrought Andi currently is that she, even mentally, refers to Sally and Clare as the Trailer Trash Sisters, a derogatory term she in the past has criticised Bryony for using.)

'Carli, if you're hiding somewhere, come out! We haven't got time for playing hide and seek right now! We can play it later, okay? after we've had some ice cream!'

Turning onto the next caravan street Andi sees a man walking along, his back to her. She calls out to the man; he stops and looks round. A lanky, thin-face young man dressed in scruffy denims and a red baseball cap, Andi knows him: Jitterbug, a young rogue male so-called on account of the fact he can never keep his body still. Even when he's sitting or standing, he will not be sitting or standing *still*; his arms and legs will be twitching, his face will be twitching, his restless fingers playing allegro on invisible keyboards; and when he speaks, Jitterbug's voice jitters right along with his body.

It goes without saying that this state of constant physical restlessness is chemically-induced.

'Have you seen a little black girl?' inquires Andi, breathless and without preamble.

'Why, have you lost one?' grins Jitterbug, jittering.

'Yes!' vehemently. 'She's my little sister!'

'How'd she manage that, then?' still grinning.

'Manage what?' impatiently

'Well, I mean: she can't be *your* sister if she's black, can she?'

'Yes she can!'

'What, half-sister, is she?'

'No, she's my whole sister! Look, have you seen her or not? She's wearing a white dress, and her hair's in braids.'

'Little black girl, white dress, hair in braids...' Jitterbug ponders this, jittering thoughtfully. 'Yeah... Yeah, I reckon I did! About *this* tall...?'

'No, smaller than that: *this* tall!'

'Right: *that* tall! Yeah, yeah, I saw her alright! Came running past here not five minutes ago, she did! Like she was in an 'urry or something!'

'Which way was she going?'

'That way!' pointing a jittering arm.

'Thanks!'

Andi sets off in the direction indicated.

'Hang on! I'll come with you!'

'Well, come on then!'

They come to the end of the street and the corrugated iron fence. Andi looks up and down the length of the fence. No Carli in sight.

'Did you see which way she went after this?' she asks Jitterbug.

'Yeah... She went that way!' pointing. 'Right down to the end, she went!'

'Are you sure?'

''Course I'm sure! I was here, wasn't I?'

'I thought you were back there when you saw her.'

'No, I was here, wasn't I? An' I saw her: she went right down there to the end.'

They follow the fence all the way to the rear of the park, and Jitterbug brings them to a halt in front of a double row of portable toilets, all blue in colour, standing in the corner like a convention of TARDISes.

'Here we are!' says Jitterbug, his tone satisfied.

'Where's Carli then?' demands Andi.

'I dunno... Maybe she's in the bog!'

This seems not unlikely. 'Carli!' calls out Andi. 'It's me! Are you in one of the toilets?'

No reply.

'Come on, Carli! We can't play hide and seek now: it's time to go home!'

Still no reply.

Andi knocks on the door of the first toilet, calls out Carli's name and opens the door. Empty. She moves onto the next one. Same result.

She tries every toilet in turn. Her sister is not in any of them.

Andi looks at Jitterbug. 'Are you *sure* she came this way?'

'Well... I *thought* she did... Hang on, hang on... Now that you mention it, I think the girl I saw was wearing a red dress, not a white one... And her hair: it was loose, it wasn't done up in braids... Yeah... Oh, and she was white! Yeah, she was definitely white!'

Andi loses her last vestiges of patience. 'Then it wasn't my sister, was it?' she rages. 'You've just been messing me around, you stupid—!'

The ringing of her phone interrupts Andi and her assessment of Jitterbug's character, qualities as a human being and general manner of conducting himself remains unspoken.

The caller is Bryony.

'Hello? Have you found her...? Oh... Oh, okay... No, no, mean neither... Mm-mm... Mm-mm... Yeah, keep looking...'

She ends the call.

'Who was that, then?' asks Jitterbug.

'My sister,' replies Andi. 'Not that it's any of your business.'

'Your sister? Great! So she's alright then!'

'It was my *other* sister! My other sister who's gone to the front of the park to look for Carli; and she says Carli's not there and the man at the gate hasn't seen her, either. She's still here somewhere, so I'm going to keep looking for her!' She stomps off, and, turning back to Jitterbug: 'And don't you follow me! You just keep sending me off on wild goose chases!'

'Aw, now don't be like that! I was only trying to help, weren't I?'

'Well, I don't want your help!'

Andi resumes her search, turning into the rearmost of the caravan street, with Jitterbug, in spite of his summary dismissal, in jittering attendance. As they near one particularly small and sorry-looking caravan, they hear sounds of a violent commotion coming from within.

Alarmed, Andi pulls up. 'What's going on in there?'

'Dunno...'

'Whose caravan is it?'

'It's... it's...' scratching his baseball cap. '...Not sure whose it is...'

'Carli! Carli! Is that you in there?' she cries. Jumping onto the steps, she hammers on the door. 'Carli! Carli!'

For a moment the sounds cease, only to recommence with redoubled violence. The whole caravan shakes with the impacts against the door. It sounds like a serious fight is going on in there!

'Is that you, Carli? Say something!'

Maybe she can't, thinks Andi. Maybe she's been gagged!

Andi grabs the door handle and turns it. She tugs on the door, but it remains fast. 'You in there! Open up! I know you've got my sister! Open the door!'

She tugs the handle again and the door swings open and something shoots past her like a rocket. The freed captive is not Andi's missing sister, being a quadruped of the canine persuasion. It stands at bay, muscles tense, growling at Andi and Jitterbug.

'Oh, it's just a dog,' says Andi, unimpressed.

Jitterbug is considerably more impressed. He stares at the beast, wild-eyed and epileptic. 'It's not *just* a dog!' he tells Andi, through clenched teeth. 'It's Sam Brown's Rottweiler and it's a vicious bastard!'

'What should we do?' says Andi, now more impressed.

'I'll tell you what we do,' says Jitterbug: 'Run for it!'

And, opting to lead by example, Jitterbug turns and runs. Andi wastes no time running after him—and neither does the dog. The three of them barrel down the street, Jitterbug yelling, Andi squealing, the Rottweiler barking.

Salvation, at least for Andi, comes suddenly and swiftly. She finds herself lifted bodily off the ground, pulled backwards through the door of a mobile home and thrown unceremoniously down a sofa. Her saviour slams shut the door (an unnecessary precaution as it turns out; because the dog, apparently far more interested in Jitterbug than in Andi, runs straight on past.)

Recovering her breath, Andi sits up on the sofa. Her rescuer is a tall and rather fat man dressed in a camouflage jacket, khaki trousers and army boots; while in contrast, a very unmilitary-looking bobbled woollen hat sits atop his jowly, close-shaven head. (Perhaps his mother knitted it for him.) The man's appearance is familiar to Andi: his name is Camouflage, an ardent military geek and yet another of Marchmont's rogue males.

The interior of the mobile home shares its owner's military aesthetic, one wall adorned with a display of firearms: revolvers, pistols and assault rifles, all genuine and all (thankfully) deactivated.

'You alright?' asks Camouflage.

'Yes, thanks!' says Andi. 'That dog was after us!'

'Yeah, I saw that. What'd you go'n let old Sam Brown's dog out for? Thing's meant to be kept locked up. Was it that Jitterbug? Did he do it? Well, I hope the dog rips his ruddy throat out, ruddy drug-takin' waste of space.'

'My mum says that people like Jitterbug are more to be pitied than censored,' reports Andi dutifully (although not quite accurately.)

'Then your mum's wrong, isn't she?' returns Camouflage. 'I reckon people like him ruddy well *should* be censored; censored with extreme prejudice.'

'I'm against censorship and prejudice,' replies Andi

loftily. 'And anyway, it wasn't him who let the dog out, it was me.'

'What did you go'n do a daft thing like that for? Don't you know that thing's dangerous?'

'I didn't *know* there was a dog in there,' says Andi. 'I thought it was my sister!'

Camouflage looks confused. 'And what would your sister be doing in Sam Brown's caravan?'

Andi explains.

'Right!' says Camouflage briskly, clapping his meaty hands. 'So we've got a missing civilian, have we? Small child, possibly in danger. This calls for an immediate search and rescue!'

'She might not be in actual danger,' argues Andi. 'She might have just wandered off somewhere...'

'Of course she's in danger: where do you think we are? This is the Marchmont Mobile Home Park! Do you know what kind of people we've got around here? Riff-raff! Wastrels! Ruddy dregs of society!'

'But *you* live here,' points out Andi.

'Aye, and lucky for you I do! Look here.'

Camouflage walks over to a map pinned to a cork pinboard. He picks up a pointer stick. 'See this? This is a plan of the park, and you've got all the caravans individually marked, see? These ones that are filled in with black,' indicating several of them with a pointer stick, 'these are the danger areas; these are where the rogue elements live: your drug dealers and your pimps and your paedos and perverts. Right? So these are the places we need to search first.'

'But she doesn't have to be in one of those!' cries Andi, alarmed at the number of black rectangles on the map. 'She might just—'

'Yeah, she *might* just, but we've still gotta check the danger zones first, haven't we? Better to be safe than sorry. Right! C'mon, let's move out!'

Andi and Bryony had not parted on the best of terms when they split up to search for Carli, each sister blaming the other for having failed to keep an eye on the girl.

And Bryony, as she makes her way back from her unsuccessful trip to the park entrance, still wears a dark expression on her face. Bryony, as has already been noted, has a tendency to dwell on wrongs done to her, actual and perceived, and some of Andi's stinging words still rankle in her mind. In fact, Bryony has decided that she is fed up with being ordered about by her bossy sister; and if she wants to waste her time looking for Rinda Neves, she can do it on her own from now on! Personally, she wouldn't lift a finger to help Rinda Neves!

But all of this is driven swiftly from Bryony's head when she sees the angry Rottweiler bearing down on her.

At first, it's a yelling man she sees bearing down on her, a man she recognises as Jitterbug. But then Jitterbug shoots past her, and she sees what it is he's running away from.

And now Bryony is running at Jitterbug's heels, adding her own shrill scream to his ragged countertenor.

The end of the avenue and the corrugated iron fence loom ahead, and with them the dilemma of whether to turn right or left.

'Don't follow me!' yells Jitterbug.

Doubtless Jitterbug is motivated only by the noble aim of drawing the Rottweiler's attention away from Bryony, but alas his good intentions are thwarted by the wilfulness of the very girl he is trying to save, who, instead of running to the left when he runs to the right, sticks stubbornly to his heels.

'Stop fucking following me!' yells Jitterbug when he sees both girl and quadruped still on his tail.

His wish is no sooner spoken than granted, when rescue comes to Bryony in much the same way as it had come to her sister; but this time it is a voice rather than an actual arm that reaches out to the girl in peril.

'In here, child! With haste!'

The speaker, a man in a silk dressing gown, stands in the open doorway of his mobile home, beckoning urgently. Bryony wastes no time responding to this offer, shoots into the caravan and the man slams the door shut.

'My dear child! I trust you are unhurt? Sit down, sit down! I shudder to think at how close you came to becoming the prey of that vicious brute! You must sit down and recover your scattered wits after such a close call!'

The owner of these plummy tones is a man is of middle age, average height and stocky build, with sparse hair swept back from an aristocratic but somehow suspiciously smooth countenance. In addition to the dressing gown, he sports a loosely knotted white silk scarf, trousers with a razor-sharp creese, and a pair of well-polished leather slippers.

Bryony knows the man, at least by report: the posh-talking man who treats his caravan as though it was a stately home, known as the Poet; and the Poet, recalls Bryony, is one of the rogue males on Andi's list. (Bryony's recollection is slightly at fault in this particular: the Poet's is one of the names *crossed out* from Andi's list.)

The poet guides Bryony to a chair. 'There! Can I offer you some refreshment? A stimulating drink to restore your equilibrium after your ordeal.'

Bryony, comprehending enough of the above to realise she is being offered a drink, nods her head, grinning bashfully.

The Poet moves over to his kitchenette, takes two wine glasses from a cupboard, and from the fridge a carton of grape juice. Having filled both glasses from the carton, he returns to his guest.

Bryony accepts the proffered glass.

'Fruit of the vine,' says the Poet, holding his own glass up to the light. 'I never drink anything else.'

Bryony sniffs the drink experimentally and takes a sip. Favourably impressed she gulps it all down and holds out the empty glass.

'My goodness, you are thirsty! A second glass?'

Bryony nods her confirmation and the Poet returns to the kitchenette and refills her glass.

'Now, my child,' handing her the glass, 'if I may venture to make a suggestion, now that your immediate thirst has been quenched, with this second glass you should allow yourself time to savour the vintage. This,' holding his own glass up to the light, 'is an exquisite *Chateau de Mont Blanc*,' (or, according to the carton in the fridge, *Tesco's Red Grape Juice*); 'and to imbibe such a fine vintage is to be considered more than just refreshment; it is more than that; it is a sensual experience. Now pay attention. First one must savour the bouquet,' and sticking his nose in the glass, the Poet inhales; and then, removing his nose from the glass, he exhales. 'Ah! Such a heady, intoxicating aroma! It arouses the senses while also stimulating the higher mind; a matchless blending of the earthly and the ethereal! Now: having taken this preliminary step, we must then take just the tiniest of sips, and we do not swallow it; no, not at first! No, we roll it around the tongue, allowing the flavour full time to stimulate the pallet, for our gustatory senses to record every delicate nuisance; and then, and only then, do we allow ourselves the crowning pleasure of ingestion. Watch closely.'

Taking a large sip, the Poet proceeds to put his wine-tasting skills into practice. Bryony giggles at the display of facial contortions.

'Like so!'

Pleased with his demonstration, the Poet looks down at Bryony to watch her follow his example. Instead, Bryony holds out an empty glass. 'Oh. Finished already, have we? Another glass?'

Bryony nods her assent, grinning goofily.

'Ah, my child! When you favour me with that warm, generous smile of yours, displaying those perfect, dazzling teeth, teeth like rows of the finest, most delicate pearls…! I am your slave, my child, your humble slave! Your slightest whim is to me a royal command!'

He repairs once more to the kitchenette, takes the carton once more from the fridge, and shaking it to gauge its remaining contents, grimaces. 'However, if I might be so bold as to make a suggestion, I really think this should be your final glass, my dear. To imbibe too much of such a rare vintage at a single sitting would be to do it a disservice. With overfamiliarity the pallet would become corrupted, the senses jaded, the entire experience robbed of its poetry. Yes, just one more glass…'

Returning with the drink, he kneels down before his guest. 'Ah, my child! I feel that although we have known one another but scant minutes, I sense that a bond has already formed between us; an ethereal, immutable bond, delicate as gossamer, yet stronger than tempered steel! Do you not feel it yourself?'

Not having understood a word of this, Bryony giggles bashfully.

'Yes, yes, you need not answer, my child. *Of course* you feel it too! How could you otherwise? Such bonds between human beings are so rarely formed, and when they are made, they should be treasured! They should be nurtured and caressed! Do you not agree, my child?'

Another giggle.

'*Of course* you do! Our minds are as one! Of what need are mere words between two such as us! I am poet, my child, a poet who alas has found his creative faculties in abeyance of late, and indeed for so long a time that I feared that my fountain had run dry! But *you*, you my child, have reenergised me! I am reinvigorated! My fountain gushes once more! Clearly it was destiny that brought you to my door this day! *You*, yes *you* shall be my muse! You are the divinity for whom every stanza, every line of the sublime poetry I feel welling up within me will be dedicated! Yes, with you by my side, there is no river I cannot climb, no mountain I cannot ford—!'

At this crucial moment the door bursts open and Camouflage erupts into the room, loud, bulky and booted.

'Caught in the act, you dirty bugger!' roars the intruder. Taking hold of the Poet by the cravat, he drags him to his feet, and before that worthy can even find the words to express his indignation, a leg-of-mutton fist sends him crashing into the kitchenette.

Andi stands in the doorway.

'Hang about,' says Camouflage, noticing for the first time that the girl seated on the chair doesn't answer to the description of Carli she supplied him with. 'That's not your sister, is it?'

'No, she *is* my sister;' Andi tells him. 'She's just not the one we were supposed to be looking for.'

The three of them exit the caravan.

'What were you doing with that pervert?' demands Andi angrily. 'You know Mum told us to keep away from him!'

'I *didn't* know,' retorts Bryony. 'I thought he was on your list.'

'Oh, he'll be on quite a *few* lists,' avers Camouflage.

'Just as well we got there in time!' continues Andi.

'How come you knew I was there?' asks Bryony.

'We *didn't* know you were there: we were looking for Carli! Camouflage is helping me look for her. He knows where all the really dodgy people around here live—and we came here first, cuz he's the dodgiest out of all of them!'

'Well, he didn't have Carli; and he wasn't hurting me, either,' says Bryony sulkily.

The Poet now appears in the doorway of his caravan, blood-stained silk handkerchief held to his lower face. 'You barbarian!' he shouts at Camouflage. 'Assaulting a man in his own home! An Englishman's home is his castle! I'll have you arrested for this! Thrown into prison! Brute! Berserker! Vandal! Visigoth! Descendent of the barbarian hordes!'

'Oh, shut your noise, you!' throws back Camouflage.

'And think yourself lucky we're not reporting *you!*'

The Poet continues to hurl objurgation at Camouflage until he is out of sight.

They turn onto the next caravan street.

'Now what?' asks Bryony. 'We still haven't found Carli.'

'So, we keep on looking for her, don't we?' snaps Andi. 'Which was what you *were* supposed to be doing, instead of getting chummy with the local paedo! And you still haven't told me what you were doing with him! It looked like he was proposing to you when we came in!'

'He was just telling me one of his poems. He wasn't doing anything pervy. He gave me some grape juice. And he helped me, as well: he saved me from this dog that was chasing me.'

This pulls up Andi in her tracks. 'What dog?' she demands suspiciously.

'*That* dog,' says Bryony, pointing.

And there, at the end of the avenue, stands our friend the Rottweiler, fangs bared.

'Oh, no!' groans Andi.

But what has become of Jitterbug? Jitterbug, who was being so relentlessly pursued by this dog? Has he fallen victim to its fangs and claws, or has he somehow managed to elude his pursuer? Now, as Jitterbug will not be appearing again in this chronicle, we can't very well ask him; and indeed, some of you might conclude that this very absence does not augur well for Jitterbug's ultimate fate—but then, just look at the way the dog is glaring at Camouflage and the girls! Is this the look of a dog who has successfully hunted down its prey and is feeling rather chuffed with itself? Or is this more the look of a very angry and frustrated dog who, having been deprived of its intended victim, is ready to take on any and all comers by way of a substitute?

I will leave you to decide.

Camouflage now takes charge. 'Right, listen, you girls,' he says, voice quiet but urgent; 'when it comes at us, I want you two to run *that* away, head straight for the gates, and me, I'll run the other way an' I'll make ruddy sure it comes after me and not you.'

'How'll you do that?'

'Easy,' says Camouflage, slowly reaching a hand into his camouflage jacket and from which he produces a hand grenade. 'I'll chuck this at it.'

'A hand grenade!' squeaks Andi.

'Aye. It's not live, but I reckon it'll still do the trick.'

The dog charges.

'Now *run!*'

Andi and Bryony run, and Camouflage (pointlessly) pulls the pin from the grenade and throws it, and he throws it well, because it hits the charging dog squarely on the nose—and for a dog being hit on the nose can be as painful as a rake in the family jewels is for Monkey Boy. The dog howls and springs into the air.

'Oi, you stupid bugger! Over here!' yells Camouflage.

The dog needs no second invitation.

Meanwhile, Andi and Bryony are running for the front gates when who do they see but the Sawdust Sisters engaged in boisterous play with their sister Carli—and in the very same spot where they had left them!

'Carli!' cries Andi. She charges up to the group and drags Carli away from her playmates. Carli, who has been enjoying herself thoroughly, squeals her protest.

'Where have you been?' thunders Andi, shaking the girl; her relief, as relief often does in these cases, expressing itself in anger. 'We've been looking everywhere for you!'

Carli, hearing the angry voice and perhaps too young to appreciate the underlying sisterly concern, bursts into tears.

'She hasn't been anywhere,' grinning Clare Sawdust informs her. 'She's been here with us all the time. She never ran off in the first place, not really. She'd just crawled under that caravan,' indicating the one opposite their own abode.

'That was why you couldn't find her.'

'And you knew all along, didn't you?' accuses Andi. 'You were looking that way, so you must have seen her crawl under there! And then you didn't tell us and you let us think she'd wandered off, didn't you?'

A chorus of sniggering from the Sawdust Sisters confirms that Andi's summary of events as being correct in every particular.

'You pinheads! You complete and utter pinheads!' cries Andi, incensed. 'Right. Just for that, you can answer my questions you wouldn't answer before! I want to know if you saw any rogue males around when Rinda disappeared! Now answer!'

'What's a rogue male supposed to be?' inquires Clare.

Andi explains her definition of the term.

Clare and Sally exchange glances. 'We were being chased by one just before she disappeared,' says the former.

'Chased by one? Which one?'

'Monkey Boy.'

'Monkey Boy! Why was Monkey Boy chasing you?'

'He chased us cuz Rinda snuck into his flat.'

'What was Rinda doing in Monkey Boy's flat?'

'What were *you* doing in there?' counters Clare. 'We saw you coming out of there that day, we did. That's why Rinda snuck in; she wanted to see what you were so interested in him about. What *were* you doing with him then? Paedo stuff?' sniggering.

'No, we were not! We were just—look, it doesn't matter! So Rinda snuck in there; and then Monkey Boy chased you off, did he?'

'Yeah. Rinda came running out, laughing her head off, and Monkey Boy, he came out after her, yelling at her. He was like "Give me that fucking video camera!"'

'No, I think he just said "bloody",' interjects Sally.

'Alright, he said "Give me that bloody video camera!"'

'He wanted Rinda's camera?'

'Yeah! He chased us across half the estate, cuz Rinda'd filmed him doing something dirty…'

'Something dirty? What was it?'

Clare shrugs. 'We never got to see it, did we? Cuz that was when Rinda disappeared. She just ran off.'

'Why did she run off?'

Another shrug. 'Dunno. It was like she'd suddenly remembered something; something really important. She looked worried, didn't she?' turning to her sister for confirmation.

Sally nods. 'Like she'd thought of something really bad.'

'Yeah, and she said something was wrong: "It's all wrong," she said.'

'No, it was more like: "It's the wrong one."'

'Well, she said something like that. And then she just ran off. Didn't say a word; just ran off. And that's the last time we ever saw her,' concludes Clare.

'Last time we ever *will* see her,' adds Sally.

'No, you're wrong!' declares Andi firmly. 'Rinda's still alive! She's being kept prisoner by one of the rogue males on the Belton Estate! I bet you she is!'

'Bet you she isn't!' counters Clare.

'Well, I bet you she is!' insists Andi. 'And I'm going to prove it, cuz I'm going to find her!' She pauses, pondering just how to go about this. 'We need to know where they live… all the rogue males on the estate… We need to know where their houses are…'

'Reckon I can help you with that,' says a new voice.

It's Camouflage. He staggers along, hatless, panting, his clothes hanging from him in tatters. A black eye and swollen cheek suggest his recent antagonist has managed to land a couple of good punches.

'Are you alright?' asks Andi.

'Me? Yeah,' grins Camouflage. 'You should see the other feller!'

And having delivered the time-honoured line, his eyeballs roll up, he pitches forward, and falls flat on his face.

Chapter Thirteen
With Reference to a Purple Traitor

Jo Seton makes her way across town from the supermarket (where she has just finished another morning shift), her destination being the home of the Neves family. Yukari is naturally still absent from work, and Jo has decided to call round and see how she's coping and lend her support if needed.

Already it seems as though normal service has been resumed in Marchmont. Only one day after the story broke, the townsfolk are going about their business just as though nothing had happened. This is not to say that the public has already lost interest in the disappearance of Rinda Neves: they will continue to be interested as long as the mystery is unresolved, because there's nothing that stimulates people's attention and curiosity as much as a tantalising mystery. (A fact which is a constant source of annoyance to writers of literary fiction.) But the tense, expectant atmosphere of the day before has dissipated, and things feel like they're back to normal.

The police are still much in evidence around town, with extra officers having been drafted in from neighbouring towns, and even now Jo can see what is most likely a police helicopter buzzing around above the outskirts of town, where she knows there are also search parties with sniffer dogs out combing the ground.

In spite of what she said to her daughters the evening before, Jo doesn't have any high hopes that this situation is going to turn out well for the missing girl. Milly Leeson's assertion that youngsters who go missing usually turn up dead is cynical but it's also depressing true. Statistically, so we're told, the majority of people who go missing go missing of their own accord: but the younger the age, the less likely this is to be the case. Ten-year-olds very rarely run away from home by choice; and if Rinda hasn't run away, then as Jo sees it, there are only two other possibilities to account for her disappearance: accident or abduction.

Yes, she *could* have run away—but not run away for good. Kids that age just don't know how to take care of themselves—and they know they don't. So, if she's run away, then she will have run away because she wants her parents to worry about her—to worry about her and then come and find her. Which means she'll be hiding herself in a place she thinks her parents will think of to come looking for her. And if she's got it wrong, and it's *not* a place her parents will think of to come looking for her, then sooner or later she'll have to come out of hiding and show herself; in fact sooner rather than later.

From what she's picked up from her daughters, Rinda does sound like the kind of self-willed attention-seeker ('a right little madam' as her mum would say) who might take it into her head to run away from her parents just to cause a fuss.

Jo remembers a story from a few years back: it was an incident that happened in Japan, but by one of those flukes, the story caught on internationally. A wilful young boy had been badly misbehaving during a trip with parents to some woods; he had become completely unmanageable and the parents, driven to distraction, had decided to drive off in their car and leave the boy stranded in the woods. Of course they hadn't intended to abandon him for good, just long enough to frighten him into obedience and teach him a salutary lesson. Trouble was, when they went back (was it only an hour or so later?) the boy was nowhere to be found. The police were called in and a massive search was commenced. This search lasted a whole week, long enough for the story to be picked up by other countries' news agencies; and people all around the world were wondering what had become of the little Japanese boy and whether he would be found in time. And then after seven days he *was* found, discovered by a soldier in a place that was supposed to have already been searched; he was found and because he'd had access to shelter and access to fresh water, he was okay. (After this, the story became one about appropriate methods for disciplining unruly children.)

But as it's now two days since Rinda disappeared, so if she ran away of her own accord, she really ought to have turned up by now; she ought to have come home—unless something has happened to prevent her from doing that.

Which brings us to possibility number two: accident or misadventure; the kind of accident or misadventure that, if it doesn't kill them at once, leaves its victim trapped and/or injured in some out of the way location. And if this is what's happened to Rinda, then it's basically a just race against time: a race to find the missing girl before she dies from her injuries, from starvation, or whatever other peril might be hanging over her head.

But if Rinda hasn't run off of her own volition, and if she hasn't had an accident of some sort, then she's been abducted, and if she's been abducted then the chances of her still being alive after nearly forty-eight hours are pretty slim.

Don't get into cars with strangers. One of the first lessons drummed into your head by your parents at home and by your teachers at school. Rinda Neves is ten and she's not stupid, so most likely she wouldn't have gotten into a car with a complete stranger—but it's not only strangers who can be dangerous, and she might have got into a car with someone she *did* know, someone she knew well enough—even if only a tenuous connection like a friend of the family, or family of a friend—not to consider them a stranger. Yes, she might have done that, especially if that someone had armed themselves with a plausible story.

These things can happen, and they can happen in broad daylight. And if Rinda has been abducted it will either by someone who wants to kill her or someone who wants to sexually abuse her. If it's the former then it's a done deal: Rinda's dead and all the fuzz can do is find her remains and (if they're lucky) the killer. If it's the latter and she's been abducted for sex, then the chances are still all in favour of Rinda being dead by now. As she'd told her daughters last night, in the end, the culprit will nearly always decide in the end that he has to silence his victim; he has to kill just to cover his tracks.

So, who's the perpetrator? (Or 'purple traitor' as Andi had misheard the word the first time it came her way.) They say that with most child abductions the culprit will be someone known to the victim; but there's still a good chance that Rinda has been grabbed by a complete stranger, the victim of an opportunistic abduction.

There was the case of their babysitter's namesake, Milly Dowler, a thirteen-year-old girl who disappeared one day walking home from school. She'd been walking along a busy road when last seen and the cops had seemed to think the abductor must have been a passing motorist. But it turned out they'd been looking in the wrong direction, because it turned out that one of the houses she'd been walking past at the time happened to be inhabited by a card-carrying sociopath.

And as well as the opportunists, there are the people who actively go on the prowl, seeking victims to abduct; a classic example being the Moors Murderers, Ian Brady and Jo's antiheroine Myra Hindley. But operators like them don't come along every day; Brady and Hindley were torture-murderers and they weren't even really paedophiles; they'd just picked on kids as their victims because kids are smaller and weaker than adults, and that makes them more conveniently abductable.

Jo has always been fascinated by Myra Hindley: just what made her tick? Why had she fall in with Ian Brady's twisted schemes? There's no doubt that Brady had been the instigator; but there's no doubt either that she had become his willing accomplice. It seems like they'd just been one of those fatal combinations. Jo's pretty sure that Myra Hindley would never have gone wrong if she'd never met Ian Brady; but *he* would still have gone wrong if he'd never met her. But they *did* meet and after starting down that wrong path, it was like just by being together they encouraged and empowered each other, justified each other. And they had discovered Saddleworth Moor together, and *that* might have been as much of a catalyst for their crimes as anything else. Those lonely, wide-open spaces can have a funny effect on some people...

And what about Myra's apparent rehabilitation? That's another one the jury will always be out on. At the time, there were some, Spike Milligan for one, who believed in her repentance and pleaded for her early release; but there were others who were sceptical, claiming her repentance was just an act; and it was the cynical faction who won out in the end because Hindley died still behind bars.

Still, whatever's happened to poor Rinda, things like this always come as an unpleasant reminder to you that no matter how hard you try, you can just never guarantee that your kids are always one-hundred percent completely *safe*—not unless you keep them locked up in filing cabinets, like in that *Brass Eye* episode.

Jo reaches the street in which the Neves family live. Yesterday, there had been a small media circus outside their house, but today the street is quiet, no police cars or reporters.

She rings the bell.

The summons is answered by Yukari, her face tired but otherwise expressionless. Jo says hi, apologises for turning up out of the blue, just wants to see how she's doing, if there's any news...

'No news,' says Yukari. She steps aside for Jo to enter. 'Please come in.'

'Is it okay...?'

'Yes; please come in.'

Yukari leads Jo to the living room where Peter sits in front of the television.

'Please sit down,' says Yukari. 'I will make some coffee.'

'Oh no, you don't have to—'

'I will make some coffee.'

Yukari departs for the kitchen and Jo takes a seat. She looks at Peter. He looks awful, she thinks, as though this has hit him harder than it even has the girl's mother. He greets Jo absently.

'So, how are you both bearing up?' she asks him. 'It must be terrible for you.'

'It's been a nightmare,' answers Peter dully. 'But at least we're back home now. Yesterday, at the police station... It was a nightmare. And you know,' looking at her squarely for the first time, 'they were even acting like they thought *we* did it; acting like *we* were the suspects!'

Jo shrugs. 'Well, I suppose they've got to do that, don't they? They've got to look at every possibility... I mean, sometimes it *does* turn out to be one of the parents who's responsible...'

The observation doesn't quite have the effect the observer intended.

'Oh, yes,' sneers Peter, his voice rising in volume. 'And especially if the father isn't actually the birth father, right? That's what you're saying, isn't it?'

'No, it wasn't what I was saying, Peter,' answers Jo patiently.

'I was at work!' proceeds Peter. 'I was at work when it happened! I was at work all day! So, how could it have been me?'

Yukari re-enters the room, carrying a tray with three steaming mugs, which she sets down on the coffee table.

'So, do the police have any leads?' asks Jo when the drinks have been distributed and Yukari has seated herself beside her husband.

'Oh, too many,' answers Peter. 'About half the population of Marchmont are saying they saw Linda that afternoon. She'd have to have been in about fifty places at the same time. And then they waste their time following up all these leads...'

'Yeah, but they have to, don't they?' reasons Jo. 'I know most of those sightings will turn out to be false ones, but one of them might turn out to be true. Are they treating it as an abduction? On the news they're just saying "it's still too early to say for sure," and that they're "keeping their options open." Is that what they're saying to you? Or—?'

'They think she might have gone off with someone by choice,' says Peter wearily. 'They think the way she left those girls she was with, those Sawdust girls, so suddenly, seems suspicious. They say it seemed like she suddenly remembered she had to be somewhere, that she had to meet someone... But they're just guessing, aren't they? I mean, who *could* she have gone off with? She doesn't know anyone like that!'

'Yes, but there might have been someone,' argues Jo. 'Someone you don't know about; someone she'd met, who was grooming her...'

'Rubbish! Linda wouldn't have been doing anything like that behind our backs! I know she wouldn't! And she had her video camera with her! She wouldn't have gone off with some other man when she had that with her, would she?'

Jo fails to see the logic in this reasoning. 'What's her video camera got to do with it?'

'Well, it was brand new, wasn't it? She'd only got it the day before! It was a present from me. You see, she wanted to use our video camera—'

'*My* video camera,' interposes Yukari.

'—Yukari's video camera for her school project, but you wouldn't let her, would you? So I just ordered her a new one on Amazon. And she was so excited about it! She couldn't wait to start using it! So, she wouldn't have just gone off with someone the first day she was out using her new camera, would she?'

'Not sure I'm following your logic here,' confesses Jo. 'What about her mobile phone? Did she have that with her? They can track her down with—'

'She *didn't* have it with her,' breaks in Peter irritably. 'She went out without it that morning. Of all the days she had to forget and leave it at home… And now the police have confiscated it! They've been going through all her messages, everything!'

'Well, they would. They'll be looking for leads, won't they? They'll want to see if she was in contact with anyone, if she'd made any arrangements…'

'Well, she hadn't! And then they act like they're suspicious of *me*, just because I tried to call her up a few times that morning! I mean it's ridiculous, isn't it? If I couldn't get through to her, how could I have arranged to meet her somewhere?'

'Yes, but she might have arranged to meet someone else,' points out Jo. 'Have they found anything like that? Any contacts you didn't know about…?'

'No, there was nothing like… They just kept asking me why I kept trying to call her that morning—like it's a crime for a father to want to speak to his own daughter!'

'Step-daughter,' says Yukari.

'Alright, step-daughter!'

Jo looks at the wife and husband. There they are, sitting side by side on the settee, but there's no fellow feeling there, no sense of support or sympathy connecting them. Yukari sits rigidly, back straight, knees together; Peter slumps forward, fidgety and tense.

'So, what do you two think has happened to Linda?' Jo asks them.

'Well, *I* think someone must have taken her,' answers Peter. 'But Yukari insists that she's run away.'

'I do not insist,' says Yukari. 'I just that it is a possibility.'

'Had there been any problems, then?' asks Jo. 'Any arguments?'

'None!' replies Peter. 'None at all! We'd all been getting along just fine, absolutely fine. Hadn't we, dear?'

'Yes, dear,' says Yukari.

'No, someone's grabbed her,' declares Paul. 'Someone's taken her...' He looks at Jo. 'And he's got her video camera, as well. They haven't found it, so he must have taken it when he took her. What do you think he'll do with it...?'

'I think you should be more worried about what he's done with your step-daughter,' says Jo, frowning.

'He thinks a great deal about that video camera,' says Yukari quietly.

'I don't! I just—!'

The phone in the hallway rings and Peter jumps in his seat.

'I bet it's that bloody inspector again! Oh God! He's not going to drag me in for more stupid questions...?'

'If it was that, he would have come here, he would not have phoned,' says Yukari, rising to her feet.

She goes into the hallway to answer the phone.

Chapter Fourteen
And Now the Screaming Stops

'He won't be there,' says Bryony.

'Yes, he will! He said he'd meet us, didn't he?'

'He *said* he would, yeah. But don't count on it.'

The subject under discussion is Camouflage. Camouflage has arranged to meet the girls on the edge of the Belton Estate, promising to bring with him a map he happens to possess, a map of the estate similar to his map of the caravan park, which likewise highlights the homes of all the rogue males (or 'rogue elements' as Camouflage calls them) inhabiting the estate. Having returned home for lunch (and leaving Carli with their mum), Andi and Bryony are now on their way to this rendezvous.

'What if it was your boyfriend the Poet, then?' challenges Andi. '*He'd* keep his promises, wouldn't he? Wouldn't pass up a chance to meet up with *you*.'

'He is *not* my boyfriend,' grates Bryony, furious.

Andi has been firing a broadside of jokes about the Poet ever since they left the mobile home park, baiting her sister with comments like: 'So, when's the wedding going to be?' and 'Shall I just get you one of those "property of a specific paedo" stickers for your schoolbag?' And whether intended or not, this exercise in reverse psychology has actually done the trick: from defending the Poet as a harmless and generous host, Bryony now rises to the boil at the mere mention of his name!

And if anything was needed to further sour Bryony's mood, it is the sight of Camouflage who, true to his word, stands waiting for them at the arranged location. His shredded camouflage jacket replaced with identical one, a fresh bobble hat on his buzzcut, the injuries to his face are the only remaining emblems of his encounter with the Rottweiler. He waves to the girls as they approach, smiling as much as his swollen jaw will allow.

'Oh, look who it is!' says Andi, looking at her sister in triumph.

Bryony's reply is inaudible.

They join Camouflage

'I've brought the map,' says he, reaching into the breast pocket of his jacket. Producing the map, he unfolds it, spreading it out against the nearest wall. Executed in the same style as the map of the mobile home park, it is a clearly-drawn plan of the courts and closes of Belton Estate, each building individually delineated, and the residences of those 'rogue elements' filled in in black.

'This is great!' enthuses Andi. 'Now we can start looking

for Rinda!'

'Why has he got a map like that in the first place?' demands Bryony to her sister. 'Where did he get it from?'

'He made it himself, stupid!' says Andi.

'Aye, I did,' confirms Camouflage.

'Yeah, but *why* did he make it?' persists Bryony, still directing her words at Andi, but in a voice loud enough for Camouflage to hear. 'Why does he need to know where all the dodgy people on the estate live? Seems suspicions to me.'

'Cuz it's my job to know about these things,' answers Camouflage. 'I'm a paedophile hunter, see?'

'Oh!' exclaims Andi, impressed. 'So, what were you in for, then?'

'Eh? What was I in what for?' says Camouflage, confused.

'I mean, what were you in prison for!' explains Andi.

'I never was in prison!' indignantly.

'You must have been!' insists Andi. 'Mum says that paedophile hunters are always men who've been in prison.'

'That's a stereotype, that is!' exclaims Camouflage defensively.

'Yeah, and she also says paedo hunters are all sad-sacks who just want to make themselves look good,' adds Bryony maliciously.

'Yeah? Well, you can tell your mam—!' blusters Camouflage, nettled. 'Well, I reckon I should have a word or two with your mam about sayin' things like that...'

Bryony and Andi trade knowing grins.

'What things do you do then, to hunt paedophiles?' inquires Andi. 'Do you spy on their houses?'

'Stakeouts? No, not much of that. It's mostly online, really. You know, places like Facebook. That's where they try and get hold of kids.'

'But Facebook's only for people older than thirteen,' argues Andi. 'Mum says that proper paedos are the ones who like children primary-school age like us, and we're too young for Facebook.'

'Aye, but it's still illegal, ain't it? If it's kids under sixteen it's illegal, so it all counts. You've got them grooming gangs, haven't you? They use Facebook to get at teenage kids.'

'Those grooming gangs are always Pakistani men, aren't they?' asks Andi.

'Aye—I mean, no: that's another stereotype. Look, never mind all that. We're here to check out the rogue elements who might have abducted that Neves girl, right?' turning to the map: 'Now, I reckon we should—'

'Where's Monkey Boy's flat?' interposes Andi, studying the map. 'I can't see it...'

'You don't think *Monkey Boy* kidnapped Rinda, do you?' protests Bryony.

'No, of course I don't! I just want to talk to him. I want ask him what happened when Rinda snuck into his flat that day.' To Camouflage: 'Where's Monkey Boy's flat on the map?'   'Who's this Monkey Boy?' replies Camouflage. 'Never heard of him.'

'You must have!'

'Nope. He's not on any of my lists.'

'That's awkward. How're we going to find him then?'

'He lives in Nettleford Court,' supplies Bryony wearily.

Nettleford Court.

Andi knocks on the door of Monkey Boy's flat. She has been knocking for some time.

'Try shouting through the letterbox,' suggests Bryony.

Andi pushes open the flap. 'Hello? Monkey Boy? It's me, Andi! Are you there? We just want to talk! We don't want to film you doing anything naughty! We just want to talk to you for a minute.'

'He's not in,' says a new voice.

It's the bald, simianly top-heavy form of Straightman-

Funnyman, face displaying the bovine expression of his Straightman persona.

Andi looks at him. 'Isn't he? How do you know he's not in?'

'Been arrested, hasn't he?'

'He's been *arrested!*' exclaims Andi, flabbergasted.

'How do you know he's been arrested?' challenges Camouflage.

'Saw it. Saw the police take him away. Drove him off in a car.'

'When did this happen?' demands Andi.

'About half hour ago.'

'Had they put handcuffs on him?'

Straightman-Funnyman thinks about this. 'Don't think so.'

'I doubt he's actually been *arrested*,' Camouflage tells them. 'If it was anything serious, this place would be a crime scene,' indicating the flat. 'There'd be coppers all over the shop. They've probably just got him in for questioning.'

'But they don't think that Monkey Boy kidnapped Rinda, do they?' protests Andi. 'That's just silly! Monkey Boy wouldn't kidnap a fly!'

'Yeah, but everyone saw him,' says Straightman-Funnyman. 'Chasing that girl through the estate, he was. The one that disappeared.'

'Yes, but that was *before* she disappeared!' expostulates Andi. 'And Sally and Clare were with her! And they were still with her *after* that, after they'd got away from Monkey Boy!'

'Aye, but maybe this Monkey Boy caught up with her again after she went off on her own,' suggests Camouflage.

'Oh, don't you start!' retorts Andi. 'He was only chasing Andi cuz he was mad at her for sneaking into his house and cuz she'd filmed him doing something naughty.'

Says Bryony confidentially: 'You know that everything you're saying's just making it sound worse for him?'

'It wasn't Monkey Boy, okay?' Andi tells Camouflage,

'If you say so,' says Camouflage. Marker pen in hand, he fills in one of the squares on his map of the estate.

'So now we've got another reason to find who's got Rinda,' says Andi. 'We've got to find the real purple-*perpe*trator and clear Monkey Boy's good name before the police put him in prison!' She claps her hands. 'Okay, let's film the introduction! Come here, Camouflage. And you,' to Straightman-Funnyman, 'can go away; we don't want you now.'

Straightman-Funnyman shambles off with the unprotesting promptitude of someone well accustomed to not being wanted.

'Should you be doing that?' asks Bryony. 'How do you know he's not the kidnapper?'

'How do I know *who's* not the kidnapper?'

'Straightman-Funnyman.'

'Of course Straightman-Funnyman's not the kidnapper!' retorts Andi. 'He's two people, isn't he? If he kidnapped Rinda while he was Funnyman, he'd just let her go again when he turned into Straightman, wouldn't he?' Andi shrugs off her backpack and, taking the video camera from it, hands to Bryony. 'I'm letting you be camerawoman again; so just be grateful!'

'Whoopee-doo,' says Bryony.

Andi turns to Camouflage. 'Are you ready?'

'What do you want me to do?' asks Camouflage, feeling a sudden twinge of stage fright.

'You just stand here next to me and answer any questions I ask you,' explains Andi. To Bryony: 'Ready? Is my hair alright?'

'Yes,' sighs Bryony. She raises the camera.

'Are we both in the shot?'

'Yes, you're both in the shot.'

Technically Bryony is telling the truth here: Andi and Camouflage, standing side by side, *are* both in the shot; but in the case of Camouflage, only from the chest down. This is not incompetent camerawork on Bryony's part: she just thinks it looks funnier like this.

They start recording, Andi slipping smoothly into reporter mode.

'This is Andalusia Seton reporting from the Belton Estate, here in Marchmont. Today we are not just here looking for any old rogue male: today we are looking for a rogue male who is also a kidnapper! The day before yesterday, our classmate Rinda Neves disappeared without a trace, an event which has sent shockwaves all across the world. Rinda was last seen here on the Belton Estate, and the Belton Estate is well known for being the home of many of Marchmont's rogue males!

'Which one of the rogue males has kidnapped Rinda and is holding her prisoner in his house? This is what we hope to find out today! Even though Rinda's really annoying and acts like she's God or something, we are still going to rescue her and bring her kidnapper to justice! And hopefully we will be able to show you the rescue live and as it happens!

'To help us with our search we have here with us today Camouflage, a well-known local paedophile hunter. Camouflage will be using his army training skills to help us track down the kidnapper.' To Camouflage: 'Isn't that right?'

'Er, yeah, that's right,' says Camouflage woodenly, staring at the camera.

'And just what do you think are our chances of finding the kidnapper and rescuing Rinda Neves?'

'Erm...' says Camouflage. And then, struck by inspiration: 'If she's here, we'll find her!'

'Thank you, Camouflage. So there you have it. Encouraging words from Camouflage. And now the search begins!' Pause. 'Okay, cut! That's enough for the intro.'

'How was I?' inquires Camouflage. 'D'you reckon I should do me first line again?'

'No, no, you were fine,' Andi assures him. 'Very natural. Let's start searching now. The top suspect on my list is the Lagger, so let's go to where he lives first.'

'The Lagger?' exclaims Camouflage. 'Why'd you reckon it was him did it? He's not a paedo: aggravated armed robbery, that's what he was in for!'

'So?' retorts Andi. 'He might be a paedo *as well* as an aggravating armed robber!'

'I doubt it. I'll tell you whose place we ought to be checking out first: that Mr Deep Sigh feller, that's who!'

'Mr Deep Sigh?' exclaim Andi and Bryony in incredulous stereo.

'Aye, and why not? It's them quiet ones you've got to look out for.'

'But Mr Deep Sigh's got depression!' argues Andi. 'He's too depressed to kidnap anyone!'

'It's the ones who say they've got depression you have to look out for,' insists Camouflage. 'Them fellers, they just use 'aving depression as an excuse! They think they can get away with anything, they do, and that bein' depressed just lets them off the hook!'

'Well, we can check on Mr Deep Sigh later,' says Andi, unconvinced. 'But I still want to check on the Lagger first.'

'No!'

'Yes!'

'Look: who's in charge around here?' demands Camouflage.

'*I* am!' is the prompt reply. 'This is *my* documentary, not yours! You're just here to help. We're going to the Lagger's first, and that's that!'

Muttering, Camouflage acquiesces, and consulting his map, he leads the way across the estate.

The sound of a shrill scream issuing from one of the flats they are passing stops Camouflage in his tracks.

'What was that?' says Camouflage, alert.

'Sounded like a baby screaming,' says Andi.

'Might've been a *girl* screaming!'

The sound comes again, shrill and piercing.

'It *is* a girl!' avers Camouflage

'No, it's a baby,' says Andi. 'Our sister screams like that.'

'Yeah, but a girl your age might scream like that, an' all! 'Specially if she's scared stiff!'

'Well, who lives in this flat? Is it on your map?'

Camouflage checks the map. 'Where are we...? Buzzard Court... Yes! It's that Mr Flipperty-Flop! He lives here! Of course: I should've guessed it were him! Ruddy weirdo!'

'Mr Flipperty-Flop?' protests Andi. 'He couldn't kidnap anyone! He's just a big kid!'

'Aye, well it's them big kids you have to look out for.'

'I thought it was the quiet ones you have to look out for? That's what you said a minute ago!'

'And then it was the ones with depression,' mutters Bryony.

'Yeah, well it's them big kid ones, an' all,' maintains Camouflage. 'Look at Michael Jackson: he were a big kid, weren't he?' And look at them windows,' pointing. 'Net curtains. Never trust anyone who's got net curtains in their windows: means they've got something to hide.'

Another outbreak of shrill screaming.

'That sounds like a girl screaming to me,' says Camouflage. 'Come on, you two! Your mate could be getting murdered in there while we stand out here nattering!'

The camera rolling, Camouflage walks up to the door of the flat, and knocks peremptorily.

The screaming suddenly stops.

'Come on! Open up! We know you're in there!' shouts Camouflage, knocking even more peremptorily.

No sound from within. The door remains closed.

'Come on, you! If you don't come out right now, we're coming in!'

No response.

Camouflage tries the door handle. Locked.

'Right! I'm giving you just five seconds and then I'm gunna bash the door in, d'you hear? Just five seconds! Five...! Four...! Three...! Two...! One...! Right: that's it!'

Camouflage throws himself against the door, shoulder first. The door shakes, but doesn't give way.

'Bugger! These uPVC jobs are a bastard to break down! Have to take a run-up!'

The camera following his movements, Camouflage retreats to the end of the path, and then he charges at the door with big-booted ferocity, smashing into it with such force that not only the lock but the hinges give way, and both door and Camouflage pitch forwards into the hallway.

'Come on! Let's go in!' cries Andi.

So saying, Andi charges into the house, Bryony right behind her, both of them running straight over Camouflage (who was in the process of getting up.) They burst into the living room, the source of the screaming.

They are surprised to find the room empty, apparently devoid of occupants.

'Oh!' says Andi, deflated. She looks at her sister. 'But it sounded like it was coming from here—what was that?'

'What was what?'

'I heard something; a sort of whimpering noise.'

'What was it like?'

'Like something whimpering...'

The sound comes again and this time they both hear it: as advertised a sort of whimpering noise.

'It's coming from behind the sofa,' whispers Bryony.

Camouflage appears in the doorway, bringing an aggrieved expression with him. 'Look, you two—'

'Shh!' hisses Andi. 'They're hiding behind the sofa!'

'*Who* is?'

'*They* are!'

The three of them tiptoe across the room to the sofa.

'Alright, come on out, you,' orders Camouflage. 'We know you're hiding there.'

Another whimper, half-stifled.

Motioning the girls aside Camouflage walks up to the sofa, grabs one of the armrests and drags it away from the wall.

The sight now revealed to Andi and Bryony's innocent eyes is not one they are going to forget in a hurry. It is Mr Flipperty-Flop, huddled in the corner of the room, a mountain of blubbery folds of pasty pink flesh. Yes, pink flesh, because Mr Flipperty-Flop is almost, but not completely naked. Not completely because he is wearing a nappy, an oversized version of a traditional baby's nappy, plain white in colour and fastened with an equally oversized (not to mention outdated) safety pin. And if a nappy seems a ridiculous thing for Mr Flipperty-Flop to be wearing, it undeniably goes very well with the frilled bonnet adorning his head, and fastened in place with a ribbon tied in a bow between two of his chins. The frilled bonnet frames a face that stares saucer-eyed at the three intruders with a mute look in which guilt and mortification battle for supremacy.

It seems that Andi was a touch wide of the mark when she described Mr Flipperty-Flop as being a big kid: because in fact, Mr Flipperty-Flop is a big baby; a great big, adult baby. And a solitary adult baby at that: an adult baby minus the strict nanny (usually considered an essential part of the whole setup) to scold him for his tantrums, feed him his baby food and change his nappies for him.

For a moment, silence hangs heavy in the air of Mr Flipperty-Flop's front room. And then Bryony sniggers. And then Andi sniggers. And then both girls are laughing their heads off.

Mr Flipperty-Flop dissolves into tears.

Chapter Fifteen
Heavy Breathing

Andi's idea of the Lagger being Rinda Neves' abductor is such a good one that somebody else has already thought of it.

In fact, lots of somebody elses, judging by the size of the crowd gathered outside the row of flats, shouting angry abuse up at the Lagger who stands on his balcony shaking his fist like the defiant dictator confronting rebellious subjects who have just found out he's also the local child molester.

Such is the sight that greets Andi et al when they arrive on the scene. The crowd hurling abuse up at the Lagger, and the Lagger, amply supplied with that commodity himself, hurling his own abuse right back at them.

'Stop fucking harassing me, you cunts!' he yells. 'I'm tellin' you I ain't got that fucking kid!'

'You haven't got her *now*, maybe!' retorts a concerned citizen. 'But it was you that abducted her! What've you done with her?'

'I *didn't* fucking abduct her, you stupid prat! Christ, I don't even *like* kids!'

'You hear that? You hear that?' cries another concerned citizen. 'He admits it! He doesn't like kids! That's why he kidnaps 'em and tortures 'em to death!'

'You evil bastard!'

'Let's get him!'

Bottles and bricks are hurled at the balcony. The Lagger ducks to avoid the hail.

'Alright, for Christ's sake! I *do* like kids, then!'

'You hear that? You hear that? He admits it! He likes kids! That's why he kidnaps them and starts messing around with them!'

'You sick bastard!'

'Filthy paedo!'

Another barrage of missiles.

'Pack it in!' roars the Lagger. 'This is harassment, this is! I'll have the law on you!'

'They should've arrested you already!'

'Bullshit! I ain't done nothing!'

'Ain't done nothing? You're on the sex offenders list, aren't you?'

'No, I'm bloody not on the sex offenders list! Whoever told you that is a bloody liar!'

'Come off it! Everyone knows you've been inside!'

'Yeah, I was inside, but it wasn't for molestin' kids! It was a bank job!'

'Pull the other one!'

'It's true! Got away with twenty million in cash, we did!'

'Rubbish! Banks don't have that much in cash! It's all on computer these days!'

'It wasn't back then, you pillock! This was back in the bloody eighties! I did thirty-five years for that job! Thirty-five years inside! Wasted the best years of me life, I did!'

'So that's why he's so bitter and twisted!'

'Yeah, and now he's taking it out on innocent kids!'

'Vindictive bastard!'

'Get him!'

Another fusillade of bricks and bottles.

'Hello, what's going on here, then?' screeches a new voice, shrill and falsetto. 'You lot been slapping Sammy senseless? You been pointing Percy at the porcelain? You been beating the meat and draining the snake? You been chasing Aunt Fanny round the gasworks?'

Evidently Straightman-Funnyman has arrived.

'Come on,' urges Camouflage to the girls. 'We're just wasting our time here. It wasn't this feller.'

'Yeah...' agrees Andi. 'Let's try somewhere else...'

'What if Mr Flipperty-Flop tells the police about us breaking his door down?' wonders Andi.

'Why would he do that?' says Camouflage. 'I told him I'd come back and fix it, didn't I?'

'He might still tell the police.'

'No, not him! He'd be too embarrassed; wouldn't want his secret coming out, would he?'

'Which way to Antenna Head's house? I want to check out him, next.'

'Antenna Head? You don't think he did it, do you?'

'He might have! All those signals he keeps picking up in head: they might've made him go bonkers.'

'He was already bonkers,' says Bryony.

'No, it won't be that Antenna Head. I keep telling you: it's Mr Deep Sigh's place we need to check out. If it was anyone on this estate, it was him.'

'Well, I think Antenna Head's a better suspect than Mr Deep Sigh, so we'll check out his place first.'

'You're wasting your time—!'

'Look, *I'm* in charge here, and I say—Shh!'

They stop and listen. They hear the sound of breathing, slow and steady and curiously amplified, drawing closer.

'Covid Man!' hisses Andi.

A figure appears on the footpath ahead, a tall figure dressed in black: a black trench coat over a black boiler suit, black trousers tucked into black military boots. Most strikingly of all, a gasmask with tinted goggles covers his head; the slow, amplified breathing which announced his advent issuing from the muzzle.

Seeing he is observed, Covid Man stops and turns his masked head, regards the trio silently for a moment, and then resumes his progress.

'Now there's a suspicious feller,' breathes Camouflage. 'How about we follow *him?*'

Andi agrees. She'd forgotten about Covid Man; but yes, he is definitely a suspect!

Covid Man is an enigma. Moving into Marchmont just in

time for the Covid-19 pandemic, he was first seen during the lockdown, when he would make early morning trips to the supermarket for supplies, dressed as we have just seen him, breathing like Darth Vader as he walked the aisles of the shop, never speaking a word. His excessive precautions against the virus soon earned the newcomer the nickname Covid Man. And with his hidden features and his uncommunicativeness, people naturally wondered just who he was and what he really looked like—and people are still wondering today, because even though the pandemic is over, for some reason Covid Man has never stopped wearing his gasmask, nor to this day has he ever been known to exchange a word with anybody.

Why had he never put aside his respirator? Had the coronavirus outbreak made him paranoid and overcautious, ever fearful of the next resurgence of the ever-mutating virus? Or had the lockdown with all its imposed isolation caused him, like many others, to lose his social skills, his ability to communicate with people, and he has now become too fearful to appear unmasked before the world at large?

Or could it be that he'd *always* dressed the way he does? No-one in Marchmont had seen him before the pandemic, had they? Maybe he had *always* been paranoid about infectious disease and bacteriological warfare? Or perhaps he'd always suffered from an extreme social phobia? Or maybe it is neither of these: maybe he wears the mask to conceal hideously disfiguring facial injuries? And maybe these disfiguring facial injuries are of a kind that impairs his breathing, so that he actually *needs* to wear the respirator?

Or on the other hand, maybe the guy's just some kinky pervert with a boiler suit and gasmask fetish. And why not? It takes all sorts and we've already just had an adult baby minus his nanny, so why not a solitary gimp with no dominatrix to call him her own and walk all over him in her stiletto heels?

Keeping at a discreet distance, our three investigators

follow Covid Man to his home, one of a row of terrace houses in Redshank Court.

'Now *that's* suspicious for a start,' declares Camouflage, as they watch him letting himself into his house.

'What is?' asks Andi.

'His house,' says Camouflage. 'Why's a single feller living in a two-bedroom council house on his own?'

'You're right!' gasps Andi, seeing the light (or *a* light.) 'He could be using the spare bedroom as a prison for people he kidnaps!'

'Well, I was thinking more about the bedroom tax he'd have to fork out, actually,' confesses Camouflage. 'But aye, there's that as well. Come on.'

They approach the housefront. 'Look at that,' says Camouflage grimly, indicating the front room window. 'No net curtains.'

'But that's good, isn't it?' questions Andi. 'Doesn't that mean he's got nothing to hide?'

'Or maybe he just wants us to *think* he's got nothing to hide,' contends Camouflage sagely. 'Never trust a person who hasn't got any net curtains in their windows.'

From what they can see of it however, Covid Man's living room looks like a perfectly normal one, containing everything you would expect to see in a living room and nothing in the way of bizarre additions. The room remains empty.

'We need to see upstairs,' declares Andi. 'We need to see what's happening in that spare bedroom of his.'

Andi, perched in a tree at the end of the back garden, has a direct view through the upstairs window of the house. At present, all she can see is a dressing table with a mirror and part of a wardrobe. There is no sign of an occupant. But then, if Rinda's there, she would probably be tied up, wouldn't she? She might be lying on the bed, just out of sight below the level of the window sill, chained helplessly to the bedposts!

A door opens inwards and Covid Man, a sinister black figure, walks into the room. Turning to face the mirror, he reaches with both hands to the zipper at the back of his gasmask.

He's going to take it off! He's going to take his mask off!

'What can you see?' calls up Camouflage. He and Bryony are stationed below, at the foot of the wall Andi has climbed to reach her vantagepoint.

'Shh!' hisses Andi.

This is it! She's going to be the first person ever to see what Covid Man really looks like! What horrors are going to be revealed to her now?

Unzipped, the mask comes away. She sees the back of a head: a normal, everyday looking head covered with dark, wavy hair. But what about his face? She can't quite see his reflection in the mirror…! Come on…! Turn around, turn around…!

Covid Man turns and faces the window.

Andi nearly falls out of her tree.

No, it can't be! It can't be…! But it is! It is! It's him! It's really him!

Omigod! Omigod! She's got to get this on film!

'Quick! The camera! The camera!' she shouts down to the others.

'What is it? What's going on?'

'Just pass me the camera! Quick!'

But it's too late. She's been spotted. Covid Man walks straight up to the window and pulls the curtains shut.

'But it was *him!* I know it was him!'

Andi is virtually in tears.

'Don't be daft!' retorts Camouflage. 'It must've just been someone who *looked* a bit like him.'

'He didn't look a *bit* like him, he looked a *lot* like him, because it *was* him!'

'What, someone like him, living in a council house in a dump like the Belton Estate in a dead-end town like this one? Come off it!'

'Bryony...!' turning imploringly to her sister.

'You're just making it up,' declares Bryony.

'I am *not* making it up!'

They come to a halt outside the door of a ground-floor flat.

'Here we are,' says Camouflage.

'Ah! So, this is Antenna Head's place?' asks Andi.

'Nope, this is Mr Deep Sigh's place.'

'But we don't *want* Mr Deep Sigh's place! He's not one of my suspects!'

'Well, he ruddy well should be,' replies Camouflage. Pointing: 'Look at that! Net curtains in the window. Always means they've got summat to hide.'

'A minute ago it was *no* net curtains that meant that,' mutters Bryony.

'You know what he's got in there?' proceeds Camouflage. 'Books. Books everywhere. Hundreds of 'em. That's what I've heard.'

'But reading books is good, isn't it?' argues Andi. 'Mum reads books, and she always says people ought to read more.'

'Reading books is alright in moderation,' allows Camouflage. 'But when a feller starts reading books all the time, then it's bad. Means he's doin' too much thinking, and people who do too much thinking, they start thinking about the wrong things and they end up going off the deep end. I'm telling you: if that missing girl is anywhere, she'll be in there.'

'Excuse me, sir.'

A hand has dropped onto Camouflage's shoulder, the black-gloved hand of authority. Camouflage turns and sees that the hand belongs to a police constable, one of a matching pair of police constables.

'We wondered if you could help us, sir,' says the policeman. 'We've received a complaint from the resident of number fifteen Sea Witch Court, a report that someone gained forcible entry to the premises by breaking down the front door. You wouldn't happen to know anything about this, would you, sir?'

'Well, I...' begins Camouflage, his face blanched.

'Before you commit yourself to an answer, sir, I should inform you that your appearance matches the description of the felon given to us by the resident.'

'But we heard a noise!' stammers Camouflage. 'I mean we... we thought summat was going on in there! Ask these two!' indicating Andi and Bryony. 'They were with me!'

'Is this true?' asks the policeman. 'Did you see this gentleman break down the door of number fifteen Sea Witch Court?'

'Well, yes...' answers Andi.

'That seems to be that, then. Eye-witness confirmation. We shall have to ask you to accompany us to the station, sir. And I suggest you two,' to the girls, 'return to your homes.'

Taking an arm each, the two constables start escorting Camouflage away.

'No, but you don't understand...!' protests Camouflage. 'We were looking for that missing girl! And I told the feller I'd fix his door for him! I dunno why he had to go'n report it—!'

'Serves him right,' chuckles Bryony, as they watch Camouflage out of sight.

'Just cuz you don't like him!' accuses Andi. 'But what about us, eh? Now we can't do the search anymore!'

'We can do it without him,' says Bryony.

'No, we can't! Cuz he's the one with the map, isn't he?'

'You should've got the map off him, shouldn't you?' says Bryony, it's-not-my-faultishly.

'I would've if I knew he was going to get arrested!' Andi pauses for a sigh and head-scratch. 'Well, I suppose we can still search here...' looking pensively at Mr Deep Sigh's suspicious net curtains.

'But I thought you didn't think Mr Deep Sigh could've done it?' argues Bryony.

'I do think that! But Camouflage thinks it could be him, and what if it turned out he was right and we were wrong?'

'Yeah, but I don't want to go in his house,' says Bryony.

'Why not?'

'He's got depression, hasn't he?' shuddering. 'I don't want to catch depression.'

'We've just got to take the risk. Investigative reporters have got to take risks sometimes, or they won't get any investigating done! Come on!'

Andi walks boldly up to the front door of the flat, Bryony following less boldly. Andi knocks on the door.

'What are you doing that for?' demands Bryony.

'Well, we've got to find out if he's in, haven't we?'

Her knocking eliciting no response she opens the letterbox. 'Hello? Are you home, Mr Deep Sigh? We're doing a school project and we want to interview you! Are you there?'

Still no response.

'He's not in,' pronounces Andi.

'What now? Are you planning to break down the door like Camouflage did? Good luck with that.'

'Yes, we can't really...' Andi ponders for a bit. And then: 'I know!'

She turns the door handle. The door opens.

'He's left his door unlocked!' Andi, wide-eyed and *sotto voce*.

'Then he's got to be in! People only leave their doors unlocked when they're at home.'

'He might have gone out and forgot to lock it,' argues Andi. 'People do that sometimes.' She opens the door and leans into the hallway. 'Hello?' she sings. 'Mr Deep Sigh? You've left your door unlocked! Hello, hello, hello?'

Cautiously, they step into the hallway. The layout of the flat is identical to Monkey Boy's: bathroom door at the end of the hallway, doors to the living room and bedroom on the left and right. The bathroom door is ajar, the other two doors firmly shut.

'Mr Deep Sigh?' lilts Andi in coaxing tones. 'Are you home? You've left your door unlocked. Coo-ee!' and, turning to Bryony: 'I'll look in the front room, you look in the bedroom.'

Bryony acquiesces. She goes to the bedroom door while her sister, with a 'I'm coming in!' walks into the living room. Bryony prefers to announce herself with a timid knock, and she cautiously opens the door.

Bookshelves are the first thing she sees. Tall bookcases, packed higgledy-piggledy with books, old and new, hardback and paperback, stand against the wall facing her. It seems that Camouflage was right about Mr Deep Sigh being a voracious reader.

About to take a step further into the room, a sound freezes Bryony in her tracks: the sound of an indrawn breath! Of a single, ragged indrawn breath! The sound comes from off to the right, from the part of the room concealed from Bryony by the half-open door. Mr Deep Sigh's here! He's here in the room!

What should she do? Announce herself? Tell Andi? Run for it? The latter option seems the most appealing one...

But why hasn't Mr Deep Sigh said something? Why hasn't he come to see who's opened the door? She can't hear anything now... Is he holding his breath? Is he scared, so he's holding his breath? Does he think she's a robber or something...?

Now comes the sound of an indrawn breath being slowly released—but it sounds funny, all wheezy and crinkly and crisp-packety. A funny kind of breathing...

No! Not breathing: snoring! Noisy, grownup's snoring! Maybe that's what it is!

Recovering the courage she has temporarily mislaid, Bryony peeks round the edge of the door... Yes! She sees a bed, occupying the front part of the room, the headboard up against the inner wall. And there he is: Mr Deep Sigh, lying on the bed, with his black suit on, stretched out on top of the bedcovers.

He must have just decided to have an afternoon nap...

Mr Deep Sigh lies perfectly still, perfectly straight, legs together, arms at his sides... But there's something funny about his head... Is he wearing a hood or something...? A white hood...? She can't make it out...

The sleeper breathes in again, and again it sounds funny, crinkly and with a kind of whistling noise that makes her think of balloons...

And it moved. The thing covering his head: it moved...

Puzzled, Bryony moves around the door and takes a step towards the bed... No, it's not a hood he's wearing: it's a bag, a plastic bag... She can see the logo on it: the supermarket Mum works at... Why's he got a plastic bag over his head like that...? And what's that round his neck...? It's his necktie, except he's wearing it wrong; it's in the wrong place: it's not tied under the collar of his shirt like it should be, it's tied round the bottom of the bag he's got over his head... Why's he got it like that? It looks silly...

And the bag, it's all pressed against his face, and his mouth's open and it's all inside his mouth as well; she can see Mr Deep Sigh's lips, hid nose, his cheekbones, the hollows of the eyes; all with the thin plastic stretched over them... And now Mr Deep Sigh breathes out once more: a great big rattling breath that puffs out the bag, puffs it up like a balloon...

But it doesn't sound right. It's not snoring; it's not the way a person snoring is supposed to sound... That rattling noise, it sounds like it hurts, like it's something really painful and it's dragged itself out from deep inside him... A deep sigh from deep inside Mr Deep Sigh...

It's not right. No, it's just not right...

Bryony backs away, back round the other side of the door, away the man on the bed...

Andi appears. 'Well, there's no-one in the living room or the kitchen—'

She breaks off at the sight of the desolate look on her sister's face. Dropping her voice to a whisper: 'What's wrong? Is it Rinda...?'

Bryony shakes her head.

'Mr Deep Sigh?'

Bryony nods.

'What? He's in there—?' Andi takes a quick peek around the edge of the door. Bryony grabs her arm and yanks her back.

'He's asleep!' gasps Andi. 'Omigod! He didn't wake up, did he? He didn't wake up and see you?'

Bryony shakes her head.

'Let's go,' says Andi. 'Before he wakes up.'

Treading softly, the two girls exit the flat, softly closing the front door behind them.

Chapter Sixteen
Rendezvous at Raggedy Towers

'This is ace reporter Andalusia Seton reporting live from... from... Oh... Where *am* I reporting from...?'

She's on a ship, that much is obvious, and even though Andi doesn't know anything about ships she knows that this ship is an ocean research vessel and that it's sailing in the Red Sea somewhere between Libya and Italy.

She's standing on the deck and she's alone; there's not a crewmember in sight. But more to the point, where is Bryony? Usually when she's doing a live news report from somewhere, Bryony is there filming her with Mum's video camera; but for some reason Bryony's not here today.

Maybe she's on holiday…

All around is lots of sea and lots of sky and nothing else at all; not a single island with a palm tree in the middle to be seen; just the sea and the sky going on and on forever…

'Ahoy there, me hearty!' It's the ship's captain, a tall German woman with a weatherbeaten face and tattoos all over her arms and legs. She's dressed in a dirty t-shirt and shorts and she has her captain's hat perched on her blonde head at a jaunty angle.

Andi knows who this captain is: she is Pia Klemp the drowning illegal immigrant rescuer and they are onboard her ship, the good ship *Sea-Witch*, which sails around the Red Sea looking for drowning illegal immigrants to rescue.

'Welcome aboard the good ship *Sea-Witch*, me hearty!' says Captain Klemp. 'Who be ye a-looking for?'

'Oh, I'm looking for Rinda Neves,' replies Andi. 'She's from my class at school and she's disappeared and I can't find her anywhere.'

'Well, we'll find her!' declares Captain Klemp. 'There's no-one we can't find with the good ship *Sea-Witch*! Full speed ahead!'

They stand at the front of the ship, which is called the stern, because the bit at the back is called the bows. Captain Klemp raises her binoculars.

'Can she swim, this shipmate of yours?' asks Captain Klemp.

'Yes, Rinda's good at swimming,' replies Andi.

'Then she be still alive!' says Captain Klemp. 'All we got to do now is find her before the sharks do.'

'The Red Sea Sharks?' asks Andi.

'Aye, them be the ones,' says Captain Klemp. 'They especially like to eat up little girls, does them Red Sea Sharks.'

'Then we've got to find her before she gets eaten up,' says Andi. 'Or I won't win first prize at school.'

'Never fear! We'll rescue the wench, or my name isn't

Captain Klemp!' declares Captain Klemp. 'We've rescued many a drowning wench, we have. Why, only last week we rescued Kathleen Hanna from Bikini Kill.'

'Kathleen Hanna from Bikini Kill?' says Andi. 'My Mum likes her.'

'Aye,' says Captain Klemp. 'Signed up with me crew, she has. She be down below right now, feeding the animals.'

'You've got animals down below?' asks Andi, mildly interested.

'Aye. We've shipped onboard two each of all the endangered species, ready for when the world gets swallowed up by water,' says Captain Klemp.

A girl with intense eyes and her hair in plaits walks up.

'You're Greta Thunberg,' says Andi. 'Did you get rescued as well?'

'Yes, I was measuring how high the water was and I fell in,' says Greta. 'I was saved by the good ship Sea-Witch and now I am one of the jolly crews and I am helping to look after the animals.'

Someone starts screaming. Andi looks over the side of the ship and she sees Rinda Neves. She's treading water and screaming and sharks are swimming all around her!

'It's Rinda!' exclaims Andi, getting excited. 'We've got to rescue her before the sharks eat her!'

'Ahoy!' cries Captain Klemp. 'Splice the mainmast! Hoist the rowlocks! Shiver the timbers and full speed ahead!'

Andi leans over the rail to get a better look and someone—that Greta!—thumps her in the back and she falls over the edge! And she falls and falls and falls towards the water and Rinda is screaming and screaming and screaming…

…And then Andi wakes up and it's dark and she's in her bed and it's her sister in the bottom bunk who's screaming her head off.

***

'I've been doing some thinking,' says Andi.

'Have you? You'd better have a lie down, then,' says Bryony, indicating the bed.

'Ha, ha, very funny,' says Andi.

There have been no new developments in the Rinda Neves case, according to the news this morning. The police are said to be 'broadening their search area,' a statement which carries with it the implication that the police are no longer expecting to find a living girl, and are now just looking for a dead body. It has been announced that a local man is currently 'helping the police with their inquiries,' but he has not been named, so only a privileged few know that this cooperative citizen is actually Monkey Boy.

Today Mum's not at work and has gone off to visit some old friends who live in a town nearby; and while she's doing this Andi, Bryony and Carli are spending the day round Gran's house.

Andi has brought Bryony to the spare bedroom for a private conference.

'You know what Mum said about how you couldn't really keep someone prisoner in a house with thin walls, because your neighbours would hear what you were doing?'

'Yes...'

When they'd told her about their attempted search the previous afternoon, Mum had said that it wasn't very likely Rinda was being held prisoner anywhere on the Belton Estate. The walls the houses and flats have there, she'd argued, were so thin that you couldn't really do anything without your neighbours knowing about it.

And they have had a good working example of the disadvantages of adjoining properties with inadequately soundproofed walls at home this very morning. The James children had been running amuck from the moment they'd got out of bed, and this time the father, usually the least audible member of the household, had lost his temper and started shouting, both at his children and his wife. His voice had been loud and angry and it had upset Carli. The Seton family are glad that they're going to be out of the way until the storm has (hopefully) blown over.

'And you know how she said that if Rinda was being kept prisoner somewhere, it would have to be in a house that was on its own, away from any other houses and where nobody could see you or hear you?'

'Yes...'

'Yes. Well, I've just thought of where that house is: Raggedy Towers!'

'Raggedy Man's house? You think that's where Rinda is?'

'I *know* that's where she is,' affirms Andi confidently. 'Raggedy Man's the one who kidnapped her.'

'Yeah...' says Bryony, pensive. 'He could've—No, wait: it can't be Raggedy Man. When we were following him back to his house, it must have been about the same time Rinda was getting kidnapped; we worked that out, remember? So it couldn't have been him. We were following him all the time, and he was on his own, wasn't he? Or do you think he'd got Rinda in his coat pocket?'

'Of course he didn't have Rinda in his coat pocket, stupid! He kidnapped her by car, didn't he? And we *saw* the car! It was the car we saw driving into Raggedy Towers!'

'No, *you're* stupid, stupid. How could Raggedy Man have been driving that car when we'd just seen him go into his house?'

'And you're stupid times a million! I *know* he couldn't have been driving the car; I never said he was driving it! Somebody else was driving it: Raggedy Man's accomplice!' she concludes grandly.

Bryony frowns. 'Raggedy Man's a compass?'

'His *accomplice*. Accomplice means another person he's got working with him.'

'But I thought you said rogue males always only do things on their own,' argues Bryony.

'Well, mostly they do,' allows Andi. 'But Raggedy Man's an acception.' (Or to you and me, an *exception*.) 'We know he's got an accomplice cuz we saw that car driving into Raggedy Towers, didn't we?'

'But didn't you say that rogue males don't drive cars?'

'Did I? Well, *some* of them drive cars. Maybe the man in the car is somebody new, someone we don't know about; and Raggedy Man got him to kidnap Rinda and bring her back to Raggedy Towers! I bet that's what's happened!'

Bryony shrugs. 'Maybe you're right, then. You should just tell Gran about it, or Mum when she gets back, and they can tell the police.'

'Don't be stupid!' retorts Andi. 'It's no good telling someone else, is it? We've got to go there ourselves, haven't we? Just you and me! We've got to go to Raggedy Towers!'

'Why have *we* got to go?'

'For the film, stupid! The film! We go there with the camera and then we rescue Rinda and we film ourselves doing it!'

'When did you want us to go to Raggedy Towers, then?' asks Bryony, stubbornly uninfected by her sister's enthusiasm.

'What do you mean "when"? Right now, of course! Here at Granny's, we're right at the same end of town as where Raggedy Towers is! I Googled it and it's only twenty minutes' walk from here!'

'Yeah, but it's still raining...' looking out of the window.

'Not as much as it was this morning,' argues Andi.

'Yeah, but it'll still be wet...'

'So what? We've got our coats, haven't we?' Andi looks at her sister squarely. 'What's wrong with you, anyway? You've been acting funny since we came home yesterday. You've been all broody and quiet. And then you go and wake the whole house up in the middle of the night, screaming your head off—'

'I was having a nightmare, wasn't I?' says Bryony defensively.

'Yeah, well try having them more quietly in future,' says her unsympathetic sibling. 'When you woke me up, I was having another important dream. I dreamed that I found Rinda and she was drowning in the sea and there were sharks swimming all around her.'

'So what?'

'So the dream must mean that Rinda's in danger and we've got to rescue her today cuz otherwise it'll be too late!'

And how has Monkey Boy been coping with his first experience of spending the night in police custody? Not very well, it has to be said. But then if you'd been dragged from your comfort zone by the uniformed representatives of the law on suspicion of having abducted and murdered—with probably some sexual activity in between—a minor and taken to the stationhouse to be subjected to prolonged interrogation, you wouldn't be feeling too peachy yourself.

And on top of all that he has had to the pass the night in a police holding cell with its pallet bed and regulation itchy blanket—and a *single* pallet bed at that, an additional torture in itself to someone accustomed to sleeping in a double bed (or the mattress from one, anyway) —with nothing more to look forward to than more interrogation sessions the next day.

During his sleepless night Monkey Boy's only coping mechanism has been to retreat from reality and into the fantasy landscape of a romanticised Eastern harem and the comforting arms of its fragrantly-scented and diaphanously-attired residents. The ultimate safe haven for Monkey Boy, although Monkey Boy's harem differs from the more traditional harem in one key particular: it being a harem composed of *other people's* wives rather than his own.

But now it is day and Monkey Boy lies stretched out on

his pallet bed, staring up at the ceiling, expecting at any moment to hear the sound of approaching footsteps in the corridor outside that will signal another trip to the interview room and another session of repetitive questioning.

Forty-eight hours. Forty-eight hours. That's how long they can hold him without charging him. Forty-eight hours. He hasn't even been here half that time yet, and it feels like forever.

They're taking their time, as well. He's been lying here since breakfast...

They'd brought in Camouflage yesterday and for a moment Monkey Boy had thought his reprieve had come. Camouflage seemed just the kind of likely suspect the cops could sink their teeth into: one of those military nutjobs, like the guy they'd fitted up with Jill Dando's murder. But no such luck: turned out Camouflage wasn't a suspect at all; they'd just brought him in for kicking down someone's front door, thinking he'd found the missing girl.

Why do they think he's the one who did it? Him of all people! They haven't got anything on him, have they? Nothing they could actually charge him on suspicion with, right? Yes, so he *had* been seen murderously chasing the girl across the estate minutes before she disappeared; and yes, the girl *did* have in her possession a video camera whose contents, if wrongly viewed, could be misconstrued as showing him performing an indecent sexual act in front of the girl—but all that's just circumstantial, isn't it? They haven't got any *real* evidence; not one crumb.

And what if they decide to turn over his flat looking for that solid evidence? The possibility is an alarming one for Monkey Boy, because while he doesn't have any abducted schoolgirls stashed away around his flat, he does one or two other things he wouldn't want the fuzz finding out about.

It's those Seton brats Monkey Boy blames for all this! He wouldn't be in this predicament if it wasn't for them. Why did they have to hide themselves in his front room and start filming him like that? He'd already told them once that he didn't want to be in any stupid film they were making. And it turns out the whole reason the Neves kid had gone and done the same thing the day after was because she'd seen the Seton girls when he'd chucked them out. So, if it hadn't been for them...! Stupid Seton brats and their stupid bloody mum. Parents are responsible for how their kids turn out, so she's to blame as well. Stupid punk cow. She might have a decent taste in music, but she's a bloody lousy parent.

Why are they taking so long...? He was expecting to be dragged back to that interview room the moment he'd finished his breakfast; why are they keeping him hanging on like this? What's causing the delay...? Could it be that they're about to formally charge him...? Yeah, maybe they have to fill out all the paperwork first! And then, when they've done that, they come along and they tell him he's under arrest and they give him that speech about not having to say anything...

Oh, Christ! That's not what they're doing, is it? They can't seriously think that *he*, Monkey Boy, who (apart from one or two entirely justified assaults upon elderly practical jokers) wouldn't hurt a fly, that he would go and...? They couldn't! They couldn't think that! Christ, he doesn't even *like* kids, the little pests! He likes women, fully-grown women, fully-grown *married* women, with coffee-coloured skin and wearing burkas...

Footsteps outside.

It's them! They're coming this way! They're coming and they're going to throw the book at him... Oh, Christ! Oh, Christ...!

Bryony thinks they should tell Gran they're just going to the shops down the street, but Andi argues that this would be telling fibs and that it will be much better all round for them to just sneak quietly out of the house without saying anything at all.

Gran is in the living room, occupied with entertaining Carli, who is unintentionally aiding and abetting her sisters by making more than enough noise to cover their departure. Creeping into the hallway, they quietly don their shoes and coats and then, even more quietly, open the front door and step outside. Dropping down, they walk crouched down under the living room window and make it to the driveway, where Gran's parked car shields them from view until they are out on the street.

And now, safe from being spotted, they set off. Two small figures conspicuous in colourful waterproofs, hoods up, one with a backpack on her back, they make their way through the drizzly streets.

'Don't forget to send Gran that text,' Bryony reminds her.

'I *won't* forget,' replies Andi. 'I'll text her when we get there.'

'Might as well do it now,' suggests Bryony.

'No, stupid! What if Gran goes and calls the police? Then the police might get there before *we* do and that'd spoil everything!'

Andi has memorised the route, and they make it onto the road which will take them to Raggedy Towers. Once a main arterial road linking Marchmont with a neighbouring market town, the road has since fallen into disuse, made redundant by the building of a bypass. As the girls proceed towards the outskirts of town, the houses become sparser, older, standing further back from the road. Soon they are in open countryside.

'Look!' says Andi, pointing to the roadside opposite. 'That's the path we came out from when we followed Raggedy Man: we're nearly there! That must be his house, over there, where all those trees are.'

They proceed and soon they see the moss-grown perimeter wall of Raggedy Towers ahead of them, the crowns of the park trees visible above the coping. And now they come to the gates, which stand open just as they did on the previous occasion. At the end of the tree-girt avenue they can see their destination, Raggedy Towers. The old house looks even more gloomy and forlorn than on the previous occasion—and so would you if you'd been standing out in the rain all day.

'I bet she's not there...' says Bryony. She doesn't like the look of the house at all.

'You're just saying that!' ripostes Andi. 'We've come all the way here, haven't we? It'd be stupid not to go in now! So come on!'

'You go first,' says Bryony.

Andi passes through the gates. Bryony follows.

'They'll see us from the house if we just walk up the driveway,' says Andi. 'We'll go through the trees.'

'But it's all wet in there!' complains Bryony.

'So, it's wet. Better getting our shoes wet than getting caught, isn't it?'

'And there's all brambles everywhere!'

'We're both wearing jeans, aren't we? We won't get pricked. Now stop moaning and come on!'

Milly Leeson makes her way up the gravel drive to her uncle's house.

Aunt Beatrice answers the doorbell.

'Hello, Auntie! I've just come to see Uncle Grant about my history project again. I'll only be a couple of minutes—'

She takes a step forward, expecting her aunt to move aside and let her in. Her aunt does nothing of the kind. She stands firmly on the threshold, barring entrance, and her expression is hostile.

'You are not seeing "Uncle Grant,"' she tells Milly, brittle-voiced '"Uncle Grant" is too busy to see you.'

Milly is taken aback. 'But I need to see him, Auntie! It's about my history project—'

'Oh, I know all about your "history projects." Very expensive, these history projects of yours, aren't they? Been costing a lot of money, haven't they? Well, you're going to have to do without any help from now on, because you won't be getting your money from my husband anymore—now get out of here, you little slut.'

The words hit her like a slap in the face. She stares at her aunt, struggles for words. 'Look... You can't... I don't know what Uncle Grant's told you, but—'

'Oh, he's told me everything, don't you worry about that,' replies her aunt, and the smile of satisfied malice on her face is like a revelation to Milly. She's never seen her aunt look like this before; she'd never thought her aunt *could* look like this before. 'Oh, yes; he's told me all about your little arrangement with him—and it's stopping *right now*. Do you hear me? You're never getting another penny out of him! Not another penny, you money-grubbing little tart. So just turn around and get out of here and don't ever come back again!'

She slams the door.

'I'll tell the police!' cries Milly. 'I will! I'll tell them!'

The threat elicits no response.

Seething with rage and humiliation, Milly turns and stalks down the drive.

That bitch! How dare she? Talking to her like that! *She's* the victim here, and her aunt acts like it's her uncle! So what if she was making him give her money? He *owed* her that money, didn't he? He bloody owed her it! Better than reporting him to the cops, wasn't it? She was letting him off lightly!

Well, not anymore! She bloody *will* go'n tell the police! That's what she'll do!

No doubt Sibby will be chiding Jo about her serial dating, about her reluctance to enter into a serious long-term relationship, to find someone to either tie the knot with or live with as knot-tied, and basically settle down. You're commitment-shy, she'll say; emotionally half-available, you want to have your cake and eat it...

Yes, Sibby will chide her, and Sibby, happily-married but still a nonconformist, will be right. Jo's last blind date, the no-show, has completely ghosted her now: he has unmatched with her on the dating site and blocked her telephone number. It's a depressing experience, being ghosted like that: not just for the cruel snub itself, but also because you are left wondering *why* you have been ghosted; and you're going to be left wondering forever as well, because by the very definition of the act of being ghosted, you're never going to learn the answer.

When you get ghosted on a dating app it's natural to assume the reason behind it is that your contact has just found another person, someone who they've decided looks like a better proposition than you did. It's easy enough to assume that, but Jo, from her vast experience of blind-dating knows that there are a lot of very insecure men out there, men who will ghost you just because they've suddenly got cold feet, or because they're worried that *you* might ghost *them*. There are even men who will ghost you as revenge for having been ghosted themselves by someone else, or for lots of other equally petty and spiteful reasons.

Her no-show blind date hadn't come across to Jo as the insecure type—but then sometimes they don't; not when the communication has been done by text. Some people can be much more eloquent online than they are in person and, without wilfully intending to deceive, can come across as being much more charismatic and forthcoming than they turn out to be in real life. In her own case, Jo's the direct opposite: she's much better face to face than online.

So, was that what it was? Had her blind date had a last-minute attack of nerves and bottled out of meeting up with her? Then why couldn't he have just told her that? He could have just apologised and explained things to her, and pissed off as she'd been for that wasted evening, she'd still have been willing to give the guy a second chance... She wonders if her intimidating appearance is to blame at all… She knows she can appear stern and unfriendly to some people, but the fact is that beneath that don't-fuck-with-me riot grrrl exterior she can be as warm and nurturing enough to put any mummy's boy child-man at his ease.

But then maybe it wasn't nerves. Maybe he had just found someone else he liked better than her…

Oh, well. Onto the next one…

It's not that Jo needs to have a man to share her life with, and especially not right now, while she's busy raising a family; but what about the future? What about after daughters have all grown up and flown the coop…?

A long time ago, Jo had coined that expression 'rogue males' ('rogue' in the separated from the herd rather than the criminal sense) to denominate all those solitary misfit males you see inhabiting any city, town or village—but she knows that there are such things as rogue females as well. They may be less visible than their male counterparts, less likely to be seen walking the streets and parading their eccentricities; but they're out there nonetheless, neglected and lonely women, often middle-aged, living out their lives inside their homes, inside their heads.

Could that be her fate? Could she end up becoming one of those rogue females…?

Oh, what are you thinking, Josephine Seton? It's way too soon to be fretting about that; Carli's only three, for God's sake!

She must be getting close to it now. She glances at her smartphone, slotted in the dashboard holder, displaying her route map. Jo has taken the old B-road back out of Marchmont instead of the main road that would have got her to destination much sooner; and she has done this because there's something she wants to check. A particular place she wants to visit.

Jo has already performed one good deed today. Before setting off, after she'd dropped off the kids round her mum's, she'd called in at the cop shop and made a statement about her daughters having concealed themselves in Monkey Boy's flat and covertly filmed him.

When she'd been shown the film, Jo couldn't help laughing at Monkey Boy sitting there in his boxers smoking a joint—she'd laughed and then she'd deleted the film. But when she'd found out that Monkey Boy had been taking in for questioning and moreover the reasons *why* he'd been taken in for questionings, Jo, even without the video proof, just had to come forward, just to make sure the cops didn't end up charging Monkey Boy with a crime there was no way in hell he'd committed.

And what Jo had to tell them tied in nicely with what they'd already heard from the Sawdust Sisters and from Monkey Boy himself. The sergeant she'd spoken to—who'd seemed like a pretty decent person in spite of her being a uniformed fascist pig and lackey of the establishment—had assured her Monkey Boy, luckless victim of circumstance that he was, was going to be released that day.

That was Jo's first good deed. The objective of her second good deed, the location she wants to check out, should just be coming up ahead. It was saying to her daughters about how if Rinda Neves was still alive and being held captive by her abductor that the place of her captivity would have to be some remote, rarely visited spot that had got her thinking; got her thinking that she knows of one such place that would fill those requirements admirably.

Just up ahead; the turning is just up ahead. Her destination is still out of sight, being some distance from the main road and shielded from sight by a grove of trees. Jo swings her car onto the access road.

Although the chances seem pretty slim that Rinda could still be alive after being missing three days, it seems worth checking out. And even if the girl is *not* still alive, whatever might be left of her could be here.

It *is* such a nice, out of the way spot.

And Jo has another reason for coming to this place: she has been here before, just once before, a very long time ago. Since that one time she has never returned here; not once—so perhaps this visit is long overdue.

The road cuts through the grove, and when Jo emerges from the trees, her destination appears before her: the decaying, derelict remains of a large building, flat-roofed, industrial. The concrete structure, weather-stained and weed-grown, looks like it must have housed a factory of some kind—and a factory of kind is what it once was; an anonymous factory, shyly concealed from public scrutiny; a factory that had not cared to advertise its particular function, whose products most consumed, although few liked to think about the manufacturing process.

This derelict building was once the local abattoir.

Chapter Seventeen
Nightmare Revisited

As she makes her way home, Milly's scattergun thoughts resolve themselves into a basic need for comfort and support, a sympathetic listener, a shoulder to cry on, someone who's 'on her side'—and oddly enough her thoughts turn to her mother. As we have seen, Milly and her mum haven't been on the best of terms of late. It hadn't always been like that; when Dad was still around mother and daughter had been united in their contempt for *him*; but alas, divorce proceedings had severed that useful mother-daughter bond; and now, with just the two of them in the house, they've only had each other to despise…

But her mum is still her mum, and a mother ought to care, especially about something like this…

True, there was a promise she had once made, a promise never to tell… But that promise, exacted from a child, is null and void now…

Yes, she won't go to the cops: she'll tell her mum.

Feeling better now, Milly quickens her pace, rehearsing the scene in her mind, what she'll say, how her mum will react to the news... She can picture the whole thing and how it will feel. Now that she thinks about it, she realises what a relief it will be to finally get it off her chest. And her mum, she'll take Milly's side; this confession will bring them back together again...

But then she gets home and it looks like her mum has gone out; there's nobody in the living room or the kitchen. Funny, she didn't say she was going out...

'Mum! Are you in? Where are you?'

No answer. She goes upstairs. Mum's bedroom door, usually left ajar, is firmly closed.

'Mum?'

She knocks on the door and opens it.

Her mother is in her bed, sitting up with hastily-gathered bedclothes held against her chest in the familiar manner, and on her face the classic flustered expression of someone caught in *flagrante delicto*.

'Milly, darling! I didn't know you'd be back so soon!' The voice is spot-on as well: striving to sound calm, but way too loud.

'Mum, what are you doing in—?' Milly breaks off, eyes resting on the supine form visible under the bedclothes beside her mother. 'Oh, *that's* what you're doing... Couldn't you have waited till tonight, Mum?'

'Well, you know...!' Her mum laughs awkwardly. 'I did wait until you were out... Didn't want to disturb you... So, why are you back so soon, dearest? Was there anything you wanted?'

'Yeah, there was, but it can keep till later,' says Milly, wondering who the mystery lover might be. Mum hasn't mentioned anyone, but then that's not surprising... Well, divorced mums are entitled to do these things... Backing out of the room, Milly starts to close the door, but then she catches sight of the male attire littering the floor—very youthful-looking male attire and some of it strangely familiar...

'What the fuck—?'

Milly marches up to the bed and throws back the covers, and there huddled on the mattress and looking at with terrified eyes is her classmate Paul Straker.

It isn't often that words fail Millicent Leeson, but they fail her now. Like a landed fish she gasps for them, but they elude her, slipping from her mouth choked and half-formed.

Paul hides his face, curling up in a ball but Milly's mum refuses to quail before her daughter and, stroking the boy's hair with a soothing, proprietary hand, adopts the insouciant look of someone who accepts that 'the jig is up.'

'Well, *you* didn't want him, did you, dear?' she says, both her eyes and her naked body throwing a challenge to her daughter's look of furious accusation.

And now the words start to come.

'You...! You...! You fucking...! You're *disgusting*! You know that? You fucking—' Milly turns and makes for the door. 'I'm moving in with Dad!'

'Fine,' says her mum. 'If he'll have you.'

Andi and Bryony wade through the overgrown garden, jungle-like in its longstanding state of neglect, the rain pattering on the leaves overhead with a loudness that seems unnatural.

The house now appears before them, and the girls, dropping onto their haunches, survey it from the border of the garden where the drive opens out into a forecourt fronting the mansion. Seen at close quarters and under the leaden sky, the gabled façade of Raggedy Towers seems less inviting than even before. Its aspect is one of dark mystery, of a house apparently silent and untenanted, concealing its secrets within itself.

'You still want to go in there...?' says Bryony, looking

at her sister uncertainly.

'Well, we've got to, now,' replies Andi, of somewhat doubtful countenance herself. 'We've come too far to turn back now, haven't we?'

What her sister says is exactly what Bryony feels: they've come too far to turn back. They have to go on now, and if anything bad is going to happen, it will happen because it's supposed to happen.

'Okay, let's film the intro first,' says Andi.

Bryony unshoulders her backpack and takes out the video camera while Andi, pulling down her coat hood, adjusts her twin-tails and her fringe.

'Ready?'

'Ready.'

'This is Andalusia Seton reporting,' begins Andi, in the hushed urgent tones appropriate for the occasion. 'We are coming live from Raggedy Towers here on the edge of Marchmont, where Rinda Neves, who went missing two days ago, is being held prisoner by Raggedy Man and his mysterious accomplice. As you can see, there are no signs of life coming from this spooky looking old mansion...'

Pause.

'I said "as you can see"!' hisses Andi, corner-mouthed. 'That means you're supposed to turn the camera to show the house!' Bryony turns the camera to show the house. Proceeds Andi: 'Somewhere inside Raggedy Towers Rinda is being kept prisoner, locked up in one of the rooms, or perhaps in the attic or the cellar. We are now going to go into the house to search for her and we will continue to report live while we do the search.'

Bryony stops recording. 'How are we going to get in?' she asks. 'Do we go through the front door...?'

'No, cuz they might see us. Let's go round the back and sneak in that way,' replies Andi. (This on the understanding that if anyone inside the house *is* keeping an eye out for trespassers it will only be through the front windows.)

'Come on. Let's keep inside the trees until we're round the side. And keep the camera on record all the time now. We can edit out the boring bits later.'

Retreating into the garden, the girls follow the curve of the forecourt round the side of the building. Herea wall extends from the wall of the mansion to the edge of the garden, and in the centre of the wall is an arched gateway giving access to a yard.

'We'll go that way,' says Andi. 'Through that gateway.'

Breaking cover, they make their way along the wall, Andi in front, Bryony following and filming her. The rain has ceased completely now. Reaching the arched gateway, Andi stops and cranes her neck round the gatepost. The yard within, surfaced with bricks, weedgrown, potholed, is enclosed on one side by the wall of the mansion, and on the other by rows of crumbling outbuildings. And conspicuously out of place amongst all this age and neglect is one very modern motor car. A dark blue hatchback, it is parked close to the wall of the house.

'The car!' exclaims Andi. 'It's here! Look!'

Bryony joins her sister.

'Get some footage of it!' instructs Andi. 'This proves I'm right! It's the car Raggedy Man's accomplice drives! The car we saw the other day!'

'I don't think it is...' says Bryony doubtfully.

'What, you don't think it's a car? It's not an elephant, is it?'

'I know it's a *car*; I'm just not sure it's the same car we saw the other day...'

'*Of course* it's the same car, stupid! Look at it: dark blue; and the one we saw the other day was dark blue, wasn't it?'

'I thought the car we saw the other day was black...'

'No, it was *blue!* Dark blue!'

'I remember it being black...'

'Then you remember it wrongly, don't you? Raggedy Man's only got *one* accomplice, hasn't he? He's not going to have lots of them.'

They enter the yard and walk up to the car.

Andi takes up her commentary. 'And here we've found the car that belongs to Raggedy Man's accomplice; the car he kidnapped Rinda Neves in.'

They circle the car, looking in through the windows, Bryony with her digital eye. 'There don't seem to be any clues inside the car. Nothing on the seats or the dashboard...' Leaning over to look through the windscreen, her hand comes into contact with the bonnet. 'It's warm!' she reports, surprised. 'He must have just been out somewhere. I wonder where he went?'

'He might've been getting rid of the body...'

'Don't say that!' says Andi sharply. 'Rinda's alive! She's locked up in a room in there and we're going to find her!'

'I still don't think it's the same car...' says Bryony. 'The one from the other day was black...'

'It was dark blue!' insists Andi. 'Your memory's going colourblind.'

Close to the parked car is a door into the house. The girls walk up to the door.

Andi addresses the camera. 'We are now going to go inside Raggedy Towers to start our search for Rinda Neves—'

'If the door's not locked,' says Bryony.

The door is not locked. It opens and the girls find themselves in a small vestibule, dingy and unfurnished. Facing them, an inner doorway, through which a corridor leads deeper into the mansion. Andi closes the outer door and they find themselves in near-darkness. The vestibule has but one small window, the dirt-encrusted glass allowing very light daylight to enter.

'We should've brought torches,' says Bryony.

'That's alright: I can use my phone,' replies Andi, reaching into the pocket of her raincoat. She switches it on: 'Crap! I forgot to text Gran! She's been trying to call me!'

'Text her now, then,' urges Bryony.

The message is rapidly typed and sent. 'Done it.'

'What did you tell her?'

'Just where we are and what we're doing. Right, now let's—'

She breaks off. They hear the sound of an approaching motorcar.

The girls stare at each other, goggle-eyed. The sound draws ever closer, and now the car has entered the yard and they can hear the sound of its wheels as it comes to a halt right outside, obviously pulling up close to the other car. Now comes the sound of doors opening and closing.

'Omigod, they're probably coming in here! Come on!' hisses Andi.

They pelt down the passageway. The wildly swinging light from Andi's smartphone picks out a door on the left.

'In there!'

Lightning quick they are through the door and inside a small, windowless chamber. The door closed behind them, Andi stabs the power button on her phone and they are plunged into pitch darkness.

Backs against the door they listen. They hear the door from the yard being opened and the sound of several voices. Footsteps advance along the passageway. Voices. A male voice and answered by a female one.

'…least it's stopped raining…'

The footsteps pass on by, the voices recede. A door at the further end of the corridor opens and closes.

Silence.

Two very loud sighs of relief in the pitch-black room. Light suddenly appears as Andi reactivates her phone.

'Who was *that*?' she gasps.

'I bet it's that black car!' hisses Bryony. 'I told you that blue one wasn't the one we saw the other day!'

'But Raggedy Man can't have lots of accomplices! It doesn't make sense…!'

Bryony sees the familiar look of fierce concentration on her sister's face as she wrestles with this latest development.

And then: 'I've got it! Prostitution!'

'Prostitution?'

'Yeah, it has to be! They've kidnapped Rinda so they can pimp her out to paedos, and now people are coming here and paying to have sex with her! Yeah, that's got to be it! And they might be making her do child pornography as well!'

'But some of them who just came in were women!' protests Bryony.

'So? You get woman paedos as well as man paedos!' retorts Andi. 'And gay ones as well! Come on: if we follow them, we'll find Rinda!'

Andi takes hold of the door knob, twists, pulls—and the door knob comes away in her hand.

'Whoops,' she says.

When Jo was a little girl there had been a sad-looking man who lived on her street, and Jo had wondered why always looked so sad, and she had wondered where he went when he walked off down the footpath that went into the countryside. Nearly every day the sad-looking man would go down this path, sometimes in the morning, sometimes in the afternoon, and he would be gone for hours and hours.

And so Jo had wondered where he was going to, and one day she decided she would follow him and find out for herself.

And so Jo had followed the sad-looking man, and she had followed him down the winding path, further and further into the countryside until they must have been miles and miles from anywhere, until finally they came to a big building standing all on its own in the middle of the countryside. Jo had wondered what the building was for and when the sad-looking man had gone inside through a door in the wall she had followed him.

She had walked in through that door in the wall and had

witnessed a vision from hell that would change her life forever.

It had taken Jo years to recover from what she saw that day. But oddly enough, she doesn't regret it; she doesn't regret what happened that day. That day had been the making of her. According to her mum, up until then she had been a quiet, dreamy little girl. What happened that day had been her wake-up call. True, that wake-up call had brought in its wake a complete mental breakdown, with trauma and recurring nightmares and she had needed several years of intense therapy to come to terms with it all—but in the end she had emerged from her ordeal, transformed; a dreamer no longer, but very wide awake. To quote the old saw: what doesn't kill you makes you stronger. Or as a more recent commentator has put it: a bit of childhood trauma helps build character.

The abattoir whose horrors Jo had witnessed has long since closed down, but the building itself still stands; a derelict ruin, but still standing. Until recently Jo had always assumed it had been demolished or at least renovated and turned into something else; but she had learned the truth from Yukari, who, pursuing her hobby of urban exploration had discovered the building. She had shown Jo the pictures she had taken of it.

Nothing she saw in those photographs had struck any chord or triggered any memories, and even now, as she stands before the building on the crazed surface of the carpark, she does not feel anything. Her strongest memory of the building's exterior is of one small door in a large expanse of bare wall; the door she had seen the sad-looking man walk in through, and through which she had been able to follow him (thanks to some criminally negligent building security.) But this door and this wall, if they really exist as her memory presents them, will be round the other side of the building. It will be from that direction they had approached from, the day she had followed the sad-looking man down that country path. Where she stands now is the main entrance, which she never saw that day. (Although come to think of it, she probably *was* taken out of the building this way—but by that time she would not have been in any condition to be taking much notice of her surroundings.)

She decides to test the accuracy of her memory.

Crossing the carpark, she follows the perimeter of the building, turning one corner and then another... And then she sees it: the door in the wall. This has to be it; it has to be. Not identical to the image in her mind, but add on twenty years, take into account the encroachment of vegetation over what was once neatly-cut turf, plus the aging and discoloration of the wall itself... Yes, this is it; the door in the wall...

And over there, across this wilderness of weeds, a stretch of woodland. It would have been against one of those trees that she left her bike before she made her way to that fatal door...

Wading through the weeds and nettles, Jo reaches the door. It is closed and when she tries to push the rusty bar, at first it seems to be locked as well, but she pushes harder and the door gives way, opening reluctantly, its joints stiff from disuse.

If anyone has come here recently, they didn't use this door to get in.

And through the door which a dreamy little girl in a summer dress (Jo has no accurate memory of what she had on that day but imagines it was a summer dress) had stepped twenty-odd years ago, walks the fully-grown woman with the sky-blue hair, tattoos and piercings, dressed in boots, fishnets, shorts and a Bikini Kill t-shirt.

A concrete corridor. She remembers these concrete corridors. A veritable maze of them. She remembers cows being led by people in waterproof overalls that she had thought looked like spacesuits. And she'd followed them, she'd followed the people leading the cows and that was how she had ended up on the kill floor.

'Linda? Linda Neves? Are you here?'

Her voice echoes down the corridor. She listens, straining her ears for the smallest of sounds.

Silence.

'Linda?'

She sets off along the corridors, calling out at intervals.

There's a risk attached to calling out. If Linda Neves *is* in this place and she *is* still alive, her abductor might be here as well. But if the girl is alone, if she's been abandoned, left tied up, chained up or locked up somewhere... And anyway, Jo has come prepared for trouble: she has both her skills in self-defence and a knife in her pocket. (Disclaimer: Jo Seton doesn't carry a knife around with her all the time: she only brings it out for special occasions like this one.)

As Jo progresses deeper into the building, proof that the slaughterhouse has received other visitors since its closure soon becomes apparent. Walls daubed with graffiti, litter on the floors; not surprising, really: a derelict building like this has probably been put to many good uses over the years: a squat for the homeless, a junkies' hangout, a venue for illegal raves...

Aside from the occasional adornments, refuse and incursions from parasitic vegetable nature, the corridors are uniform and uniformly barren, forming a network of concrete passageways with doorless openings leading into vacant rooms. Jo hasn't come here to recreate her journey of twenty-odd years ago, but she can't help but think of the kill floor, the mouth, stomach and entrails of this manmade monster, as her ultimate destination, the fatal zone to which this network of concrete arteries will inevitably take her.

'Linda? Can you hear me? I'm Jo Seton; Andi's mum! I'm here to help you!'

She looks into every room she passes, surveys every corner with the light from her smartphone, persuading herself she is searching for a living girl and not a corpse.

She smiles to herself. She needs to pump herself up with some of her eldest daughter's determined optimism, that unflagging belief of hers that Rinda is still alive somewhere...

And as for Bryony... She needs to have a talk with that girl. Since she came home yesterday afternoon she's been subdued, like someone or something has upset her or something is weighing on her mind. And then waking up screaming in the middle of the night! something she hasn't done for years. She can't help thinking there must be a connection... According to Andi nothing had happened yesterday that could account for her sister's sudden change of mood... But something must have gone wrong somewhere; something must have upset her, even if it was only something in her own mind...Yes, she needs to have a good heart-to-heart talk with that girl...

And now, quite suddenly, Jo comes upon the kill floor. She knows it the moment she sees the doorway, much bigger and more important-looking than any other doorway she has passed... This is it: the doorway she'd seen the cows being pulled in through by the men in the waterproof suits...

And me, the little girl who followed them in there.

And now here she is, following in her own footsteps.

She stands in the doorway. The kill floor. Or what was once the kill floor. Now it's just a big empty room: a vast high-ceilinged chamber, narrow windows close to the ceiling and one or two doorless emergency exits allow light enough to enter to reveal a concrete floor littered with cans, bottles and other detritus, graffiti-covered walls, and a whole lot of empty space.

This is the place alright; but she doesn't feel anything; it doesn't all come flooding back.

She tries to superimpose past memory over present reality, to match those images of blood and butchery seared on her mind with this silent dingy room. The blood and the butchery, the stench and the noise...

...And the horrified look on the face of the sad-looking man.

Jo has always wondered what became of the sad-looking man. He was Jo's first rogue male. He was the one who sparked her interest in the genus, in her naming and defining of them. True, this particular rogue male hadn't conformed to type in the respect that he did have a job of work—he had a job alright, but it was the worst job on the whole planet, and she has always believed that the sad-looking man thought so himself and that it was the reason for that look of horror on his face when he saw her there on the kill floor...

She's never been able to find out what became of him. Her mum and dad couldn't (or wouldn't) tell her anything. He just moved away, they said. By the time she came back home he was long gone... She never even knew his real name...

Was he blamed in any way for what happened that day? Did he move away because he had to move away? Or was it just a crushing sense of guilt that drove him away?

And what happened to him after that? Could guilt and remorse have driven the poor man to suicide? The possibility has haunted Jo for years. If he had taken his own life, it would have been because of her, because she decided to follow him that day... He would be like the jockey who trampled Emily Davison...

Why had she been so interested in the sad-looking man as a child, anyway? Doleful, uncommunicative, he'd been in every way the complete reverse of the kind of grownup that kids the age she was then generally warm to... Only goes to show what an odd one she had been back then...

Jo advances slowly into the chamber. Of the winches and pulleys, the hooks and chains, all the appurtenances of a production line for the killing, flaying and dismemberment of animals, nothing remains. From the profusion of graffiti, it seems very likely raves and parties have been held here in the not-to-distant past. The kill floor turned into a dance floor ...

As she draws closer to the far wall of the chamber, she decries a familiar phrase, sprayed in loud, angry characters:

MEAT IS MURDER!

One visitor at least knew what this place used to be.

'Linda? Linda?'

Jo's voice echoes around the cavernous chamber. She quarters the room, calling out Rinda's name while probing dark corners for huddled remains wearing a flower-patterned dress, a fluffy angora cardigan, white knee-socks and buckled shoes.

She searches without success and returns to the corridor entrance.

She stops. She hears a noise. A faint tapping. Not from in here, but from outside, somewhere down the corridor. She listens. It comes again: a pattern of tapping sounds. The sound comes from some distance away, off to the right; the direction opposite from that by which Jo had arrived.

'Linda? Linda Neves? Is that you?'

Another series of taps, faster this time, an urgent affirmative.

And Jo Seton's face lights up; it lights up so much that her piercings almost seem to sparkle in its reflected radiance. Joy, disbelief, excitement, relief, all blended together.

'I can hear you!' she shouts. 'I can hear you, Linda! Keep tapping and I'll come and find you, okay?'

Another rapid series of taps.

Ecstatic, Jo sets off down the corridor, only to be brought up in her tracks moments later. A new sound, a sound coming from outside the building: the sound of an approaching motor car.

Her smile vanishes.

The kidnapper...? No, no, it can't be...! If he abandoned

Rinda here, he wouldn't be stupid enough to come back, to return to the scene of his crim...!

Hang on a mo. What if the kidnapper *hasn't* abandoned her? What if he's been here, entertaining his victim the whole time, the last three days...? And she, maybe she just happened to turn up at the moment he'd nipped out to the shops...

She hears the car stop. He's out there, in the carpark... And *her* car's there, sitting there in plain sight! He'll know he's got a visitor...!

Jo starts running. Whatever else happens, she has to get to Rinda before he does. And after that... Well, she's got her knife, hasn't she?

'Keep tapping, Linda!'

Has *she* heard the car? Does Rinda know that her tormentor has returned, that the clock is ticking? She might not; where she is, she might not have heard the car; she might not realise how urgent things have suddenly become.

Jo runs along the corridors, hitting the walls as she corners without breaking, homing in on the tapping sound. She's getting closer... It's getting louder, clearer... A wooden sound, knuckles rapping on a thick wooden surface...

Another corner brings Jo into a much wider corridor, a corridor lined on both sides with heavy wooden doors. The doors are composed of thick wooden planks, age-darkened, each fitted with a slide-bolt lock, and with a barred aperture at the top. Some of the doors are open, some of them closed and bolted.

Stalls. The stalls for the animals awaiting execution. Jo remembers now. She was here that day, in this corridor or one like it, and she saw the cows being brought out of the stalls by the men in the spacesuits and wellingtons.

'Linda? Are you here! Where are you?'

Three urgent knocks bring Jo to one of the closed and bolted doors. She pulls back the bolt, grabs the loop handle and pulls open the door.

'Linda!'

The girl has fallen backwards onto the floor just inside the stall, gasping and spent with exhaustion. Bobbed black hair untidily frames a face pale under dirt-smudges, and hollow red-rimmed eyes look blearily up at Jo: a haggard ghost of the smiling young portrait reproduced in so many newspapers and television news bulletins. Rinda Neves. She still wears a flower-patterned dress, a fluffy angora cardigan, white knee-socks and buckled shoes, her 'last seen wearing' attire, now rumpled and stained and filthy with dirt. The room reeks of urine and excrement.

Jo drops down beside the girl, cradles her head in her lap.

'You poor thing...' She strokes the girl's disarranged hair. 'Who did this, sweetheart?' she asks urgently. 'Who did this to you?'

Rinda's mouth, working painfully, forms a single cracked syllable, barely audible: it sounds like the word 'man.'

'A man? You mean a man you don't know? A stranger?'

An impatient shake of the head in Jo's lap. She repeats the word, wincing with the effort.

'What's happened to your voice, love? Christ, you've shouted your throat ragged, haven't you?' A nod. 'Have you been shut in here on your own, all this time then?' Another nod. 'My God... So the man who kidnapped you: he never came back?' A silent negative. 'Did he say he was going to come back?' Another negative.

'Then maybe I was wrong about that car...' says Jo, thinking out loud. 'Maybe it's someone else...'

Jo surveys the stall that has been Rinda's prison these past few days. This doesn't take long. Spacious yes, but lacking in the amenities. In the far corner resides the source of the stench, two small stools and a puddle of urine. In the opposite corner a copper pipe runs down the wall and extruding from it a faucet, most likely fitted to fill a water trough. But there is no trough there now; apart from cold water and the improvised toilet facilities, there is absolutely nothing: no bedding, no food left for the prisoner; and no sign of the video camera, either, the video camera Peter Neves had seemed so concerned about. Just an empty container for condemned livestock; concrete underfoot and overhead, breeze blocks at the rear and wooden partitions on either side; partitions which, rising to only seven feet in height, communicate with the neighbouring stalls—but seven feet is too high for any ten-year-old child to hope to reach.

'Come on, let's get you out of here, sweetheart,' says Jo. 'I'll carry you back to my car; it's just outsi—'

She breaks off. Footsteps! Footsteps echoing down the corridors.

'Shit!' hisses Jo. She looks at Rinda. The girl's eyes are wide with fear. 'Listen: another car pulled up outside, just after I first heard you knocking. I didn't see who it was, and it could be anyone; but it might *him* come back for you.' Jo listens. The footsteps are definitely drawing closer. Jo reaches into the pocket of her shorts, pulls out her knife, flicks open the blade. 'If it *is* him, I'm not going to let him harm you, Linda, okay? I've got you now, and there's no fucking way I'm going to let him harm you.' She contrives a smile. 'Even if it *does* get me done for manslaughter.'

Setting Rinda down against the partition wall, Jo positions herself in front of the girl, crouched with knife in hand, facing the open doorway, muscles tensed, ready to spring.

The footsteps are in the corridor outside. A pause and then come on again. He's seen the open door... He knows something is wrong...

Closer... Closer...

A shadow falls across the floor and then a figure appears in the doorway.

Jo stares, astounded, hardly believing her eyes.

It is Yukari. Rinda's mother.

For a moment the two women stare wordlessly at one another—and then Yukari drops to her knees and, uttering a groan, buries her face in her hands.

Chapter Eighteen
Like a House on Fire!

A close up of Andalusia Seton's face, lit from below by an unseen source (her smartphone.) Behind her, inky darkness.

'We've had to hide in this room,' she whispers, 'because another car has arrived and some people have just come into the house. We now know for sure that Rinda Neves is a prisoner here, and we know why, as well: she has been forced into forced prostitution by Raggedy Man and his mysterious accomplice, and people are coming here to have underage sex with her and watch her do child pornography. The people who just arrived are her latest customers. So now we're going to search the house to find out where all this is happening, and then we can rescue Rinda and expose this evil conspiracy!

'As well as the door we came in through, there's another door in this room that leads to a different part of the house—'

'Which is just as well since you broke—'

'Shut up, camerawoman! There's another door and we're going to go through this door to explore further into Raggedy Towers.'

Tracked by her sister's digital eye, Andi walks over to the door in the far wall of the room. She passes into the next room, Bryony following. Phone held out like a torch, Andi scans her surroundings. The light from the screen falls upon nothing save for bare floorboards.

'This seems to be a very big room, a big room with nothing in it. We'll follow the wall and see if we can find another door...'

They follow the wall and reach a corner. The next wall

extends much further in length and is as featureless as the first until they come to a set of double doors. Andi tries the doors, but neither of them yielded.

'We'll be in trouble if these are the only other doors,' says Bryony.

'They *won't* be the only other doors,' retorts Andi. 'A big room like this should have lots of doors leading from it.'

The girls proceed and reach the next corner without encountering any further means of egress; but along the next wall they find another door, a single door this time. Andi is just in the act of reaching for the doorknob when they hear a sound: the sound of a door being closed, followed by heavy footsteps approaching from the other side of the door.

'Hide!'

The girls retreat from the door and Andi switches off her phone. For a moment they are involved in utter darkness, but then the door opens and a light appears through the door and behind the light comes a man: the Raggedy Man! A lantern in his hand, a genuine oil-burning antique, he walks across the room, moving away from where the girls stand petrified and over to the locked double doors. Taking a key from his pocket he opens one of the doors and passes through. The door closes, darkness returns and the girls hear the sound of the key turning in the lock on the other side.

The Raggedy Man's footsteps retreat.

'Come on!' hisses Andi.

Switching her phone back on she leads the way back to the door Raggedy Man came in through. Beyond the door is another empty room, smaller, but with several doors. The first two doors Andi tries proves to be locked. They move onto the third. Locked as well.

'Oh great; we're trapped here,' says Bryony. 'And Raggedy Man might be back any minute!'

'There's still one more door,' says Andi.

It's not a promising door. Smaller than the others, it has the appearance of a cupboard door. Andi pulls the handle.

The door opens and it's not a cupboard after all. A narrow flight of stairs ascends into darkness.

'Stairs!' gasps Andi, as though these useful architectural features had been until now nothing more than an urban legend. 'Now we're getting somewhere! It's bound to be upstairs where they're keeping Rinda Neves prisoner!'

'Why is it bound to be upstairs?' challenges Bryony. 'Before, you said she could be anywhere in the house.'

'Yes, but that was before we knew that they were making Rinda do prostitution and pornography!'

'So?'

'*So*, you need a bed to do prostitution and pornography, don't you? And the bedrooms are always upstairs!'

Try arguing with logic like this!

The girls ascend the staircase and at the top they find themselves at the beginning of a very narrow corridor. Andi shines her phone around; its light picks out rough wooden walls, a bare floor and a ceiling festooned with cobwebs. The air is close and musty and thick with dust.

'This looks all wrong,' says Bryony. 'It's like we're on the wrong side of the walls or something...'

'*I* know what this is,' declares Andi. 'It's a secret passage! All these old mansions have secret passages. *This* is where Rinda will be: hidden away in a secret room; somewhere that a normal search wouldn't find. Come on!'

The girls start along the passageway, which is just wide enough to allow them to walk side by side.

They come to an intersection, where passageways branch off to the left and right.

'Shh! Listen!'

A faint sound of music reaches their ears. It sounds familiar to the girls...

'It's Beyonce!' exclaims Bryony.

Not in person, but it is undoubtedly one of her songs, the sound floating towards them from the left-hand arm of the passageway. Cautiously, the girls advance towards the music, which becomes clearer as they proceed, and with it they begin to discern the sound of voices; several human voices engaged in conversation. Both music and conversation sound muffled, and seem to be emanating from the other side of the passageway wall.

And then another sound manifests itself, one that seems to be coming from further down the passageway than the music and chatter. The sound pulls the girls up in their tracks. It's the sound of voices, his and hers; but these are not his and hers voices engaged in conversation; these are his and hers voices engaged in something else entirely; his and hers voices making the kind of noises Andi and Bryony sometimes hear coming through the wall from Mum's bedroom on the nights of one of her more successful blind dates.

The girls stare at each other.

'Omigod!' gasps Andi. 'It's Rinda! We've got to save her!'

'She doesn't sound like she wants to be saved,' says Bryony.

'You can't always tell by the noises,' declares Andi sententiously. 'Where's it coming from…?'

They proceed very cautiously, looking for a door, but there's no sign of one or of any other means of ingress; just bare wooden boards.

But then:

'What's that?' Andi points. 'Look! Up there on the wall! A light!'

Andi extinguishes her phone. In the darkness, they see it clearly: a small circle of light high up on the wall above them, and through it the sounds of the music and conversation (but not the sex noises) seem to be reaching them. There are several voices, some male, some female, frequent laughter.

'It sounds like they're having a party,' says Andi, reducing her voice to a whisper. She puts her ear to the wall.

It doesn't help: the voices are still muffled, individual words indistinguishable.

She steps back, eyeing the circle of light speculatively. 'You know... If one of us was to get up on the other one's shoulders, they'd be able to see through that hole...'

'Okay,' agrees Bryony. 'I'll get up on your shoulders.'

'How about *I* get up on *your* shoulders?' retorts Andi. 'Who's in charge here?'

'Yeah, but I weigh less than you do.'

'Not *much* less!'

After some more *sotto voce* squabbling they agree to take turns looking through the hole, and after further parley resolve upon applying the democratic process of rock-paper-scissors to determine who goes first.

Bryony wins best of three. After she has also won best of five, Andi concedes with very bad grace. Feeling that the natural order of things has been turned on its head, she hunkers down to let Bryony straddle her shoulders, and then, very precariously, raises the girl aloft.

Bryony applies her eye to the hole.

She is looking into a room. The room is windowless and lit by electric light, an old filament lightbulb hanging unadorned from the ceiling. The walls and floor are bare and drab in keeping with the rest of the house, only this room is furnished and the furniture looks new. There are three settees, and two armchairs, none of them matching, as well as a minifridge and a table littered with food and drink. The Beyonce song is playing on a tablet resting on the arm of one of the settees. The room has two doors, both closed, one on the wall facing Bryony, the other on the wall to the right. The room has six inhabitants, three girls and three men. The girls are all teenagers, and look to Bryony to be about the same age as Milly; the men are all older than the girls, grownups not teens, and they are all Asian (brown Asian rather than yellow Asian) and they all have moustaches. Cigarettes are being smoked by both the girls and the men, and bottled beer is being drunk. One of the girls is busy snogging one of the Asian men. A second girl is bent over the table and she appears to be inhaling what looks to Bryony to be sherbet, introducing it to her nostrils via the medium rolled-up banknote. This seems odd to Bryony, because has never heard that sherbet tastes better taken nasally.

'What can you see?' whispers Andi.

'Shh!' says Bryony.

The snogging girl breaks away from her partner. She looks toward one of the closed doors, a frown on her face.

'God!' she says, irritable. 'How much longer are they going to be?'

Getting up from the settee, she walks over to the door and knocks loudly.

'Oi, you in there!' she shouts. 'Hurry up! People are waiting!'

'Get down!' hisses Andi, backing up this demand with a violent shaking that very nearly sends them both tumbling, Bryony climbs down from her sister's shoulders.

'What did you see?' demands Andi.

Bryony tells her.

Andi frowns in the darkness. 'Big-school girls and Pakistani men with moustaches? That sounds more like a grooming gang. Why would big-school girls want to have sex with someone like Rinda?'

Bryony remarks that it takes sorts.

'And what about Raggedy Man? Isn't he there?'

No sign of him.

'And they've got Rinda in the next room?'

That's what it sounds like.

'Right. Now it's my turn to look.'

Andi climbs onto her sister's shoulders and, raised to the spy-hole, takes in the room and its occupants. Barely has she assimilated this interesting view when the door to the adjacent room opens and from it emerges a fourth moustachioed Pakistani man and arm-in-arm with him a fourth teenage girl. This Pakistani man looks older than the other three, and Andi thinks she's seen him before... Yes! Isn't he Mr Mohyedlin from the One Stop Shop on Silver Street?

But where's Rinda Neves? It was supposed to be *her* in there having sex, not this teenager.

'Good one, was it?' asks the impatient girl. 'Hope you haven't left a mess in the bed.'

'Shut-up, Carrie!' says the girl on Mr Mohyedlin's arm, blushing crimson.

'Look at you! God, you're a total baby! "Oooh, don't *talk* about it, Carrie! I've been doing dirty things and I'm *so* embarrassed!"'

The girl with the powdered nose starts giggling.

And now the second door bursts open and another player appears on the scene: another teenage girl, a girl with dark frizzy hair. Andi knows this girl... Yes, it's Milly's schoolfriend! The one who went off on one that day on the estate! Nicki! That's her name: Nicki!

Nicki's arrival is clearly an unanticipated event to the other people in the room.

'What are you doing here?' demands Mohyedlin angrily.

'What are *you* doing here?' retorts Nicki, fixing wild accusing eyes on him. 'You said you weren't coming here today! That's what you told me! And what are you doing with *her*?' pointing at her of the bashful countenance, who, quickly lets go of Mohyedlin's arm, becoming her of the completely terrified countenance.

'What do you think she's been doing with him?' inquires Carrie, wearing a smile that advertises her enjoyment of the situation. 'Playing snakes and ladders?'

A fit of helpless laughter from powdered-nose.

Nicki ignores this, her accusing eyes still fixed Mohyedlin. 'You lied to me!' she accuses. 'You told me you weren't coming here today! And here you are, with *her!* I *thought* there was something funny going on!'

'Stop making a scene, girl!' barks Mohyedlin, angry because his chums are all grinning at him.

'For fuck's sake, Nicki, what does it matter if Jilly went with him?' says Carrie. '*You* can still go with him as well, can't you? It's just sex, isn't it? It's not like you're in a serious relationship with him!'

'I *am* in a serious relationship with him!' fires back Nicki.

'Don't be ridiculous, girl!' from Mohyedlin.

'Oh yeah?' says Carrie. 'His wife might have something to say about that.'

'He's going to *leave* his wife!' throws back Nicki.

Clearly this is news to Mohyedlin. 'Don't talk nonsense, girl! I cannot just leave my wife!'

'But you've *got* to!' insists Nicki. 'Because we're... you see...' and, summoning all her resolve: 'We're going to have a baby!'

Carrie chokes on her cigarette and powdered-nose falls to the floor in convulsions of laughter.

The men are grinning as well, but one person is not so amused. 'What are you talking about?' roars Mohyedlin. 'Are you insane or are you lying? You told me you were taking precautions!'

'Yes, but I... I might have forgotten a couple of times...'

'You're lying!'

'I'm *not* lying!'

'Then get rid of it!'

'I don't *want* to get rid of it!' wails Carrie, pressing a maternal hand over her lower intestines. 'It's *our* baby! We can be a family!'

'You stupid child! Get rid of it! Get rid of it, or you'll get us *all* into trouble! All of us! Your friends as well!'

This wipes the smile from Carrie's face. 'Yeah, he's right! You're gunna spoil this for all of us, you selfish bitch! So stop pissing around and if you really have got a bun in the oven then go'n get a fucking abortion—and if they ask you who put it in there, say it was some boy from school!'

'No, I'm not having an abortion!' insists Nicki. 'I'm going to keep it!'

'You will not keep it!' roars the prospective father. 'I forbid you to! I order you to get rid of it! At once!'

'No, I'm not getting rid of it, I'm going to keep it, and you're going to accept your responsibilities and you're going to stop seeing that cow Jilly and you're going to tell your wife who doesn't love you as much as I do anyway cuz you said so yourself and you're going to leave her and then I can move in with you and I'll work in the shop with you and we can have our baby togeth—'

A hearty slap round the face from Mohyedlin brings Nicki's word-picture of domestic bliss to an abrupt end.

'What's going on in there?' whispers Bryony.

'Shh!' retorts Andi impatiently, her eye glued to the spy-hole. This is better than *East Enders*!

A hand to her crimson cheek, Nicki stares at her assailant, dumbstruck.

And then, finding her voice: 'You... You... How could you...?' Her expression resolves into fury. 'I'm going to make you pay for that!' turning to face the others: 'All of you! You're all going to regret this!'

And Nicki is gone, slamming the door behind her.

Mohyedlin now breaks into a rapid stream of Pakistani, directed at his three associates. A heated conversation ensues.

'Oi. No talking in jibber-jabber!' cuts in Carrie. 'That's the rule here, remember? No fucking jibber-jabber!'

Meanwhile, either from impatience to know what's happening, or else weariness from carrying her sister's weight on her shoulders for so long, Bryony starts to totter, which in turn causes Andi to sway alarmingly.

'What are you doing, stupid? You'll—' She breaks off. 'Eww, what's that horrible smell?'

And then Andi realises she knows only to well what said

horrible smell is. She looks fearfully over her shoulder. Standing behind them, is Raggedy Man, his features wild with mute rage, eyes glaring murderously.

Andi screams, Raggedy Man roars, Bryony screams and loses her balance, Raggedy Man lunges and the partition, old and rotten, gives way, and all three of them are precipitated into the room, crashing to the floor amid a shower of splinters, plaster and sawdust.

Andi, recovering, raises herself onto her elbows and, wiping the coating of plaster dust from her face, meets the eyes of the room's eight occupants. The room is silent, the music having been switched off. One and all, the four men and four girls stare at the new arrivals with matching expressions of slack-jawed immobility. The Raggedy Man, being the owner of the establishment, is no stranger to them, but his sudden advent through a solid wall, and in the company of two primary school girls is not an event they could have easily anticipated. Had the ceiling above their heads suddenly been lifted away by a giggling giant girl who then started dropping lighted matches on them, they might have been more surprised, but not much.

A pregnant moment and then the eight witnesses emerge from their stupor, with exclamations of 'What the fuck?' from the girls, and some presumably similar sentiments expressed in Pakistani by the men.

Accusing eyes are fixed upon Raggedy Man. He, springing to his feet, points an accusing dirty finger-nail at the unseated Setons. 'Caught 'em! Caught 'em spyin' on yer, I did!' he vociferates.

'He's lying!' exclaims Andi, standing up she helps her sister to her feet. 'I mean, he's *not* lying: we *were* spying on you; but *he* must have been spying on you before we were! *We* didn't make the spy-hole! It was too high up the wall!'

'She's lying!' explodes Raggedy Man agitatedly. 'She's lyin', she is! It's them what made them 'oles in the wall, not me! They weren't there afore! I never made them 'oles! It's them what did it!'

'I bet it *was* you, you dirty old fart!'

'Who are these kids, anyway? How did they get here?'

'Yeah, I never trusted him!'

One of the men, a man wearing wraparound shades, claps his hands, bringing the room to order. 'Stop, stop, stop!' he says and, addressing Raggedy Man: 'I want to know what you mean about *two* spy-holes! These girls only spoke of one. Which is it: one or two?'

'There was just *one* that we saw,' answers Andi.

'Oh yeah, yeah,' agrees Raggedy Man quickly. 'I meant it was just one spy-'ole they made, not two. Yeah, it was just one…'

Wraparound shades regards Raggedy Man suspiciously; then he turns and speaks in Pakistani to two of his companions. They pounce on Raggedy Man and taking an arm each, try to restrain him. Raggedy Man struggles wildly, but the two men grapple him to the ground and pin him down, one of them planting a knee on his back.

'Go and look in the other room.'

Mohyedlin disappears into the adjoining room, switching the light on as he passes through the door. In less than a minute he returns, and his expression is grim.

'There *is* a spy-hole in the wall in there,' he says.

Jilly, Mohyedlin's recent partner, stifles a scream. 'Omigod! You mean he's been watching us! All this time, when we've…!'

'You filthy…' says wraparound shades. Marching up to Raggedy Man, he looks ready to kick him in the face.

'It weren't me, I tell yer! It were them girls made them spy-'oles!' he protests, trying to squirm free.

'No it wasn't!' retorts Andi. 'We didn't even know about that second one!'

'What's behind there, anyway?' Carrie wants to know. 'Is it another room?'

'No, it's a secret passage,' Andi tells her.

'And how did you two get in there? You're the Seton girls, aren't you? What are you doing here?'

'We were... we were just exploring the house and we found the staircase that leads up to the secret passages...'

'What if he wasn't just watching us?' speaks up the fourth girl. 'What if he was filming us as well? I've heard about perverts doing stuff like that!'

'Omigod, omigod...!'

'Was he?' Carrie asks Andi. 'Was there a camera set up out there? Anything like that?'

'No! There was nothing like that...' says Andi, her voice trailing off as she suddenly remembers their own camera; they'd put it down on the floor when they started looking through the spy hole. And there it must still be...

'Yeah? You don't sound too sure,' observes Carrie, eyeing her narrowly.

'No, there was definitely no cameras there!' declares Andi brightly.

'Hm. I'm gunna have a look for myself.'

So saying, Carrie steps through the demolished wall.

'There fucking *is* a camera!'

And she returns, brandishing the video camera.

'Look! The bastard's been filming us!'

'Oh God! I wanna go home...!'

'So you've been filming us, you bastard! What is this? Blackmail? You want money?'

'What if he's posted them online...?'

'That ain't my camera! I never seen it afore!'

'Don't give us that crap...!'

'Actually, he's telling the truth,' interposes Andi. 'That's *our* camera.'

Wraparound shades turns on her. '*You've* been filming us?'

'No, we weren't filming *you*,' says Andi. 'We were... we were just filming us exploring the house. We never filmed you in here. Give it back, please. It's our mum's...'

Carrie flips open the display screen. 'Let's have a look... Last recording... Ah! Oh yeah, it is just her...'

Andi's voice, shrunken like her image on the screen, issues tinnily from the device: 'This is Andalusia Seton reporting. We are coming live from Raggedy Towers here on the edge of Marchmont, where Rinda Neves, who went missing two days ago, is being held prisoner by Raggedy Man and his mysterious accomplice. As you can see—'

Carrie pauses the playback. 'You thought it was *him* who kidnapped that Neves kid?'

'We *did* think it was Raggedy Man, yes,' says Andi.

Bryony tugs at her coat-sleeve. 'I'm confused here,' she says. 'Where's Rinda? I thought she was in the other room.'

'No, Rinda's not in the other room,' explains Andi. 'She was never here at all. We were wrong about that,' (generously allowing her sister half-shares in the incorrect deduction.) 'Rinda's not here: it's just these people having their grooming gang parties.'

'We are *not* a grooming gang!' snarls Mohyedlin.

'That's what the fuzz would call you!' jeers Carrie.

Powdered-nose laughs.

'Now, look you—!'

'What's that smell?' asks Jilly, sniffing the air.

'What do you mean what's the smell? It's *him*, isn't it?' says Carrie, pointing down at Raggedy Man.

'No, I don't mean *him*. I can smell something else, as well... Like burning...'

'I can smell it too! Smoke!'

Mohyedlin rushes to the door, throws it open. Smoke pours into the room. Lots of it.

'Fire! The house is on fire!'

'Oh, Christ!' says Carrie. 'It's that mad bitch Nicki! She's fucking torched the place!'

'NO!' roars Raggedy Man. Coming to savage life, he breaks free from the men pinning down, springs to his feet, charges across the room and out into the corridor.

Says wraparound shades: 'Never mind him! We've got to get the hell out of here! Come on!'

And now it's every man for himself and no standing on ceremony as everyone runs for the exit, the men, not waiting for the teens, are first through the door, and the teens are right behind them, equally negligent of the preteens, Andi and Bryony, who find themselves bravely bringing up the rear.

They come out onto a wide corridor and at the end of the corridor a balustraded landing and staircase descending to the ground floor; and from the ground floor rise dense plumes of smoke. The Asian men are already running down the stairs.

Coughing and holding their sleeves over their noses, Andi and Bryony race down the corridor. They reach the head of the staircase. Below them is the main hallway of Raggedy Towers, crackling flames climbing the walls on either side. The main entrance is still blessedly clear.

Coughing, Bryony drops to her knees.

'Come on!' cries Andi, grabbing her arm. 'We can still make it!'

'Leave me!' sobs Bryony. 'Just leave me here!'

'What are you on about? Get up, stupid!'

She tries to pull her sister to her feet, but the girl stubbornly resists. 'No! Just leave me! I'm *supposed* to die here today! I know I am! It's my punishment!'

'What are you *on* about?' screams Andi. 'Punishment for what? Stop pissing around! I'm getting out of here and so are you!'

Literally dragging Bryony to her feet, Andi starts running down the staircase and Bryony, her wrist tightly gripped, is compelled to run with her. The front doors beckon but the flames are closing in fast on both sides. The heat is intense. The girls race across the hall and out through the doors into the blessed fresh air.

Clear of the heat from the burning house, they drop

coughing and exhausted onto the forecourt. Away from the noise of the conflagration they now discern the sound of approaching sirens. Across the forecourt are the girls, all of them, including arsonist Nicki, who dances giddily with her of the powdered nose, enjoying the fruits of her labours. The other three girls are making for the side of the house, from which direction two cars, one black and one navy blue (so Bryony was right!) now appear, travelling at speed. The girls run towards the cars, but neither vehicle has any intention of stopping to pick up passengers, and the girls are all but run down as the vehicles sweep past them and accelerate down the drive.

But alas! they do not get far. A quartet of police cars turn in through the gates and resolutely blocking the way out, cut off the fugitives' retreat. The cars skid to a halt, and uniformed officers rush towards them.

Andi, still coughing, rises to her feet, and turns to look at the burning house. The front doorway is now ablaze, and flames have appeared in the upstairs windows. Smoke rises thickly into the overcast sky. Raggedy Towers is doomed.

And then something suddenly occurs to Andi, something alarming. She looks down at her sister.

'Bryony...?' she says, controlling her voice with an effort. 'Where's the video camera...?'

Epilogue
Closing Remarks

'...has been found safe and sound. After running away from home, ten-year-old Linda became lost in the countryside, and finally found her way to a derelict factory building some three miles from her home, where yesterday she was discovered by a member of the public...'

'…They're lying. They're lying about something: I bloody know they are.'

'Who's lying?'

'The whole lot of them: the kid, the parents, and that Seton woman. There's something they're not telling us, and between them all they've cooked up this story to cover it up.'

'What're we going to do about it, then?'

'There's nothing we *can* do. The kid's turned up safe and sound and they've given her a clean bill of health. It's case closed, isn't it…?'

'…and he'd been lying there for five days before they found him…'

'Who was it that found him? One of the neighbours, was it?'

'No, it was the cops. They turned up and broke the door down.'

'So, who told *them*…?'

'…and she won't get rid of it?'

'That's what I heard. Wants to have her half-Paki brat so she can take him to visit his old man in prison.'

'Silly bitch. Who else was doing it, then? There was Carrie Bowman, yeah? And Jilly Grade…'

'Yeah, and Cindy Allen. She was doing it.'

'And Milly Leeson…'

'Fuck off! Milly Leeson wasn't doing it!'

'Oh yeah? Then why hasn't she been in school, genius?'

'It never was…!'

'It *was*, I'm telling you! It was *him*! That's why he was always wearing that gasmask: it was so people wouldn't recognise him…!'

'…Nobody's seen him since the house burned down…'

'But they haven't found a body, have they…?'

'…Hello, there! You're a lovely cat, aren't you? Come here… Lovely fluffy white cat… Here, what's going on? You're all over me…! And Christ, you're *purring*…! I knew there had to be one somewhere! I knew there had to be one…! Let's have a look at your collar… "Courtney Love…" Well, that explains it, then! It's the lumberjack shirt, isn't it…?'

'…and the first prize goes to Martina for her video diary about her rabbits Flopsy and Dropsy. But I'd also like to give a special mention to Andalusia for her "Rogue Males" documentary, which we all enjoyed watching, even though she did technically cheat by using a video camera instead of her mobile phone…'

Samurai West

disappearer007@gmail.com

Printed in Dunstable, United Kingdom